# ONCE UPON A TIME IN KAZIMIERZ

Barbara Pearman

Copyright © 2022 Barbara Pearman

The moral right of the author has been asserted.

Apart from any fair dealing for the purposes of research or private study, or criticism or review, as permitted under the Copyright, Designs and Patents Act 1988, this publication may only be reproduced, stored or transmitted, in any form or by any means, with the prior permission in writing of the publishers, or in the case of reprographic reproduction in accordance with the terms of licences issued by the Copyright Licensing Agency. Enquiries concerning reproduction outside those terms should be sent to the publishers.

This is a work of fiction. Names, characters, businesses, places, events and incidents are either the products of the author's imagination or used in a fictitious manner. Any resemblance to actual persons, living or dead, or actual events is purely coincidental.

Matador
Unit E2 Airfield Business Park,
Harrison Road, Market Harborough,
Leicestershire. LE16 7UL
Tel: 0116 2792299
Email: books@troubador.co.uk
Web: www.troubador.co.uk/matador
Twitter: @matadorbooks

ISBN 978 1803130 514

British Library Cataloguing in Publication Data.
A catalogue record for this book is available from the British Library.

Printed and bound in Great Britain by 4edge Limited
Typeset in 11pt Minion Pro by Troubador Publishing Ltd, Leicester, UK

Matador is an imprint of Troubador Publishing Ltd

For Rebecca, who provided the spark that ignited my passion for writing, and subsequently made it impossible for me to do nothing during lockdown!

# Author's Note

It was during a visit to the historic city of Krakow that I was inspired to write this story. Our hotel was situated in the lively Kazimierz district and surrounded by quirky cafés and bars. One evening we chanced upon the unlikely named Once Upon a Time in Kazimierz, a bijou restaurant serving authentic Polish dishes.

A carpenter's workshop, grocer shop and tailor's, unchanged since pre-war years, have been integrated into one space and furnished with an eclectic mix of fixtures and artefacts from the original interiors. A duo of young musicians played violin and accordion, and in the beguiling atmosphere of that unique and intimate space the seed of an idea was sown and two years later my first novel was begun.

# Once Upon a Time in Kazimierz

It's 1930 and Poland's economy is beginning to suffer as a result of the Great Depression. Kindhearted but naïve Marianna lives with her parents in the rural village of Zalipie in Poland. This small farming community is all she has ever known and she dreams of a different life in the city. A whirlwind romance with Leon, a dashing but egotistical musician, leads to a hasty marriage providing her with an opportunity for change.

Leon's father, Stanislaw, runs the local grocery store in Kazimierz, a busy district of Krakow. His fellow shopkeepers and their families are a close-knit, diverse community and they welcome the couple with open arms, but the lives of the inhabitants of this small row of shops will be changed forever by the arrival of the newly wed couple. By nightfall, the seeds of new relationships will have been sown and the shattering of others begun as family rifts, unfulfilled dreams and personal resentments are tested by their presence.

# Autumn

*Zalipie 1974*

Marianna sits gazing out of the open window at her garden and the familiar landscape beyond. Her notebook lies open on her lap, her pen poised above a blank page. She's eager to start writing and has much to tell, but where to start?

A sudden gust of wind blows, shutters slam and the pages of her book flutter in the draught. She pins her platinum hair into an untidy knot and begins to write.

# Spring

*Krakow, Poland 1932*

# One

The wind rattles dilapidated shutters as it passes the rundown shop fronts and crumbling facades of Szeroka Street and rushes onwards to the open space of the square beyond. Here in this street of grey cobblestones and faded doorways lives a diverse community of traders and their families who collectively cater for the day-to-day needs of local residents. Outmoded and faded signboards display the shop owners' names: Nowak, Stolarz, Krawczyk, Weinberg.

First in the humble row of businesses is the carpentry workshop of Stefan Stolarz. His father taught him everything he knows and his passion for wood lives on in his eldest son. Tucked in the corner of the window is a small sign with an arrow pointing to the entrance. *Bespoke Furniture/Chair Doctor*. A beautifully restored rocking horse is barely visible through the dusty window, the interior being dimly lit by a single light bulb. Some effort is required to push the door open as ripped lino in the hallway causes it to jam, but once inside a dingy hallway leads to the rear of the property and narrow bare-boarded stairs to Stefan and Truda's flat. The steady thump-thump of Truda's kneading can be heard from above and the comforting aroma of freshly baked bread blends with the warm earthy scents of worked oak, pine and spruce.

At the far end of the hallway is an open arch hung with a heavy curtain that leads to the studio where Stefan's brother Feliks, an artist, lives and makes a meagre living. A fleeting glimpse of a bare leg, draped over one end of a shabby sofa, is reflected in the black-freckled glass of an ageing mirror, and the barely audible sounds of an intense, melancholic tango tune drift from inside.

The workshop is small and packed with tools neatly hung in rows behind an oak bench. A battered sawhorse is strewn with sandpaper and assorted leftover wood is piled beneath. Screws and nails in rusty tins are neatly stacked on a long shelf alongside glues, clamps, discarded paperwork and plans from long-past projects. A beautifully carved sign commands *Measure Twice – Cut Once*. As Stefan works, carving and shaping the hidden life of some object still to be born from his hands, the stone floor is littered with spring-like curls of shaved wood in all the hues of cream and brown. He loves the slowness of his craft, the absorbing joy of cutting and joining, turning and smoothing and the smell of fresh sawdust as it scatters from the teeth of his saw. Allowing himself an occasional break, he relaxes in a rocking chair made by his father over fifty years ago, its arms worn smooth by work-weary hands. It's here that he feels most at ease and where he first sets eyes on Marianna.

*

Newlyweds Marianna and Leon have spent the first few weeks of married life with her parents in the small rural village of Zalipie, but today they begin a new phase in their life as they travel to Krakow. Leon's father, Stanislaw, runs a small grocer store in Kazimierz, a suburb of the town, where Leon has lodgings above the shop and where they will set up home together.

The bus journey from Tarnow is going to be long and uncomfortable and Leon is already bad tempered. They've struggled to carry the heavy leather suitcases held tight with her father's old belts, and Leon's treasured violin, in its unwieldy case, has been bumped and bashed along the way.

The bus appears full, but the driver has already stacked their luggage on the roof and they manage to squeeze on. Leon has insisted his violin stays with him, despite disapproving glances from the other passengers.

Squashed close together, rocking and swaying with every bump on the road, they travel in silence. The bus stops frequently for travellers to alight at their journey's end and be replaced by others at the start of theirs. Marianna's head leans uncomfortably against Leon's shoulder as they are jolted back and forth, but the steady monotonous droning of the engine eventually sends her to sleep. The heavens open to coincide with their arrival in Krakow and it's a good half an hour's walk to Szeroka Street.

'Can't we wait a while?' Marianna asks as Leon strides out in front. 'We're going to get soaked.'

'No. Come on, let's just get there. I've had enough of this journey and it could be pouring like this for hours.'

They turn their collars up, but rain drips from their hats and trickles down their necks. Marianna's shoes are soon sodden as they negotiate the cobbled pavements, their luggage becoming more cumbersome with every step. She lags behind Leon, wondering how far it is and wishing he would slow just a little.

'This is it,' he announces suddenly as they stop outside his father's store. A bell tinkles somewhere out back as they enter and the delicious smell of fresh coffee and bread greets them. Stanislaw comes from behind the counter, arms outstretched, smiling broadly.

'Here you are at last! Look at you, soaked to the skin. Come in and take those wet coats off.'

Leon breaks free from his father's bearlike hug, embarrassed by the unusual display of affection, and introduces his new wife. Stanislaw takes both her hands in his and shakes them enthusiastically. He adjusts his glasses, sliding them to the end of his nose, peers over the top and exclaims, 'So we meet at last, Mrs Nowak, and my goodness, you're just as beautiful as Leon said.' His fleshy chin quivers as he guffaws an exaggerated laugh and she is immersed in the combined smells of brilliantine and carbolic soap as he pulls her to him. Marianna returns his warm embrace, blushing a little, but is relieved to find that her new father-in-law appears to be a cheerful character.

He ushers them to two sagging armchairs on either side of a table piled with old papers and magazines. 'Come and sit here. Make yourselves comfortable while I fetch some coffee,' he urges, fussing around Marianna.

This is where he encourages his customers to rest and pass on the local gossip while he makes up their orders. A consummate salesman, he makes the most of every opportunity to sell his regulars a coffee and maybe something tasty from his daily supply of freshly baked pastries.

The store is an emporium of all things dried, preserved, pickled, packeted, tinned and bagged, although recently, with shortages becoming the norm, his shelves have been somewhat depleted. Stanislaw's pride and joy, an oversized brass till with heavy keys and flag signs that pop up with a clunk as the cash drawer springs open, sits on one end of the counter and a set of iron weighing scales with its tower of weights takes the space at the opposite end. A series of wooden shelves are stacked neatly with tins and jars displayed in identical pyramids and a glass-covered counter houses bowls of fresh pickles, sauerkraut, vegetable salads, pickled fish and other delicacies, the like of which Marianna has never seen before. A gilt plaque advises that a prime selection of smoked meats and sausages is available at all times, but this is a promise he can no longer guarantee. On a side table are the leftover items from Truda's daily delivery of home-baked goods and in front of the counter sit a dozen hessian sacks, their open tops displaying a varied assortment of dried goods.

The bell rings as the door opens and Michal, Stanislaw's neighbour, hurries in, shaking rain from his jacket. His face lights up in surprise as he spots Leon. 'Ah! Leon! So you're back? I hear you're a married man now and this must be Marianna?' He steps forward and a cool thin hand grips hers enthusiastically.

Michal introduces himself while Stanislaw stands aside looking annoyed. 'What can I get you, Michal?' he asks, irritated by the interruption. Michal has a habit of leaving his shopping till last thing and although Stanislaw doesn't usually mind, today it's inconvenient. Michal rummages around in his pocket and produces a scrappy piece of paper.

'I'm sorry I'm so late. I won't bother you for long. I just need half a dozen items. If it's not too much trouble.'

Stanislaw tucks a hand under Michal's elbow and steers him towards the door. 'No problem at all,' he says, taking the list from Michal. 'If you wouldn't mind calling back, I'll put these items together for you and we'll have a chat later.'

He slaps Michal on the shoulder affectionately and closes the door firmly behind him, hangs the closed sign in the window and resumes his conversation.

'Come on, you two, help yourselves to coffee, you've had a long tiring day and you must be exhausted.'

He pulls up a chair and listens attentively as Leon relives the journey in tedious detail, exaggerating the number of hours it's taken to get here and making sure to dramatise how heavy the cases were. Stanislaw listens patiently.

Leon has always been predisposed to dramatising events. Once refreshed by the smoky-flavoured coffee Marianna is keen to see the apartment, and their shoes click clack on the narrow boarded staircase as they make their way in convoy up to the first floor where Leon's former musician friend Amelia occupies a room.

'And how is Amelia?' Leon asks. 'Still playing her accordion?'

Stanislaw pauses to catch his breath. 'She's well enough I think. I see little of her but she'll be joining us later. She's really looking forward to seeing you.' Leon doesn't comment but a smile curls the corner of his mouth.

Stanislaw adds quickly, 'Oh, perhaps I should have said earlier, but I've arranged a small get-together this evening with our neighbours. They're all excited to meet you, Marianna.'

The stairs become increasingly steep and narrow the higher they go. On the top landing a skylight floods the space with light. 'Here we are!' Stanislaw says, puffing with the effort of the climb. Marianna is surprised as they enter a large, well-lit room.

'Don't look so shocked,' Leon says. 'I told you it was a nice flat. I certainly wouldn't have lived here if it wasn't.'

Stanislaw throws him a glance Marianna is unable to read, but he refrains from commenting and the moment passes.

'The best thing about the flat is this,' Leon says, wandering to the window. The view takes in Szeroka Street and the rooftops beyond all the way to the centre of

Krakow, where church spires rise majestically above the town. It's a view Leon has described many times.

'It's beautiful,' Marianna comments. 'I can't wait to explore.'

Stanislaw is eager to give them a guided tour of the flat. A sagging sofa dominates the living room and fills the space along one wall. Hanging above is an assortment of naively painted portraits and Stanislaw waves his hand towards them dismissively. 'Rogues' gallery,' he laughs. 'Otherwise known as family members.' Opposite is a wooden dresser painted a garish shade of green and filled with books and a random collection of china. To the right of the window there's a deep square sink with a rudimentary wooden drainer and a functional black iron stove. A selection of worn pots and pans hang from a wooden contraption fixed to the ceiling above.

'You should be able to cook up a storm on this little beauty,' Stanislaw says, slapping his hand on the side of the oven.

Marianna is pleasantly surprised that Leon has kept the place so tidy, although this myth is dispelled when Stanislaw grumbles about having spent too much of his precious time cleaning the place.

The bedroom is dark and small with an unimpressive view to an enclosed air well that allows little natural light to enter. A dressing table with triple mirrors and a solitary cupboard in the corner provide the only storage space. The bed with its heavy iron bedstead, sagging mattress and faded cover looks decidedly uncomfortable.

'I'll leave you to it then. You'll probably want to change,' Stanislaw suggests, indicating their bedraggled state. 'Something a little,' his finger taps against his nose, 'fancy perhaps.'

*

Truda, a friend of Leon's has left him a note.

*I heard you were back today. If you've*
*got time call by. Can't wait to see you. T x*

'And who is Truda?' Marianna asks.

'Just a friend. We've known each other since school. You'll like her I'm sure. Come on, leave the unpacking and we'll go now,' Leon says. His obvious enthusiasm is unexpected and although she's tired there's no point upsetting him by objecting.

Stanislaw lifts a hand in acknowledgement as they pass through the shop. Michal has returned and the two are deep in conversation about the ever-deepening financial crisis in which the country finds itself. It's all very worrying they agree and ponder over how long their respective businesses will survive, share opinions on the Government's handling of the situation and console each other with various philosophical ramblings along the lines of 'contentment is the only real wealth' and 'a little thought and kindness are worth more than money'. But each of them has more than an eye on where the next zloty is coming from.

It's still raining and the overflow from a broken pipe pours down Marianna's neck as they scurry out of one door and through the other. Stefan's workshop is closed but they can hear muffled voices from within.

'Sounds like he has a customer,' Leon says, 'we'd better leave it for now. We'll call in on the way out.'

'Up here,' he gestures, and they climb the narrow stairs to the first floor. Truda has heard them coming and appears in the doorway, flustered and wiping flour from her face.

'Leon! Oh dear, do excuse the state of me. What a way to greet guests!' She's annoyed she looks such a mess and fumbles about behind her back untying her apron. 'Come on in. It's so good to see you again after all this time. I've missed you so much.' Leon takes both her hands in his and swings her round enthusiastically.

Marianna stands back awkwardly, waiting to be introduced, but Leon seems in no rush to do so and as the pair exchange prolonged greetings Marianna uses the opportunity to have a good look at his friend. Truda is plain. It's a harsh observation but knowing Leon as she does she's surprised his best friend isn't more glamorous. She's pale-skinned and everything about her from her clothes to her hair to the way she moves lacks vitality. Smiling proves to be an effort despite Leon's enthusiastic greeting. He fusses over Truda for a while then, at last, puts an arm around Marianna's shoulder.

'Truda, I'd like you to meet Marianna.'

Truda looks Marianna up and down and mutters

a curt hello. 'Well, you'd better come in. I'll make some coffee. It would have been nice if Stefan was here but he has a new client and they're negotiating the price of a piece of furniture. They've been at it for hours. Goodness knows what's taking them so long. I would have thought they'd be finished by now. Most people only want repairs done these days and Stefan does these for a pittance, but this is a proper commission job and likely to earn us some much-needed cash. Apparently Mr Cohen is a wealthy man, but you know what Stefan's like, Leon. He's more interested in perfecting his workmanship.'

'I do indeed,' he agrees. 'Never mind, we'll catch him on the way out perhaps,' Leon says.

Marianna is perched on the edge of her chair looking round the room. Three wicker baskets covered in cloths catch her eye and she sees this as an opportunity to make conversation. 'Have you been baking something nice Truda? Leon tells me you're an excellent cook.'

'No. Nothing fancy,' she replies. 'Just an order of pastries for the shop.'

'Let's have a look,' says Leon, standing up, mug in hand. But the baking is for the party and Truda wants it to stay a surprise. 'Not now, Leon, they're cooling. Sit down and tell me all about your trip.'

Truda listens attentively as he launches into a long dialogue, although Marianna notices he doesn't mention her or her parents, preferring to enthuse about the new songs he's written, how much he's missed the bustle of Krakow and how good it will be to see all his old friends again. Not a word about their romance or marriage. They have barely begun their life together and she's already becoming tired of Leon's ego-fuelled one-sided conversations. She sits quietly sipping her coffee, feeling decidedly uncomfortable as she looks from one to the other, completely excluded from the conversation.

The room is sparsely furnished and there's nothing that gives it a homely feel. *If this was mine,* she thinks, *I'd have pretty china on that dresser, some flowers in a jug on the table and maybe some coloured cushions on a rocking chair in front of the stove.* She's brought back from her daydreaming by Leon's voice instructing her, 'Come on, M. We should get going.'

'I assume you'll both be at the get-together this evening?' he asks Truda.

'Yes of course. We're looking forward to it,' she replies unconvincingly and avoids eye contact with Marianna who concludes that Truda is unfriendly to the point of being downright rude.

The workshop door opens as they reach the hallway and a tall, distinguished gentleman wearing an expensive pinstripe suit appears. He's carrying an expensive leather briefcase with a brass plate bearing his initials, and when he smiles his immaculately groomed Clark Gable-style moustache frames perfect white teeth.

'Thank you very much, Stefan, for explaining it all in such detail. It's been fascinating.' He shakes Stefan's hand enthusiastically with an impeccably manicured hand. 'I look forward to seeing the finished piece in due course and thank you for settling on such an agreeable price. My wife will be thrilled. I'd like to see how the work progresses if I may? Could I call on you again in, say, three weeks?'

'Yes of course,' Stefan replies. 'Hopefully by then I'll have finalised the proposed design and we can discuss the detail for the carving.'

Over Mr Cohen's shoulder, Marianna stares trance-like into Stefan's steel-grey eyes. He holds her gaze as he closes the door behind his visitor and shows them into the workshop.

Leon introduces her as 'my lovely wife' and refers to Stefan as 'our local expert craftsman,' but Marianna notes a touch of sarcasm in his voice.

'Hello. It's lovely to meet you,' she says, a pink flush spreading across her cheeks.

'Likewise,' Stefan replies, a smile creasing the corner of his mouth as he takes her hand in his and squeezes it gently.

Marianna returns the smile and turns redder.

They appraise each other for longer than is comfortable. Leon looks from one to the other, his expression questioning.

Stefan removes his work apron in a sudden burst of activity and unconvincingly blurts out, 'Goodness, Marianna, you have an uncanny resemblance to somebody I used to know.' This obvious lie appears to have gone unnoticed as they exchange pleasantries for a few moments until Stefan, suddenly brusque, appears to want to close the conversation.

'Perhaps we can have a longer chat this evening. I'm sorry to cut you short like this but I must clear up this mess. I don't like to start a new day in an untidy workshop.'

As Marianna pulls the door to behind them she glances back but, disappointingly, Stefan has turned away.

*

Back at the shop, Stanislaw is counting the day's takings, stacking coins neatly on the counter-top, his double chin wobbling as he swipes them one by one into his open hand. 'It's been a bad day,' he says, shaking his head, 'but at least Truda has sold all her baking. People will always need bread I suppose. Ah well, one can only hope things get better,' and he slams the till shut.

'Right, you two,' he says, glancing at the clock on the wall behind him. 'It's six o'clock and our little get-together will start at seven thirty so you'd better freshen up and get yourselves back down here. It's going to be a great evening. We could all do with some fun. It'll take our minds off this awful depression and I, for one, intend to make the most of it.'

*

'I could do without this party,' Leon grumbles when they're back in the flat. They've collapsed onto the bed and Marianna eases herself alongside him, one leg seductively sliding up and down his, her hand inside his shirt, stroking his chest, her face close to his ear, nuzzling. 'But it'll be lovely to meet everybody and they're clearly excited about meeting me,' she says.

'Yes I expect they are,' he agrees reluctantly. 'We'll just have to make an excuse and leave early if we've had enough.'

Marianna is annoyed. 'I'm tired too, you know, but it sounds as though Stanislaw has gone to a lot of trouble to arrange this evening so I'm determined to look my absolute best and have a thoroughly lovely time.'

Their suitcases lie on the floor unpacked, but Marianna has already removed her outfit for the evening. 'Shall I show you what I'm wearing tonight?' She pokes him in the ribs. 'Leon, are you listening?'

Leon is lying on his back, eyes shut, arms folded over his chest. 'Mmm?' he mutters, half-heartedly. 'Not that green dress I hope. I always think you look like a frog in that.'

Marianna looks aghast. Leon sniggers and covers his head with his arms, expecting the pillow that shortly flies through the air. 'Pig!' she snorts. 'I'm going for a bath.'

The bathroom is dimly lit, its grimy cracked window partially hung with a limp net curtain providing only a semblance of privacy from the overlooking properties. A low enamel bath with chunky legs occupies the wall under the window. The freestanding water boiler, smelling suspiciously gassy, is squeezed into a space beside it.

There's a large ornate sink on a stately-looking pedestal with a wooden cupboard above containing personal items. Each shelf has been allocated to a member of the household, but the names are illegible where condensation has blurred the ink. Leon's shelf is filled with the tools of his vanity. A shaving brush with a bone handle and a block of soap; some eau de toilette arrogantly named All Man; a matching fake tortoiseshell comb and hairbrush set; and half a bottle of skin balm, the cardboard container of which states *Be Fair to her Face and Yours.*

Marianna's nose wrinkles with disgust at the musty smell emanating from a selection of faded towels that hang on a row of hooks behind a rickety chair and makes a mental note to replace them as soon as possible. An oval mirror, its surface cloudy and spotted, is hung inconveniently behind the bathroom door. Green lino is stained around the sink and bath areas, clearly the result of overenthusiastic bathing. There is no toilet facility, this being housed in an outbuilding at the back of the shop.

A scum mark around the bath is evidence of previous use by a less than fastidious bather. Marianna takes a cloth and some powder cleaner from the windowsill and having removed the scum line, fills it, one bucketful at a time, from the simmering boiler.

She undresses and folds her clothes neatly, places them on the chair and wipes the mirror's steamy surface. *I wonder what they'll make of me,* she ponders, raking her hair back from her forehead and contemplating her reflection. Her nose is neat and straight and lightly freckled, her mouth full and seductive. She's never been vain but if there's one thing she does like about herself, it's her hair. It's glossy and deep amber like a ripe conker, and a heavy side fringe and natural wave draw attention to her defined eyebrows and warm brown eyes. She presses her lips together, runs her fingertips along the faint shadows under her eyes and sighs. She could do with a good night's sleep.

She steps tentatively into the steaming bath, lowers herself in and lies back. An hour passes by and Leon is becoming impatient. He grabs a towel and goes to the bathroom grumbling. 'Oh, do come on, M. How much longer are you going to be?'

The hot water has made her lethargic. 'Leon, give me a hand will you, I've gone all limp.'

'I'll give you limp,' he replies, but takes her hand anyway. She wraps herself in the least offensive of the towels, gathers her discarded clothes and leaves.

'And don't forget to clean the bath!' she yells from the landing.

Perched on the bed she rubs her hair vigorously, flicking her fingers through to give it some semblance of shape, then stands naked in front of the mirror turning slowly this way and that, contemplating her reflection. There was a time when Leon would tell her what a beautiful body she had, but those days are already gone. Sighing, she slips into her undergarments and sits at the dressing table, chin resting on her hands. For some time she stays like this, deep in her own thoughts, until the sound of Leon returning galvanises her into action.

Marianna's skin is unblemished and she rarely wears makeup, but tonight she wants to look sparkling so will make an exception. She tips the items from her makeup bag onto the dressing table surface. A compact decorated with the profile of a hatted woman contains a blue powder puff that resembles the delicate feathers of a baby bird. A fine cloud of powder is released as the mesh covering is unclipped. Rouge, in a tiny red tin with a bluebird and pansies on the lid, remains unused. The contents are greasy and too pink for her, preferring as she does the pale-complexioned look that is fashionable. A rectangular tin with a block of mascara and a tiny brush reminds her of a miniature artist's palette. But the item Marianna thinks most decadent is a cherry red lipstick in a sophisticated gold case.

Leon enters the room. He looks displeased.

'Not dressed yet? You'd better get a move on, we need to be downstairs in ten minutes.'

Marianna doesn't respond but quickly applies green shimmery eye shadow to both lids below her beautifully arched eyebrows. A thin layer of Vaseline is smeared carefully over this – a trick of the Hollywood stars. She spits onto the mascara cake and scrubs colour onto the tiny brush, applying it heavily to her upper lashes. Powder is applied sparingly to her flawless cheeks. The final essential touch, lipstick, is dabbed on with a fingertip then she blots her lips together with the corner of a handkerchief, brushes her hair vigorously and sits back to admire her reflection.

The pale green dress complements her colouring, its boat-shaped neckline accentuating her sleek shoulder line.

She adds a wide belt and heeled shoes and completes the look with the emerald glass drop earrings Leon bought her as a wedding gift.

'What do you think? How do I look?' she asks.

'You'll do,' replies Leon. 'More to the point, how do I look?'

'You'll do,' she retorts.

*

Stanislaw has hinted there may be dancing. It will be the perfect opportunity for Leon and Amelia to play. He's an accomplished and enthusiastic musician, and when his slim elegant fingers fly nimbly over the fingerboard and the bow strokes the strings, he and the instrument are in effect in conversation. Leon is proud of his violin, although he has made a poor job of painting it, somewhat bizarrely, a glossy blood red. Drips run down the back and spatters dot the turning pegs and bridge but, despite its defacement, the sound it produces is rich and warm. The first time he showed the instrument to Marianna her nose wrinkled with distaste.

'That looks horribly macabre. What on earth made you do that?'

'Ah, now that's an interesting story. It was my attempt at recreating a Marco Berlusconi.'

'And he is?' she asked, intrigued.

'He was a greatly revered violinmaker who had just finished his latest masterpiece of craftsmanship when his wife and child both died during childbirth. He was distraught with grief and became a little mad apparently. I read an account of how he came to varnish the violin red. It's a fascinating read. It was written by the man himself and reads like a confession.'

Leon searches amongst his papers and finds the article. 'I'll practise my latest piece while you read it. It will set the scene.' Marianna is suspicious this is yet another of Leon's unlikely stories but she reads anyway.

*The violin was perfect in every detail yet remained unvarnished, although I'd played it a hundred times. Its neat waist and long slender neck were like those of an elegant woman and it played effortlessly with a sweet, plaintive sound. After Anna's death and acting irrationally I dragged her lifeless body to my workshop and slit her waxy flesh at the wrist with a razor. I watched, numb, as blood oozed down her hand and dripped from between her slender fingers, like a clock ticking away the seconds. I collected the sticky blood in a copper bowl and mixed it with clear varnish until it became silky and glowed red like burning embers. I varnished that instrument many times. The sweet metallic smell made me nauseous, but after each layer was applied the sound magnified and became stronger and deeper. I played and played, caressing the strings with yearning. It was like holding Anna in my arms. I was speaking to her through the music. Over time the heartbreak within me eased and the notes turned to comforting words in my head. The violin had become my saviour. I sold it to a grieving friend and in time it became his saviour too. Eventually it was given to an orphanage. I like to think the children who played it benefited in some way but I don't suppose I'll ever know.*

Leon sits on the edge of his seat, eagerly awaiting her opinion. 'Well, what do you think?'

'My God, Leon, it's gruesome and certainly tragic. I'm not sure what to say. I feel quite sick thinking about it. I suppose my initial reaction is that I should be grateful yours was coloured with the contents of a pot of cheap paint.'

*

Downstairs, Stanislaw has arranged trestle tables for the food, and in his living quarters, at the back of the store, chairs have been placed in a circle leaving a small space for dancing. His friend Elena bustles about lending a hand. She is short with a matronly figure, a round face with dimpled cheeks prone to blushing and dark eyes that sparkle like shiny black buttons. Her black hair is fashioned into tight curls below her ears and wherever she goes she leaves a waft of lily of the valley perfume in her wake. She has a flower stall in the square and consequently her chubby hands are red and scratched from hours of preparing, wiring, taping and arranging flowers. She laughs at all Stanislaw's jokes and everything about her wobbles as she does so. Stanislaw calls Elena his flower and can't keep his hands away from her voluptuous, huggable body.

The first of the guests to arrive is Stanislaw's great friend and neighbour Michal. He has a reputation for being a perfectionist and is expert in the art of constructing, altering, repairing and modifying garments for his customers, based on their personal specifications, needs and preferences. *Nothing but the best* is the heading on the leaflets he distributes each Saturday at the local bric-a-brac fair. This weekly event has grown from the few random stalls of years ago to the hordes of sellers and bustling crowds who now fill the streets, and there's no doubt the market has been a key factor in expanding his business.

A life-sized mannequin in the workshop window is the only clue to his trade, whilst the cramped dingy interior is piled high with bales of fine worsted, wool, tweed and mohair. Oversized reels of cotton are lined up in colours from light to dark, and cardboard boxes of buttons and buckles spill out onto shelving above a substantial cutting table.

Sara, his disgruntled wife, complains constantly that he spends more time sewing than he does with her, but Michal is a mild-mannered man who listens patiently and then goes about his business unperturbed. They have been married for twenty-five years, during which time she has changed from a quiet, coy young girl to a gossiping busybody whose days are filled with mundane ramblings about the weather, household chores and the latest local gossip. Her favourite phrase is 'I probably shouldn't be telling you this... but...' Intellectual stimulation for Michal comes from talking with his great friend Stanislaw over a glass or two of vodka, and despite his quiet demeanour Michal relishes the lively debates they share, usually at Stanislaw's shop where there's less likelihood of Sara eavesdropping on their conversation.

Michal is always well dressed. 'I am my own advertisement,' he tells Sara when she mocks him for being so fussy about his appearance. 'What would my clients say if I was unkempt?'

'Well, it smacks of vanity to me,' she retorts, although she secretly enjoys his immaculate turnout. 'Perhaps you should have a new sign made for the door. *House of Dapper*.'

Michal smiles a slow smile in response to this unexpected attempt at humour but responds sure of his convictions. 'You may mock, my dear, but, on this particular subject, you are wrong. Looking good isn't about self-importance, it's about self-respect.'

His working garments consist of grey tailored trousers, a collarless shirt with the sleeves rolled up to his bony elbows and a fitted waistcoat lined with navy silk. He wears a tape measure round his neck and has a square block of tailor's chalk tucked into the small pocket on the front of his waistcoat.

Michal and his wife shuffle into the room. Lidka, their timid daughter, follows close behind. He removes his hat and nervously turns it round and round in his hands. Lidka stands behind him like a mute shadow, preferring to be near her father and keeping her distance from Sara and her inane chatter. She is tall and slim with lank mousy hair worn shoulder length. She has her father's aquiline nose, small mouth and pale grey eyes that seek approval for every move she makes. She's a timid young woman overpowered by her domineering mother and living a mundane life that alternates between household chores and the unpleasant job she has washing down the sinks, gutters and floors at the local abattoir. She hates working where the air is thick with the nauseating smell of warm blood and bleach but has no confidence to look elsewhere. Life is passing her by and she knows it.

Out in the wider world, beyond childhood, Lidka found life more of a challenge than she imagined it would be and it daunted her. Her mother's smothering influence grew as her teenage years approached and, undermined by constant scrutiny and criticism, her self-confidence was crushed. The local boys added to her lack of self-esteem with their relentlessly cruel comments about her appearance.

'There goes Quasimodo,' they would jeer as she scuttled along, head down, shoulders hunched. Pale and thin, she would sit with her knees glued together and her arms folded high across her chest in an attempt to disguise her boyish frame.

'Keep away from boys,' Sara advised. 'They're nothing but trouble.'

As she approached her teenage years she contemplated 'trouble' might be a welcome change, and although her pace quickened as she passed them by, she was unable to resist looking back in the hope of receiving even the most fleeting of glances. These were never forthcoming and at night she lay awake fretting about the hurtful words they flung at her.

The girls were worse. Their unkind name-calling was relentless. 'You look like a rat. A skinny rat.' But the comment that hurt the most and got Lidka thinking was 'You look like an orphan in those awful grey clothes. Are you an orphan?'

Lidka hated wearing grey but when she begged her mother for something brighter the response had been predictable. 'Certainly not!' her mother yelled at her. 'Grey is practical and vanity can easily overtake wisdom, Lidka, something I have to remind your father of constantly. It's best not to be noticed.'

Excluded from any social contact with her peers she became withdrawn and antisocial. She needed to break free from the constraints Sara put upon her but didn't have the courage. Irrational thoughts filled her mind. *Am I adopted? Should I run away?* It became increasingly difficult to talk to her mother about anything that mattered. Contradiction was met with 'Don't talk back to me like that, Lidka.' Suggestions with 'Why on earth would you think that's a good idea?'

Her mother would have none of it, dismissing her with a final 'Do as I say and you won't go far wrong.'

She despised herself for responding with 'Yes, Mother' this or 'No, Mother' that, so stopped talking altogether.

'You can take that sullen look off your face, my girl,' Sara bullied.

'Give the girl a break,' her father would urge. 'Give her some leeway for goodness' sake.'

Small attempts at rebellion like hiding a lipstick under her mattress or looking at 'unsuitable' magazines were only partially satisfying. She stole one of her father's cigarettes once in an attempt to appear grown up, but didn't get away with it because it made her hair smell. Sara forced her to wash it in cold water, in the depths of winter, as a punishment. And so the resentments grew.

She kept a secret diary full of her grudges, especially those referring to her mother, but what was the point in 'rebelling' if nobody knew you were doing it? She poured her dissatisfaction about her looks, her clothes, her lack of friends but especially her job, onto the empty pages. 'I hate everything about life,' she wrote. 'Everything.' Afterwards, as she lay back on the bed exhausted, she promised herself that when the time was right, she would rebel.

*

Stanislaw is hosting with enthusiasm, ushering people to their designated seats and encouraging a mood of celebration. Everyone is feeling the pinch as the depression takes hold, but his neighbours have been generous and agreed they will each bring a dish of food. Sara has made potato dumplings stuffed with pork. They're cold but would be better heated so Elena bustles about with pans, transferring the meaty delight to the stove at the back of the shop.

The door closes with a bang as Chajim, proprietor of Weinberg's General Store (everything you need and more), wheels his ageing and overweight mother, Sofia, in from the street. Wheelchair-bound for many years, although nobody can remember why, she says little but nods a lot even when asleep. When she does speak, the room fills with the pungent smell of eucalyptus lozenges, a bag of which she permanently clutches in one hand. Chajim is about to apologise for forgetting to bring anything for the meal when Sofia suddenly produces a large jar of bottled plums from under her lap blanket and nodding uncontrollably hands it to Stanislaw.

Her son is a big strong bear of a man – gentle and kind – a do anything for anybody type of man. Thick brown hair and an untidy bushy beard give him the appearance of a Neanderthal hunter, but despite his somewhat alarming appearance he's a bit of a pushover, some would say soft. He was married once but his wife left him for the local butcher. She was apparently unable to resist his extensive selection of cold cuts and enormous sausages.

Chajim loves his mother very much, but not quite as much as his own impressive collection of assorted hardware. His shop is his life, and he boasts that his stock of soaps and cleaning products, cooking equipment, crockery and pans, keys, locks, hinges, paint, tools, ladders, buckets and brooms provides everything a household needs.

Stanislaw has put aside a variety of dishes from his somewhat depleted delicounter along with those he's been unable to sell to his increasingly hard-up customers. Herrings in aspic – pickled cucumbers – a huge bowl of surowka (a delicious mixture of shredded root vegetables with lemon and sugar) – a small amount of sausage and smoked cheese. He has allocated a bottle of his best Polish vodka for the toast to the newlyweds but has hidden it behind the counter in the hope that somebody else will bring some, in which case it will stay there.

Six guests sit expectantly now. Sara chatting to whoever is prepared to listen while Michal looks on patiently. Sofia nods away and Chajim holds onto his mother's wheelchair as if his life depends on it. Lidka is still standing. Should she sit or not?

Elena is arranging chairs when Stefan and Truda arrive. They're laden with baskets containing various dishes for the buffet including a roulade of chicken with mushrooms, an apple cake and a poppy seed cake with raisins and nuts and, of course, a selection of freshly baked bread. Truda likes to put on a good show and enjoys the compliments her cooking receives, but on this occasion she has had to pawn one of her mother's pearl necklaces in order to be able to afford the ingredients.

'My dear Truda,' Stanislaw exclaims, 'you've excelled, as usual. How generous you are and it looks delicious. And what a pretty dress you're wearing. Come, Stefan dear boy, come in and make yourself comfortable. Our guests should be down any minute. Where's Feliks? Have you seen him today? Is he coming?'

Stanislaw is gabbling now and Stefan places a reassuring hand on his arm.

'Don't worry. He'll be here.'

Right on cue Feliks breezes in, wide-legged flannel trousers flapping round his dapper brogue shoes. He has dancing in mind and has brought a partner. She is wide-eyed, smiling Amelia, dressed in a cinch-waisted halter-necked multi-coloured dress and sporting a large ornate hair clip in an attempt to tame her wild auburn hair. Despite her flamboyant appearance she is a quiet, private person with little to say.

'We're here! Ta da. Let the fun begin!' Feliks announces with his arms held wide. He slaps Stefan on the back. 'If I wasn't an artist I'd be a performer. Or a master of ceremonies,' he adds, as an afterthought. 'In any event, something flamboyant!'

Stefan grimaces. *God help us all,* he thinks.

Marianna and Leon enter the room, arms linked. There are one or two oohs from the ladies and the gentlemen stand, mouths agape. Marianna is a vision in her green 'frog' dress. Sofia nods so fast her head is in danger of falling off.

Marianna smiles broadly as she looks from one to the other and takes in the welcoming scene. The guests mingle and chat. Truda is talking animatedly to Lidka who has relaxed a little and taken the bold step of removing her coat. Elena is bustling about serving drinks. Leon makes a beeline for Amelia, and Stefan appears to be admonishing Feliks about some misdemeanour or other.

Marianna is momentarily left alone and Feliks, quick off the mark, pulls her towards himself and Stefan.

'My brother and I are discussing art,' he lies. 'Maybe you can add something to this debate?'

'Oh! No, I'm afraid I know very little about art but I love to write. That's an art form in itself, I believe,' she says.

'And?' Feliks urges. 'Anything else?'

'Well, I do like to sing a little.'

Stefan says nothing, seemingly intent on staring into his beer glass.

Feliks leans towards Stefan. 'And what do you say to that, brother? It seems we have a songbird in our midst.'

Stefan looks amused. 'Then I look forward to hearing you sing later,' he purrs, holding her gaze.

Marianna's stomach turns to liquid. She swallows and mumbles an indecipherable reply.

He leans forward feigning deafness. 'I'm sorry I didn't quite catch that.'

'I said I'd feel more comfortable reciting a poem.'

Stefan smiles and nods. 'Then a poem it is,' he says and turns away to speak to Sofia who is sucking away on a lozenge and nodding wildly.

Marianna is becoming impatient with her husband who has left her more or less alone since they arrived. He seems completely oblivious to her presence and is instead holding court with Truda who looks at him with undisguised devotion, Amelia who is hanging on his every word and Lidka who says nothing but looks in turn from one to the other wondering if she'll ever have anything to say that will be of interest.

*He's a peacock preening himself*, thinks Marianna and turns away.

Stanislaw claps his hands.

'The food is ready. Please come and enjoy and I'd like to thank you all for your generosity. As the old saying goes, the more we share, the more we have.' Stanislaw chuckles, pleased with his own wise words.

Feliks sidles up to Marianna as she moves towards the table and, resting one hand on the small of her back, leans in close to whisper in her ear. 'I must say Leon has picked himself a real looker. I hope we get to see a lot of each other from now on.' His hand brushes her behind as she moves aside, smiles sweetly and responds by handing him a plate that misses its target and smacks him full in the chest.

'I'm so sorry,' she says, disguising a grin and turning to Truda who is serving food. 'This all looks delicious, Truda. It's kind of you to go to so much trouble.'

'Thank you, but it's no trouble. I love cooking. Chicken? Or dumplings?'

Leon is flirting outrageously with Amelia in the queue behind Marianna, one arm draped intimately across her shoulder. 'We must get together again soon and see if we can recreate that old magic,' he says and Amelia blushes.

'Oh yes, I meant to tell you, Amelia. Starcja restaurant are looking for musicians to perform three nights a week and I was hoping you'd come along to the audition. We always made a great duo, me with my suave good looks and you with your mad hair.' This is as good as music to

Amelia's ears and she giggles like an adolescent. 'They're not paying much,' he adds, 'but it's better than nothing.' He flicks her hair and it sticks up like candyfloss.

Marianna has heard him and turns to ask, 'What's this, Leon?'

'I was going to mention it later. Amelia, her of the mad hair, and I are thinking of forming a duo and auditioning for the job at Starcja. We've played together before and make a great team.' He leers at Amelia and she blushes. 'You can see what you think of us when we play later.'

Stefan is nearby. Listening.

'Do you play an instrument?' Marianna asks, wishing to engage him in conversation and detract attention from her husband.

He shakes his head. 'Me? Good heavens no. I'm not musical at all. But I do believe the sounds of turning and sanding wood fall into that category, although I imagine there are few who'd agree.'

'Well, we're all different after all. Some people seem unable to exist without noise of one kind or another. Sometimes the sound of silence is like music to my ears but I suppose living in the country I've been used to that.' She looks sideways at Leon who is in full voice. 'And sometimes I like to be alone.'

'Yes. It's good to take yourself off somewhere quiet and peaceful occasionally,' he agrees and moves aside as Leon gives Marianna a gentle push in the back.

'Move on, slowcoach,' urges Leon. 'I'm hungry.'

Amelia giggles behind him.

Truda and Sara are discussing the best way to remove stains. Truda has spilt food on her pale blue dress and she rubs at it, irritated. 'Damn. Look at this mess. I should have worn an apron.' Sara provides her with a dozen different remedies for stained clothing and assures her that if it ever stops raining she'll be able to hang it on the line and it'll be fine and dry in no time. She witters on endlessly about washing and rain, and even Truda who thinks Sara is misunderstood looks bored. Behind her back Lidka raises her eyebrows in exasperation and with a sudden uncharacteristic urge to contribute something to the conversation asks Feliks:

'Do you dance tango?'

All around, the chatter stops. 'Why, Lidka, you can speak after all,' teases Feliks. 'Yes of course I can dance tango. I'm the best in Kazimierz. The question is, Lidka, can you?'

Since tango captivated the nation it has become increasingly popular and everyone can dance it at one level or another. Lidka blushes, stammering, 'Er. No. And I couldn't. I'm sure.'

'Couldn't? Wouldn't? Can't? Won't?' He glances at Sara who has her arms folded across her chest and has heard every word. 'Whoever gave you that idea? Come on, I'll show you. D'you fancy giving it a try?'

Lidka is beside herself with fear and self-doubt. 'What? Now?'

'Yes of course now,' Feliks laughs. 'Come along. I can teach you everything you need to know. For instance, did you know it's considered to be the vertical expression of horizontal desire?'

Lidka looks horrified and within seconds her neck has blotched red. She has always believed it to be a display of male macho domination, a dangerous coming together of bodies. At least that's what Sara told her. She catches a glimpse of her mother out of the corner of her eye and notes that Sara has produced a fan from her bag and is waving it frantically in front of her appalled face.

'Oh. I can't,' Lidka insists, shaking her head vigorously. But Feliks is determined and takes her hand.

She pulls back. 'No, Feliks, please.'

'Come, my little mouse-kin,' he insists, 'I won't take no for an answer,' adding, 'no lady ever turns me down.' He takes her hand and turns to Stanislaw. 'Get those records of yours. You know. The ones you've stashed away. I've heard you have quite a collection. Lidka and I are going to astound you all.'

The cumbersome record player sits on a chest of drawers in the corner. Feliks lifts the lid and inserts a small needle into the stylus. He chooses a record from Stanislaw's collection and slips it from its worn cardboard cover, polishes the vinyl disc on his sleeve, huffs on the surface, polishes again and deftly places it on the turntable. The arm is lifted and the stylus is placed gently on the record. It makes a scratchy sound as the needle finds the groove and the music starts to play with a rhythmic shushing sound as it travels round and round in an ever-decreasing circle towards the centre.

'Have a listen,' says Feliks. 'Feel the rhythm. Get in the mood and then we'll have a go.'

Lidka is mortified. What has she done? She can't back down now. She looks at her mother.

Sara hisses, 'Lidka, stop. You're making a fool of yourself.'

Lidka's heart sinks, but the deal is done. It's now or never. There's no time to run up a silky, slit-to-the-thigh dress or exchange her flat-laced shoes for seductive heels, but damn it, she'll have a go at this tango if it's the last thing she does.

But how will she get through this audacious pretence? There is only one way. She must imagine she's an expert about to perform in a dimly lit nightclub and take on the persona of a seductive, confident woman. To his amazement, Lidka grabs her father's beer glass, downs the contents in one go and looks Feliks in the eye.

Lidka closes her eyes and takes a deep breath. 'Let's do it!' she says, and entering into a fantasy world she never believed she could even imagine, takes his hand. The comfortable, homely surroundings of Stanislaw's sitting room fade as she allows herself to indulge in the fantasy.

The lights are dim. The room is musty with stale cigarette smoke; the dusty, scuffed floor covered in a crisscross of tape marks, the faded scars of a previous production. It's an empty stage awaiting their performance.

Her skin is chilled in the thin dress. She smooths the wrinkled fabric down over her hips and thighs. The dress makes her feel good. Fastening the ankle straps on her black leather shoes she senses someone standing close. She straightens slowly and turns to meet his gaze. Chiselled features and dark brooding eyes stay serious as he casually pushes a strand of black hair behind one gold-pierced ear and extends a hand. He is tango personified. She brazenly meets his gaze. The baggy hems of his loose-fitting trousers drape on black and white spat shoes. Scarlet braces restrain a silky black top and a broad chest.

'I am Giovanni,' he purrs. 'I am your partner for this evening. Come.'

She moves towards him.

He reaches towards her, his strong arms bronzed and sinewy. As he places one broad hand on her back and draws her closer, the other slowly, seductively closes around her right hand. A flop of hair falls over one eyebrow as he lowers his chin. His brooding eyes are fixed on hers. He smells of sweat but she doesn't mind. From somewhere in the gloom the music starts to play hauntingly, scratchily.

Her feet are her anchor now as he slowly swivels her round. Their backs are ramrod straight, all movement confined to their lower bodies. Their faces intent, they dance in a wondrous world of their own. Amid staccato moves and gentle swaying, they swirl and kick, their feet like flickers of light pulsing the air. She is rocked and cradled as he instructs her in the moves of a *cunita*. He strokes her leg with his foot and finally drags her on her toes to the crescendo of their dramatic dance.

The music stops. Their blood is pulsing. There's sweat on their brows. Their mouths are a whisper away. He stares at her intently. She stares back seductively.

'Not bad for a first attempt,' grins Feliks.

Lidka's head is spinning. She feels a little sick. The room comes back into focus as she's brought back to reality. She returns to her seat between Sara and Sofia. Glowing.

There was a time, before her peers ostracised her and she was downtrodden by her mother, when Lidka dreamt of being famous. The draughty third-floor landing of her childhood home was her personal stage where she performed for her own pleasure. She was happy as long as she was dancing, singing, reciting her own poems or playing her beloved secondhand recorder. The high ceiling provided excellent acoustics and the tall sash window a good supply of fresh air. Her elderly grandfather occupied one room on the same floor and spent most of his time either lying on, or sleeping in, his bed. It was fortunate for her that he appeared not to be bothered by her amateurish efforts. Lidka adored her grandfather and held his opinion in high esteem. Sometimes she would prop his door open so that he could watch her. He rarely commented but would occasionally give a nod of encouragement or stick a thumb above the covers as a sign of approval.

Interruptions to her rehearsals were usually rare but lately they had become more frequent. Something was going on. Sara would bring plates of food to Granddad's room that she would later collect, the meal having been untouched. Dr Wozniak visited regularly, but despite Lidka pressing her ear to the door, their muffled conversation was indecipherable. A sour smell seeped from the room and his temper was uncharacteristically belligerent. After one particularly disruptive morning, whilst perfecting the finale of her opera-singing debut, Granddad had thrown his hernia truss at the door and shouted for her mother to 'Get this wretched kid downstairs.'

That evening as the family sat unusually subdued around the kitchen table, her mother told her she would have to practise elsewhere.

Lidka adopted a sulky face. 'Oh, that's not fair.'

'I know. But I think that just for a little while, you could take yourself somewhere else to practise? For your grandfather's sake.'

'What's wrong with him?' Lidka had asked, folding her arms in a huff. Sara didn't answer but piled more carrots onto her plate. Lidka hated carrots.

'There's always the park,' her mother said. 'You're old enough to go there on your own.'

'I'm only nine!' Lidka exclaimed. 'And it's too far away. Why do I have to?'

Her mother stood abruptly to clear the dishes away. 'It's only for a short time. Stop making a fuss.'

Unexpectedly, the dilapidated park bandstand had proved a satisfactory alternative despite being a good half hour's walk away. Armed with a bottle of Oranzada and some pastries, she would disappear for hours at a time to perfect her pirouettes, magic tricks and monologues about the unfairness of being misunderstood in a world filled with adults.

One day she returned to find an ambulance parked on the driveway, its rear doors wide open like a huge mouth waiting for a meal. Her grandmother and parents stood like a silent guard of honour in the hallway, watching moist-eyed, as Grandfather was manoeuvred downstairs in a wheelchair, his emaciated body wrapped in a red blanket and held tightly by a wide strap. Lidka was mesmerised by the sight of his stick-like legs and swollen feet squeezed into giant slippers, his wispy white hair framing his shrunken features.

Her grandfather held her bewildered gaze with his pale dying eyes as he passed by on his journey towards another world. The ramps were lowered and as he was hauled backwards Lidka saw the red blanket move and a thin, wrinkled thumb appear.

Lidka's aspirations had died along with him, but tonight there was a spark of hope that the fire of her former self had been relit.

*

The music plays on. Elena and Stanislaw, their bulky forms in perfect harmony, astonish with their dancing skills. Feliks and Amelia show off some fancy moves. Leon and Marianna are together for the first time that evening but their dance is awkward and inhibited. Michal and Sara are doing a sedate two-step, side-to-side version of their own.

Truda is clearing the dishes, organising plates of leftovers for the guests to take home. Lidka is drinking beer. Chajim sits with one arm around his mother's shoulder, the other tapping his knee as she nods rhythmically in time to the music. Stefan leans against the wall casually, a glass in his hand. Watching. The record ends but is soon replaced with another.

'All change,' directs Leon, making a beeline for Amelia.

'Shall we?' Stefan's hand gently presses against Marianna's waist. She turns, caught off guard, as he pulls her towards him.

'Oh goodness. I don't know. I'm not very good at this,' she stutters.

'You'll be fine. Just follow me,' he says.

The music has slowed and they dance perfectly attuned, their faces so close she can feel his breath on her cheek. They don't speak but he looks into her eyes as though seeking the very core of her. She is frozen in time and unable to look away as they sway in time to the music. Marianna feels lightheaded and her stomach is performing somersaults. She can feel the heat building on her neck and ears and for a moment forgets to breathe. The sounds in the room fade and blur into one until suddenly 'That's enough!' Leon shouts, appearing from nowhere and grabbing her roughly by the arm. 'I'll have my wife back thank you.' He dances like a man possessed as the rhythm changes. Marianna watches as Stefan moves away, hands in pockets and goes to find his wife.

Truda looks peeved. 'Where've you been?'

'Enjoying the party. Come and join in.' Stefan offers her his hand but she fusses with stacking dishes. 'Come on, Truda, come and enjoy yourself for once.'

But Truda is stubborn. 'I can't, there's lots to do here,' she insists, 'clearing up and so on.'

Stefan takes her by the hand. 'Leave it. Don't be a martyr. The others will help later,' he says crossly and leads her away.

'You should have seen your husband dancing,' Feliks says as they re-join the party. 'It was quite something.' Feliks nods towards Marianna. 'I had no idea my brother could dance like that! Veeeryyy sexy.' Truda looks annoyed but says nothing as Stefan throws him an exasperated look.

Leon has drunk too much beer and his speech is slurred. 'Come on, Amelia, let's play. You can accompany me on your magnificent accordion and you, Stanislaw, perhaps you would give us a tune on that old mouth organ of yours.' Stumbling, he removes his violin from its case with a flourish, tucks it under his chin, lifts the bow with a dramatic sweep and begins to play a lively folk tune. Amelia joins in, her slender fingers skimming over the accordion keys, her auburn hair flying free as she moves her head vigorously in time to the music, all the while smiling that big smile of hers.

Stanislaw plays with gusto; his cheeks redden and sweat breaks out on his forehead as he tries to keep up with the other players. The room is hot and alive with movement, whooping and hand clapping. Marianna grabs a rejuvenated Lidka and swings her round with both hands. Everyone joins in and an hour later, Stanislaw, red-faced and with a dark patch of sweat spreading under his armpits, calls for some quiet.

'Please stop. I'm an old man. It's too much. Hush now, everyone. I think it's time for a change of pace. I believe Marianna promised us a poem?'

'She did indeed,' confirms Stefan, taking the seat closest to her. Marianna stands with her hands clasped in front of her. 'Well, I suppose I should explain why I wrote it first. It was inspired by something my mother said when I was quite small and was the first poem I ever wrote. I hope you like it.' The room is silent and she closes her eyes for a moment. 'Okay. Here goes.'

*She was only five years old*
*A dream come true*
*Bright like a star in the night sky*
*That's what Mum said she was*
*Glittering.*
*One in a million*
*No, more than that*
*Unique in her own way*
*Longed for and given, like the sun after rain*
*The calm after a storm*
*The bright of day after night*
*Precious, like a diamond taking shape*
*Waiting to be discovered and treasured forever.*

Marianna sits down, glad it's over, feeling a little self-conscious.

'Oh, well done, Marianna. That's lovely,' Stanislaw

enthuses. Lidka beams and searches for her handkerchief as a tear rolls down her cheek. If only her mother had ever said anything remotely as lovely as that about her.

Elena hugs Marianna. 'Oh please can we have another?'

'Not now,' barks Leon with a sneer. 'One is enough.'

Marianna is crushed by his indifference, her self-confidence shaken, and instinctively she looks to Stefan for approval.

'Beautiful,' he mouths silently.

Stanislaw appears, carrying a tray filled with small glasses. 'I think it's time we toasted the happy couple,' he says, handing round vodka shots.

'A long prosperous and happy life to you both.'

The cry goes up for a speech from Leon. He waves his glass above his head, spins on the spot, spilling the contents, and falls against Stanislaw.

'Pull yourself together,' Stanislaw hisses between gritted teeth. 'Don't embarrass me. You've only been back a few hours!'

'It's a bit late for a bridegroom's speech I think,' Leon retorts, turning his back on his father. He downs a glass of vodka in one and continues, 'Strictly speaking we're not really newlyweds. We're old hands at this marriage game now, though at least we are still speaking, just about. Which I suppose is something. I expect I'll get used to her eventually,' he slurs, swaying dangerously.

Marianna's heart sinks. He mutters on for a minute or two, making little sense. Stanislaw takes his arm and steers him to a chair to avoid further embarrassment, but Leon pulls himself free and staggers towards his new bride, draping himself around her neck.

Elena has brought fragrant roses and painstakingly separated the petals to make confetti. A shower of blancmange pinks, red and white descends as they're thrown high into the air. Truda looks in horror at the mess and goes for a broom. Everyone else gathers round. Kisses are exchanged. Stefan shakes Leon's hand.

'Congratulations, I hope you know how lucky you are.'

He kisses Marianna on the cheek.

'Be happy,' he whispers and touches her hand.

Truda reappears and pulls at Stefan's sleeve. 'Can we go now? I've a splitting headache and have to be up early tomorrow.' Turning towards Marianna she lifts her hand briefly. 'Congratulations by the way,' she adds. But it sounds like an afterthought.

'Call into the workshop tomorrow,' Stefan says, his voice lowered. 'We have a gift for you. I'll be there all day.'

# Two

Leon has a thumping headache and is making a fuss about it.

'It's self-inflicted, Leon,' Marianna tells him. 'I have little sympathy and Elena did warn you about Stanislaw's vodka, but you just had to have one more, didn't you?'

'Don't start, Marianna. It was a party, what else d'you expect?'

She fills a mug with steaming black coffee and thumps it on the table under his nose. 'Stop moaning and drink. If you get moving you'll feel better and don't forget we have to call into Stefan's workshop this morning.'

'I'm really not in the mood. Must we?'

Marianna shakes her head. 'Yes we must, it would be rude not to. Now hurry up. You may not be bothered, but I can't wait to see what it is he has for us.'

Scraping his chair back Leon stands, his hand against his forehead. 'Ooh my head. It's so painful.' He presses his fingers to his temples and squeezes his eyes closed. 'Oh, how I suffer.' Marianna ignores him.

Stefan is unlocking as they arrive. Leon's pale face prompts him to ask, 'How's your head this morning, Leon?' He looks at Marianna briefly, winks and smiles. 'Not good I bet.'

'Yes I know. Don't you start,' Leon replies. 'I've already had a ticking off from madam.'

In the workshop there's a large item on the workbench, mysteriously covered with a cloth. Stefan removes it with a flourish. 'I hope you like it.'

Marianna's eyes widen. 'Oh my goodness. That is so beautiful, Stefan.'

Leon, hands in his trouser pockets, nods approvingly. 'Very nice indeed. Thank you. That's very generous of you.'

The small chest has been lovingly smoothed and varnished to accentuate the sinuous lines of the wood's natural grain. The drawer fronts are carved with small birds, berries and leaves, and the finishing touch, Stefan's signature bumblebee motif, has been intricately carved on one corner.

Truda appears covered in her usual dusting of flour. 'It's taken him hours,' she says resentfully, prompting Leon to comment further.

'I can see that, Truda. It's a work of art.'

Stefan smiles. 'Well, it was a pleasure to make and I've really enjoyed indulging my passion for carving.'

Marianna leans forward and kisses him lightly on the cheek. 'Thank you, we'll treasure it.' She fiddles with the buttons on her top and her face flushes pink. 'I'll find the perfect place for it, Stefan. It will look wonderful.'

Truda can't help herself and adds, 'It's a good job you've finished it. Stanislaw has been asking for some new shelving and now you can get on with it. Anyway I must go, my bread will be overdone and I've more baking to do.'

'I'm going to be helping Stanislaw a little in the shop,' Marianna says in an attempt to be friendly. 'Perhaps I'll see you there?'

'Yes. Perhaps you will,' Truda replies tersely.

*

It's the day after the party and Lidka has returned from a morning at the abattoir to a kitchen full of steam. Monday is washday and Sara is up to her elbows in soapsuds as she agitates the clothes with a wooden dolly. The room reeks of the acrid smell of soda, and condensation from the boiling copper streams down the walls and window. A heap of sodden washing is piled in a metal bath waiting to be squeezed through the mangle.

Michal is reading his newspaper and, looking up, he greets her with a warm smile. 'Hello, love, had a good morning?' Lidka leans down and kisses him lightly on the cheek.

Sara wipes her face with her apron. 'Oh good, you're back and about time. You can give me a hand with this lot. I'm getting too old for this.'

Lidka sighs. *Another day in paradise,* she thinks resentfully but replies meekly with 'Yes, Mother,' sensing that Sara is upset about something.

They work as a team for a while, Lidka turning the mangle handle, Sara hanging the squeezed items over a clotheshorse next to the kitchen stove.

'And what do you think you were playing at, young lady?' Sara suddenly blurts out.

'Whatever do you mean, Mother?' Lidka pretends to be puzzled.

'You know full well what I mean, madam. That ridiculous carry on with Feliks.'

'And exactly what was ridiculous about it?' Lidka is becoming uncharacteristically angry.

'Behaving like a slut with that no good womaniser.'

'I'm not a slut and Feliks is a sensitive, passionate man!' She flushes at the thought.

Sara's mouth drops open. 'What would you know about passion?'

'I'm just saying he's a real man,' she replies, defiant for once.

Sara snorts. 'As if you'd know what a real man is. If you must know, it made me feel... well, uncomfortable.'

Michal gives his newspaper a shake and ducks his head out of sight. Lidka, on the verge of tears, heaves the handle round, squeezing every ounce of water into the bucket below. 'Please don't treat me like a child, Mother.'

Sara tuts. 'I only have your best interest at heart. You know that.' She shakes a sheet with gusto before hanging it on a makeshift line above the stove.

'Maybe,' Lidka dares, 'but I would appreciate it if,

just for once, you'd give me a little credit for something. Anything in fact.'

'You've always been so quiet and reserved. It was a shock to see you behaving like that.'

'I was dancing for goodness' sake! Have you never danced!'

Michal folds his paper and leaves the room. Sara flops into his vacant seat, blows out a long breath between pursed lips. 'Alright, I admit I would have loved to dance when I was a young woman but your father wasn't into that sort of thing.'

Lidka, calmer now, takes her mother's hand. 'Then you should try it some time. It really is quite exhilarating.'

'I'm too old for all that. Exhilaration and the like.' Sara chews her bottom lip, pats her damp face with a handkerchief. 'Let's forget about it. I'm too tired to argue. As long as you're sure you've nothing else to tell me?'

'Yes, Mother, I'm sure,' Lidka responds. She turns her back on Sara and, muttering under her breath, declares to herself, 'Well, not yet anyway.'

*

An early riser, Stefan is already working when the majority of Szorak Street is still asleep. The workshop, in semi-darkness, has an air of calm at this hour. Stefan loves this time of day and calls it his thinking time. He doesn't turn the light on but sits quietly in his father's old rocking chair contemplating the day's work, surveying his wooden empire in the semi-gloom, pleasuring in the slow reveal of his tools as the sun slowly lights the room.

Today Stanislaw is coming to collect the shelves he ordered. Stefan is nothing short of a perfectionist, and his customers know that whilst he may take his time, the end product, be it a new item or an expert repair, will be worth the wait. He is honest and fair when pricing his work but this does not, however, please Truda. 'Why can't you be more like my father?' she whines. 'He never sat around doing nothing. He would have completed three jobs in the time it takes you to do one. You're like an old man daydreaming in your rocking chair. If you worked faster, perhaps you'd earn more.'

Her comment rattles him. 'Well, believe me, that isn't going to happen. Rushing would be detrimental to the quality of my work.'

Today, Stefan doesn't feel inclined to dwell too long on Truda's endless criticisms. Outstanding bills are the focus of his attention when the sudden appearance of Feliks startles him. Stefan groans inwardly. There are times when the promise he made to his father to look after Feliks has sorely tested his resolve and the proverbial bad penny is here again.

'Feliks.' Stefan glances at the clock on the wall. 'It's early for you. Something the matter?'

Feliks stands in the doorway, raking his unruly hair back from his face. 'I need to speak to you.'

Stefan knows full well what's coming.

'I know it's only a month and I don't know where the money goes but here I am, once again, with nothing to live on.'

'Disappears how exactly?'

'I have expenses. You know that. I can't work without paints and canvas.'

'But I make your frames and Chajim provides you with cheap canvas. So what exactly have you spent it on?'

'It was a friend's birthday. I had to get her a gift.'

Stefan spreads his large hands wide on the workbench, tapping impatiently as he glares at Feliks.

'Well, you'll just have to pull in your purse strings. For goodness' sake, man, it's high time you took more responsibility. Truda and I are finding it hard to make ends meet as it is and we can't keep handing out money like this.' He runs his fingers through his hair, pacing about the workshop. 'Is there any chance of you earning anything in the foreseeable future?' Stefan's tone has softened.

Feliks seizes an opportunity to make his case. 'I have a couple of interested clients; it's just a matter of time before they order. I'm sure of that and I promise you this is the last time.' It's a total fabrication of course, but he has survived on the promise of imagined patronage for years.

Stefan sighs, defeated by Feliks' constant manipulating.

'Alright, wait here, I'll speak to Truda. But I'm telling you now, this is the last time and I mean it.'

At that moment Stanislaw arrives.

'Would you mind waiting for a bit. I won't be long,' says Stefan, taking the stairs two at a time.

'Don't worry,' Stanislaw calls after him, 'I just wanted to drop this off.' He waves a brown envelope at the departing figure and places it on the workbench.

'Paid on time for a change,' Stanislaw says, winking at Feliks. He leaves and Feliks leans against the workbench with his hands in his pockets to await Stefan's return.

Truda is washing up the pans from her early morning baking session when Stefan bursts into the room. 'You made me jump,' she says, momentarily alarmed. 'Is something wrong?'

He looks uncomfortable. 'It's Feliks.'

Truda screws her tea towel up and throws it on the table. 'Oh, let me guess. He's on the scrounge again.'

Stefan lets out a deep sigh and runs his hand through his hair. 'Look, Truda, don't start. I've told him this is the last time.'

'Huh! I've heard that before!'

Stefan lowers his voice. 'I mean it.'

She raises her eyes to the ceiling. 'Really? Honestly, Stefan, this has got to stop!'

Downstairs Feliks, hearing Truda shout, moves to the hallway to eavesdrop. *Here she goes again,* he thinks and wonders how his brother lives with her constant nagging. Their voices suddenly go quiet and he turns his head, straining to hear.

Stefan takes Truda by the arm and pulls her closer. 'Listen to me,' he says, placing his hand gently on her shoulder. She turns on him, her face distorted with anger.

'I'm sick of listening to you. He has you round his

little finger. He only has to ask and you give in. Oh yes, Feliks, anything you want, Feliks.'

Downstairs, Feliks sighs, questioning this analysis. *It's not true,* he concludes. He has to fight for every zloty.

'It's not that simple and you know it,' Stefan continues.

'He's a manipulating bastard that's what he is!' Truda explodes.

It's the first time Feliks has heard this particular accusation voiced out loud and he's shocked. 'That's a bit strong,' he objects to the empty hallway.

Stefan is losing patience. 'Be reasonable, Truda, he's my brother and I promised Father I'd help him.'

'That was years ago for God's sake. It's high time he looked after himself.'

'But he's passionate about his art and I know what that's like. I can't deny him the chance to realise his ambitions.'

'But not at our expense!'

Feliks grimaces. It sounds like she means it. Feelings of affection for his brother surface unexpectedly. Oh well, at least he's tried.

Stefan continues, 'He tells me he has commissions coming his way and I'm sure that if he was your brother you'd help him.'

'You're a soft touch, Stefan Holcer, and it sickens me to know it. *I'll* speak to him. We're not going to lend him a single zloty more and that's an end to it.'

Truda's footsteps stomp across the floor above. Quick as lightning Feliks slips into the workshop, removes some notes from the brown envelope, stuffs them in his trouser pocket and is out on the street and gone before she reaches the stairs.

*

Five minutes before opening time Stanislaw takes his overall from its peg, squeezes his arms into the sleeves and with difficulty buttons it up, patting his belly satisfyingly with both hands as the last one holds fast. He licks his fingers, smooths his hair, checks his watch and waits. On the stroke of seven he unbolts the door, eases it back, steps out onto the threshold and, hooking his thumbs under his lapels, takes a deep breath. He looks up into another overcast sky full with the promise of more rain. The persistent wet weather is bad for business as fewer customers mean fewer sales and even less profit and goodness knows there's little of that at present. He turns to re-enter the shop but slips and has to grasp the doorframe for support.

The pavement and doorstep are covered with bird droppings and soggy bread. A club-footed pigeon is pecking around pathetically and more of the pesky creatures flap about two floors above, wings squeaking, as they vie for position on a narrow window ledge and cling on precariously like an amateur trapeze act. A slender hand appears and scatters more crumbs.

'Oi! What are you doing?' Stanislaw shouts but there's no reply. He disappears into the shop and returns moments later with a bucket and broom just as Feliks appears. Stanislaw is busy swearing under his breath and sees Feliks too late to avoid the inevitable. He swings the bucket and the ensuing deluge of soapy water soaks Feliks' legs and feet.

'What the hell!' Feliks cries, flapping his trouser legs. 'I'm soaked to the skin. Damn! It's just not my day!'

'Your day? What about mine? I wouldn't call it an ideal start, clearing up mucky bird shit. Well, don't just stand there, come in if you're coming.' Feliks steps over the threshold. 'Whoa!' Stanislaw exclaims, 'That's far enough with those filthy shoes and what do you want anyway?' He slams down the bucket but grips the broom and sweeps furiously around Feliks' feet. 'Well? Speak up!'

Feliks is sheepish. His earlier confrontation with Stefan has unsettled him. 'I just wondered if you've any bread left from yesterday.'

'On the cadge again?' Stanislaw tuts and, turning away, waves his hand towards the counter. 'Have a look. There may be something left over.'

Feliks glances over Stanislaw's shoulder but the table is empty. 'I don't suppose you could spare a little cheese maybe. Or some sausage?'

His last few coins were squandered on a bottle of beer, shared last night with the delightful but rather intense Wanda from the bookshop, although he had concluded on reflection that it had been worth every złoty.

It's the last straw for Stanislaw. 'You know what, Feliks? You're a damn disgrace. I've seen the way you take advantage of your brother and Truda even though you know they're struggling to make ends meet. Living rent-free, constantly relying on other people's goodwill, spending what little money you earn on women and beer. We all recognise your talent but you're not bloody Van Gogh or,' Stanislaw waves his arms about, 'or... what's his name. Michelangelo. It's high time you got off your artistic backside and got a job. Be more self-reliant, man. Have some self-respect.'

Feliks, open-mouthed, is too shocked to respond.

'And another thing, I didn't get all this,' an arm gesticulates wildly, 'without working damned hard for it. Your long-suffering brother does the same. You would do well to spend less time holding women and more time holding a paintbrush.' Stanislaw shakes his head and slams down the bucket and broom.

Feliks looks crestfallen. An uncomfortable silence follows until suddenly, head down, he rushes from the shop empty-handed, his shoes squelching as he goes.

'Right,' Stanislaw mutters to himself, 'now for that Marianna.'

*

Marianna's cheeks are flushed. Never since her childhood has she eavesdropped on a conversation. She's heard everything from her position on the first-floor landing and is surprised at Stanislaw's anger. What can Feliks have done to deserve such a dressing-down? She tiptoes quietly back to the flat, shuts the door, pours herself a mug of coffee and waits.

'Where did you go in such a hurry?' asks Leon.

'Oh, Leon, I feel terrible. I was feeding the pigeons. You know I can't resist doing that, but they made a terrible mess and Stanislaw is angry and he shouted at Feliks and it was my entire fault. It was only stale bread left from yesterday. I really didn't think to ask if it was alright to take it and why was he so cross with Feliks? What has he done to deserve that?'

'Oh do stop worrying, woman. You know how fastidious Stanislaw is about his shop front. He calls it the grand entrance to his emporium. Not that there's anything grand about it. He's just obsessed with everything being just so. He'll get over it.'

He returns to his newspaper for a moment then, frowning, adds, 'Mind you, it was a mistake to take the bread. If Truda finds out you gave her precious baking to the pigeons she won't like it one bit. She'll no doubt say those crusts could have been put to better use. She hates pigeons. When we were kids we used to chase them, but she always had a sly kick if nobody was watching.'

Stanislaw climbs the stairs to the top floor with difficulty and stands puffing, bent over with his hands on his knees waiting for his heart to stop thumping. Re-buttoning his overall that has come undone with the effort, he straightens and taps at the door.

Marianna immediately launches into her apology. 'I'm

so sorry, Stanislaw. I had no idea the birds would make such a mess. Is there anything I can do to make amends?'

Behind her Leon raises his eyebrows. 'Grovel, grovel,' he mutters.

Stanislaw's intention had been to launch into a lecture about feeding the birds but Marianna is so repentant he hasn't the heart. 'Okay, okay, apology accepted, young lady, and if you want to make yourself useful you could give me a hand for a couple of hours while I work on my accounts. That would be a great help. Is ten o'clock okay?'

'I hope you're going to pay her, Father,' quips Leon.

'That's enough from you. I've had a bellyful of nonsense from you young chaps for one day.'

Stanislaw finds it impossible to be cross and winks at Marianna. 'A word of advice. Don't tell Truda you took the bread.'

# Three

Stanislaw's difficulty sleeping has been exacerbated by the stifling heat of the last week. He lies awake for hours searching for ways to make the shop more profitable, worrying about Feliks and his lack of ambition and mulling over conversations he's had with his customers during the day. The only advantage to these sleepless nights is the amount of time he has to think about new money-making ventures. It's been this way since his wife died, along with so many of his friends and neighbours, when she succumbed to the rampant and deadly spread of Spanish flu. Stanislaw considers himself a lucky man to have survived the war and then the pandemic that ravaged the world shortly afterwards.

The Saturday bric-a-brac and furniture sale is due again in two days' time, but despite the number of visitors it attracts, they seem more intent on buying junk than his groceries. This interminable heat has meant he has fewer customers and daily takings are down. People eat less when it's hot, he concludes, but this can't be said of Stanislaw who has an excellent appetite. Lately his consumption of leftovers has reached epic proportions and realisation has dawned that he is gradually eating his own profits.

That night he is lying awake as usual, the bedroom window wide open in a vain attempt to cool the room, when he hears a loud clatter from below. A late-night drunk has dropped a bottle and swayed on down the street, but Stanislaw's brain is working overtime and in an instant he's struck with an idea. That's it! Drinks! People will be parched and desperate for a cooling drink. He throws back the cover, leaps from the bed as quickly as his ample torso will allow and makes his way to the storeroom.

Switching on the light he scans the room for his stock of Oranzada and Kvass. Good, there's plenty. He calculates that he can get two drinks from each bottle and that'll more than double his takings. There are enough glasses if they are washed and reused and they can be repacked for sale afterwards. He rubs his hands together and, chuckling, sits on a sack of lentils to run through his plan. Drinks may not be enough to draw them in but with a display of Truda's bread and pastries the customers should be queuing. First thing tomorrow he'll speak to her and hopefully, if she agrees, she will have two days to prepare. She can keep her profit and he'll keep his. The plan seems foolproof.

Stanislaw manages to sell the idea to Truda who is keen but nervous at the thought of having to sell her own goods and engage with the customers. She'll have to spend all day in the frazzling heat of her kitchen, but it should be worth it as her baking is well sought after by the locals and the visiting crowds should make it a financially successful venture.

Satisfied that he's about to make a substantial addition to the weeks' meagre takings Stanislaw returns to bed and sleeps like a baby for the first time in months, although his dreams are a confused chaos of cold meats, cheese and bottles of Oranzada swirling in a tornado of coins.

He usually opens the shop later on a Thursday, so with a little time to spare he rushes to see Elena who lives two streets away on the ground floor of a tall narrow house tucked between the abattoir and a sheet metal workshop.

'Get inside, flower,' he hustles as she opens the door still dressed in her nightwear. 'I've something to tell you.'

'What's all this about?' Elena looks concerned.

'It's nothing to worry about. I've had an idea and I want to ask you a favour. I wonder if you'd mind spending your Saturday morning with your hands in a washing-up bowl?'

Stanislaw shares his plan and Elena is more than happy to oblige. She'll do anything to spend more time with him.

'Of course I'll help. I can't run the stall this weekend; the heat has shortened the life of my lovely blooms and by Saturday I'll not have enough stock to make it worthwhile.'

Stanislaw is one step ahead.

'Why don't you use any leftover flowers and foliage

and make up some bargain bunches. You might at least recoup some of your outlay.'

'Stanislaw my lovely, you aren't just a pretty face,' she says and, giggling, grabs him round his ample middle and kisses him full on the lips.

He chuckles and slaps her bottom. 'The thing is, flower, I have all my best ideas in bed!'

'Get away with you, you cheeky devil. I must get going. I need to sort my stock out before their poor heads drop off with thirst.'

Stanislaw's idea is running away with him. By lunchtime he's enlisted Leon and Amelia to play some tunes. 'You might get some extra work when people hear how good you are. They'll stop to listen and we'll sell them a drink and a pastry. It'll be a group effort.'

'We're not sitting out in this heat for hours,' Leon objects. In Stanislaw's opinion music and beer go together and he's eager to accommodate them.

'No, of course not. There's no question of it. I'll rig up an awning. Perhaps you would give me a hand, Leon. I've plenty of canvas and I'm sure we can do something to provide you with a bit of shade, even if it's only a temporary structure.' Leon reluctantly agrees and, that settled, Stanislaw spends the rest of the day humming and calculating how much his takings will increase.

It's Friday morning and Feliks calls in for his usual picking of leftovers.

'I wondered when you'd appear,' Stanislaw grumbles, but he's feeling generous today so offers Feliks some leftovers. 'Here, take this cheese. It's practically running off the counter anyway. Eat it today and you'll be fine. Any longer,' he makes a face, 'who knows!'

Stanislaw winks but Feliks doesn't laugh.

'I'll make it up to you when I'm famous and the gentry are flocking to my studio to be immortalised in oils,' he says seriously.

'Well, I won't hold my breath, though one can hope, and while you're here you can give me a hand with this awning.'

'What's it for?' Feliks asks half-heartedly.

'We're having a bit of a stall outside the shop and I'm hoping it will drum up some extra business. I'm providing the drinks, Truda is baking and Elena is bringing some flowers. Amelia and Leon are going to play for a couple of hours.'

Feliks perks up. 'Amelia? I might call by then. I usually work on Saturdays but if Amelia's going to be there I could make an exception.'

'Oh. You work on a Saturday, do you?' Stanislaw questions. 'Doing what?'

'Thinking about my next masterpiece.'

Stanislaw is moving sacks around the shop and he pauses to stand and look Feliks in the eye. 'Thinking won't get you far, young man. I think I've an idea for you. How about setting up a mini studio in the shop. It'll be a bit of a squash, mind. Bring along your easel, some paper and your charcoal or whatever you use and charge people for a quick portrait sketch. If you do one every fifteen minutes, from nine until lunchtime, that's sixteen paying customers, and why not have a bit of a display of your unsold artwork. You never know, you might sell something.'

Feliks shuffles his feet around and looks at the floor. It's an early start and sounds like hard work but he desperately needs some cash. The new waitress at the café on Jakoba Street is showing an interest. 'That's not such a bad idea, though God knows who can afford to waste money on drawings at the moment. Still, I might take you up on it.'

'Good lad. There you are you see. All it takes is a bit of forward thinking.'

By the end of the day Stanislaw has everything in place. He's pleased with the response to his idea but the rushing about has tired him. He goes to bed earlier than usual and is asleep before he can start counting sheep.

*

It's been quieter in the shop as the sweltering days have continued with little respite and Stanislaw's orders for Truda's baking have become less demanding. It's been a struggle to find all the items she needs for the amount of baking she'll do for the fair, but she's managed to source what she needs and is ready for a new challenge. Stanislaw's enthusiasm that she sell her own baking has surprised her. She prefers to leave that side of things to him, as he is a consummate salesman, jollying the customers along and persuading them to make unplanned purchases. It's not that she can't talk to people but by her own admission she can be a little abrupt and she's afraid she is more likely to scare them off. She's proud of her baking skills so perhaps it's time she gave selling a go. There's nothing to lose by trying.

Two dozen poppy seed cakes are first on her list. A deliciously crisp layer of shortbread pastry topped with a poppy seed, honey and breadcrumb filling and topped off with a drizzle of sweet sugar glaze. Seed cakes in the oven, she starts on her *faworki* – a light fried pastry sprinkled with powdered sugar to be served in brown paper cones. Truda's apple strudel is legendary, her filo pastry sheets so thin it's possible to read newspaper print through them. Scattered with thin slices of tart apple and sprinkled with sugar, cinnamon and raisins, the long sausage-shaped pastry is carefully rolled, brushed with melted butter and baked to crisp perfection.

Other delicious goodies are added to the selection as she weighs and mixes and bakes throughout the day, crossing each item off satisfyingly. The kitchen has become unbearably hot, the humidity frizzing her hair, but her passion is baking so she labours on beating, blending, rolling and glazing. Next is Krakow's own version of gingerbread, soft and spicy on the tongue. Then *paczki,* with a filling of fruit jam and dusted with soft powdery sugar and, last but not least, a half-dozen large dome-shaped *babka,* to be sliced into hand-sized wedges.

The used baking tins pile up. Packets of ingredients have become a pile of flattened card and paper, and finally, eight hours later, she sits exhausted, admiring the display she has created. She piles the pastries into large flat-bottomed baskets and covers them with clean white muslin cloths. There's barely time to tackle the mountain of dishes before Stefan appears.

Lifting the cloths he emits a long slow whistle.

'My goodness you've excelled yourself, Truda.'

'Why thank you. It'll be fun tomorrow. Are you going to help?'

'I don't think so. Elena and Stanislaw will be there. You won't need me, will you? You know how I look forward to a good browse through the junk, and remember that antique table I found last month? It made my searching worthwhile and earned us some extra money, didn't it?'

'Yes, that's true. It will be good though if you could drop by for a drink at some point?' Stefan doesn't answer and, removing her apron with a flourish, she cheerfully adds, 'I'll just freshen up and we'll have something to eat.' Humming, she goes to the bathroom.

Stefan smiles to himself. Funny how happy Truda is when she's had her hands in a mixing bowl. What a pity her enthusiasm for baking doesn't extend to other areas of their life.

*

Traders have been arriving in horse-drawn carts and scruffy open-backed vans since early morning. The air is filled with the sound of wheels rumbling on cobblestones and vendors shouting and banging as furniture and wooden crates are unloaded and displayed on the dusty road. People arrive by packed tram, by bicycle and on foot. Every buyer is looking for a bargain and they fill the street, wheeling and dealing over the price of everything from tap handles to rugs, mirrors, old sinks, lamps, pots and pans, clocks, metalware, trinkets, crockery and furniture of every size and description.

Stanislaw, awake since dawn, has already set up a long trestle table, covered it with a cloth and lined up the glasses and drinks in military fashion. Today sees the start of his new venture and he's already decided that if it's successful it could be a weekly occurrence. A rudimentary awning has been erected. If the wind gets up it'll collapse within minutes but he's prepared to overlook that possibility. 'Always be positive,' he told Feliks and Leon as their doubts about its suitability were voiced repeatedly throughout the haphazard erection process.

Elena, resplendent in her best floral dress and with a flower in her hair, arrives laden with bunches of assorted blooms wrapped in brown paper and tied with string. Stanislaw greets her and stands back in admiration with arms outstretched. 'My very own flower, just look at you. Such a beauty and so elegant.' Elena blushes and Stanislaw sorts around for a half-dozen metal buckets. The overall effect is impressive once the flowers have been displayed.

Leon and Amelia are inside the shop chatting and drinking Oranzada. 'Two drinks each,' Stanislaw tells them. 'After that you pay. This isn't a charity function.'

'Tight sod,' Leon whispers to Amelia.

They're discussing their repertoire for the morning. 'We need to keep things upbeat. Get their feet tapping. If anybody asks tell them we're available for all events even if we aren't. Better to get their interest and then say we're fully booked. Don't miss a trick, Amelia, just smile that lovely smile of yours and they won't be able to resist stopping.'

Truda is unloading her baking with Stefan's help, and the delicious smell of freshly baked bread and pastry is mouth-watering. There is hardly room for it all, but this makes for a more impressive display and once she has attached her price list it all looks very professional. Truda finds endless tasks for him, but Stefan is keen to get away.

'I'll leave you to it then,' he says. 'I'd better start browsing before all the best bargains are taken.'

*

The stream of sellers continues to pour into the square and the surrounding streets. The fair grows every week as its reputation as the place to find a bargain grows. Rumours that the odd Fabergé egg and the work of revered but forgotten artists are to be found amongst the junk from other people's attics draws specialist traders, but you are more likely to find an old bicycle than a piece of royal jewellery. Kazimierz is in no way a refined flea market experience. It is brash, full-on and truly immersive.

The fair has been in full swing for two hours, the sale of drinks at Stanislaw's stall is increasing with the intensifying heat and Truda's baking is a huge success. One lady has put in an order for her son's bar mitzvah and a grocer shop in the main market square has enquired about a regular supply of bagels.

Amelia and Leon have had several enquiries. Most promisingly, the owner of the restaurant Starcja in Jakoba Street has asked them to call in and discuss the possibility of a few hours' work each week.

Inside the shop Feliks has a queue of young ladies waiting to be immortalised on paper. It's a long wait, but considered worth it for a close-up of Feliks in all his green-eyed artistic intensity. He's dressed for the occasion and his cotton shirt, undone to the waist, gives a tantalising glimpse of his lean muscular chest. Baggy trousers hang loose around his hips. He periodically rakes his hands through his unruly hair purely for effect. Propped against the counter his recent paintings of jugs are attracting no buyers, although one or two people have expressed an interest in his work. But this is a junk market and they are after a bargain. Feliks expresses faux outrage when he is offered derisory amounts. 'I'm not a cheap street vendor. I'm an artist! No deals!' he exclaims dramatically.

Stanislaw overhearing this clucks and raises his eyebrows. 'I'd have thought anything was better than nothing.'

But Feliks is holding his ground.

Around the central rotunda, food stalls are set up selling sausage with a crusty roll, and the Cracovian pizza-like specialty, *zapiekana*. Hungry stallholders are the first to partake, despite the stench from the butcher shops trading alongside the poultry slaughterhouse and a plague of pestering flies.

Stefan has spent a couple of hours browsing and so far, despite the thousands of items on display, has found nothing of interest. Contemplating the purchase of a cracked oval-framed mirror he is suddenly distracted by the rear view of a woman in a striking red dress. Her glossy dark hair falls across her face as she studies something in her hands. He's admiring the gentle curve of her buttocks and her slim belted waist when the stallholder snaps, 'D'you want that or not?'

'Er. No. It's not quite right. Too small,' he adds, placing it on the floor.

Marianna is looking for cheap decorative items for the flat. As she searches amongst the piles of bric-a-brac, grubby china and dull glass, the sun glints on a small round silver bowl with a lid. She is pushed and shoved by passers-by as she bends to retrieve it.

The stallholder moves closer. 'Very pretty item that, love. Solid silver. Feel the weight.' Marianna looks dubious.

'It'll clean up a treat. Can't go wrong with that,' he says, looking her up and down. 'As you're such a pretty lady I'll give you a special price.'

Marianna ignores him but carries on searching amongst the piles of bric-a-brac and finds a battered square box with a fancy brass clasp.

'Oh! I do like this. It's so pretty,' she says, holding it towards him. 'How much is it, please?'

He gives her a price. She hesitates and he can sense losing a sale. 'Tell you what. I'll do you a deal if you buy both.'

She turns the items over in her hands and stands aside to make room for other customers. 'Let me think about it.'

'You don't need to do that,' Stefan says from behind her. 'You buy the pot, I'll buy the box, give it a good clean-up and it'll be yours.'

Marianna is surprised to see him and taken aback by his suggestion. 'Oh, I'm not sure about that. Perhaps I should just choose.'

'Not at all, it'll be my pleasure,' he insists.

'Well, thank you, that's very kind.'

'Well, I believe that when you see something you like you should have it,' he replies, suppressing a mischievous grin.

'Are you looking for anything in particular?' she asks as he bends to rummage in a large wooden crate.

'No.' He straightens and carries on scanning the junk on the ground. 'Just keeping my eye open for old tools. I get satisfaction in bringing them back to working order but I'm not having much luck today.'

The stallholder grabs an opportunity. 'I've got just the thing for you.'

He reaches into the crate and pulls out a chisel with a chipped blade and a loose handle. 'This here chisel was used to carve the pews in the synagogue right there,' the trader says, pointing across the crowded road.

'Really?' Stefan says, unimpressed. 'So what's your best price?'

'For you, as you're already a valued customer,' he points at Marianna's items, 'I'll let you have that for the same price as the box. Then we'll both be happy. Deal?'

Stefan takes the chisel, rubs the edge of the blade against his thumb, reaches into his pocket and hands over the money.

Pleased with their purchases they move on.

The street is crowded with people jostling and vying for space by the stalls. A small boy pushes past them at full speed.

'Oi! Stop that kid! He's nicking stuff!' A red-faced seller puffs up behind them but stops in his tracks gasping for breath. 'Damn him! Always on the nick that one!' and gives up the chase. The boy disappears into the crowd.

The fair is in full swing now. A pretty woman haggles over the price of a mirror; an old gent tries a walking stick for size; and small boys argue over a box of balsa wood planes. On the pavement two men play a hurried game of chess and agree that whoever wins gets to buy the set.

The sun is high above Szeroka Street and the heat is oppressive as they wander amongst the stalls. Marianna's cheeks have turned red and Stefan's shirt is wet with perspiration. 'We should get a drink,' he suggests.

'That would be lovely. I'm parched. Stanislaw is selling refreshments at the shop, perhaps we should see how they're getting on.'

'Not there.' His hand rests gently on her back. 'I know a better place. It's not far.'

She barely notices where they're going as he walks

beside her, effortlessly weaving through the crowds, directing her down one street and then another, until turning into a narrow alley they stop in front of a pair of battered green doors. There are chalk blackboards on the wall either side displaying a limited menu of potato dumplings stuffed with curd cheese, cabbage soup and warm beetroot with potato salad. Stefan pushes the door open into a small room crammed with people.

'Not in here,' he says. 'Through here, it's quieter and cooler.'

They pass through another set of doors and out into a dingy enclosed courtyard. The towering walls of the surrounding buildings give the space a closed-in secretive feel. Straggly ivy clings to their crumbling surfaces and weeds grow in the cracks in the cobbles underfoot. There are two or three empty metal tables with chairs and they choose one in the furthest corner.

'This will do,' he says. 'What will you have to drink?'

'A beer, please,' she replies.

Marianna feels a little uncomfortable. It's the first time they've been alone and she wonders if they'll find enough to talk about and whether she should be here at all, quickly dismissing such thoughts as fanciful. Where's the harm in having a drink with your nearest neighbour after all?

'Are you pleased with your box?' Stefan asks, shuffling his chair closer to the table.

'Yes of course,' she says, taking the box from the bag and studying the detail.

'Then I'm pleased too. But I think it would be best not to mention it to Truda.'

Marianna nods in agreement. 'I won't mention it to Leon either. He has a tendency towards jealousy,' she lies.

Stefan raises his eyebrows and smiles. 'Then you'd best be careful what you say. I don't want my nose punched.'

She smiles. 'It's a deal.'

Examining the box again she says, 'I love the little bird on the lid. I've always loved birds. The garden at home is full of them and we have chickens and geese too. I love to see them pecking about.'

'I've never known a garden,' Stefan tells her, 'having always lived in the city.'

'Country life can be hard despite the beauty of the surroundings,' she says, 'particularly at the moment. My parents are lucky they have enough land to grow vegetables and keep hens.'

'Your parents must miss you very much,' Stefan says.

'Yes, I'm sure they do and I miss them, of course. They were upset when I left home but I longed for town life and I think they understood. It's early days I know, but I do miss the countryside and it's so busy here in comparison. Have you always lived in town?'

Stefan sighs. 'Yes, I'm afraid so. Growing up I thought living in the country would be good, although I knew nothing of its realities of course. My parents said we were better off here, so we stayed. And now I'm married to Truda and she has no desire to move away, won't even consider it, so I don't bother to mention it anymore. It's a closed subject.' Stefan leans back and folds his arms across his chest.

'So tell me. How did you meet Leon?'

Marianna avoids answering by asking, 'How long have you known him, Stefan?' You seem to know each other fairly well.'

'I've known him since we were youngsters, although he was a few years younger. We never really hit it off. I sometimes wonder if he was jealous of Stanislaw's relationship with me and my brother. He and Stanislaw seemed to clash on a regular basis.' He rests on his elbows and clasps his hands together. 'Anyway you carry on and tell me about you and Leon. How you met and all the gory details.'

Marianna laughs fleetingly and then pauses to consider her answer. 'I think you'd call it a whirlwind romance. How silly does that sound when you say it out loud?' She hesitates. Stefan smiles and for a moment or two she is distracted by the way his lips part and his tongue flicks to the corner of his mouth. 'Go on,' he prompts.

'I met him in a café in Tarnow when he was visiting his aunt. She lived there alone after her brothers moved away when they were young and apparently Leon visited her from time to time, usually when he'd fallen out with his father. It seems they had a difficult relationship.' She lowers her eyes and rests her chin on her hand before continuing. 'Anyway we started meeting. I guess you could say he swept me off my feet. He was fun and I'd never met a musician before. The village boys were dull and unambitious by comparison. His personality was addictive and everything he said seemed interesting. Three months later he asked me to marry him and wouldn't take no for an answer. I've since learnt that what Leon wants, he usually gets. I was a little unsure and had never imagined myself with anyone like him and in hindsight I'm sure the lure of a new life in the city was part of the attraction.'

'How did your parents feel about him?'

Marianna laughed. 'My mother was unsure. "He's not right for you, Marianna," she told me on more than, let me see,' she pretends to count on her fingers, 'ten occasions.' She laughs nervously again. 'My father was more considered in his judgment. He did warn me that I'd struggle to compete with Leon's ego but felt I was old enough to make up my own mind. Said he was sure I'd make a go of it.'

'And are you making a go of it?'

She taps her fingers against her cheek and looks away. 'I'm doing my best.' Talking about Leon is making her uncomfortable and she's keen to change the subject.

'Here's to bargain hunting,' she says, lifting her glass and chinking it against his. 'That's enough about me. How about you? How long have you and Truda been married? I think longer than us novices.'

'It'll be three years in a couple of weeks.'

'Oh. Not that long at all. I assumed longer.'

'There are times when it certainly feels it.' Stefan averts his eyes and sweeps his hair back from his forehead.

'I'm sorry. That was unkind but things aren't always easy. We've known each other since we were teenagers. Truda and her parents moved into the house next door. Despite the age difference we were friends from the start, like brother and sister.' He takes a mouthful of the cool beer. 'Truda's father died in the war and her mother only fairly recently. Both mine died when I was eighteen and Feliks a little younger. Luckily I was able to earn a living and Stanislaw, who had been my father's greatest friend, became our father figure. He kept an eye on us. Leon was younger and we had little in common. Like I said, he and Stanislaw argued constantly about little things.'

'So you and Truda have known each other for a long time?' she says.

'Yes indeed, a long time. We got on well enough but if I'm honest I think we married because it seemed the next logical step.'

Marianna touches Stefan's forearm briefly with her fingertips. 'And will it be a happily ever after story?'

Stefan sighs. 'That remains to be seen. She's been used to being spoiled and the death of her mother was a great loss. I think I'm a pretty tolerant person but I don't respond well to sulks and tantrums. We're very different. But her pastries *are* particularly good.'

They both laugh.

'I love this place because of the people but I'd swap these monstrosities', he gestures at the buildings around them, 'for a simple cottage any day'. Now tell me about life in the country, about quiet, leafy lanes and open spaces.'

'Where do I start? It's idyllic on sunny spring days when the trees are coming into leaf and in summer when the canopies shade the lanes with dappled light.' She pauses but hasn't finished. 'Oh, and autumn is lovely too, the colours are fantastic.' Her imagination is running riot now. 'Oh yes, and winter can be wonderful, especially on days when the snowfall is marked only by the footsteps of birds and icicles drip like lollipops in the warmth of the early morning sun.' She laughs nervously. 'So it seems they are all my favourites! Perhaps when we all know each other better you could visit and judge for yourself.'

'I'd like that very much. Shall we indulge in another beer?'

They talk and laugh and swap stories as café life carries on around them.

'Tell me about your writing,' Stefan says, leaning closer. 'I loved your poem. It was beautiful. Do you write often?'

'I write when I can but not as often as I'd like. I've written a number of short pieces about random subjects that appeal to me for no particular reason. I wrote a story about a chair once and a fairy that was found asleep in a walnut shell with a stamp for a cover. Totally silly, but fun to write.'

'Sounds fun but as you say, silly.' He laughs and pats her hand. 'So what's your favourite piece?'

'It's a description of an imaginary cottage on a clifftop by the sea. I love the sea, although I've only been to the coast once. My mother says I have too much imagination but I believe it's essential if you want to write. Sometimes

I think my head is so full it will burst. When I think of an idea I'm impatient to get the words onto paper. I grab the nearest pencil and paper and write and write until I'm empty, so to speak, and then when it's all written down, I'm content. It's very therapeutic. I keep all my stories in a folder. I suppose there are about sixty now.'

'Has Leon read them?'

'He's read a few. I don't really know what he thinks about them.' She pauses, fiddling with the wedding ring on her finger and he notices how her nose twitches ever so slightly when she's nervous. 'He says they're good but doesn't elaborate in any way. Still, I write them for myself so it doesn't matter.'

'I'd love to read them,' he enthuses, but in case she thinks he's being overfamiliar adds, 'it's a shame to leave them hidden away.'

'Maybe. One day. Perhaps the shortest one, so you don't get bored.'

'I think boring me is something you're never likely to do,' he replies, holding her gaze for a little too long.

A flush spreads across her cheeks. 'And you. Do you have any interests?' She leans in towards him, widening her eyes deliberately. 'Any secret passions in your life?'

'Well, since you ask.' He looks around as if checking for eavesdroppers. 'Nothing of interest to anybody else, just my ridiculous obsession with anything and everything to do with wood.'

'It shows. The chest you gave us was beautiful.'

'I'm pleased you like it. I really enjoyed the carving.

I spend most of my time doing repairs these days and I'd like to do more designing but there are fewer people around who can afford to spend the money. My father always insisted that everything we make should be of the highest quality. We owe it to the tree, he'd insist. I have this fantasy that I'm carving something that will be revered for generations to come. In an amazing building, or a palace maybe. Or somewhere like the Sagrada.'

'The Sagrada? Where's that? I've never heard of it.'

Stefan explains. 'It's a monumental Roman Catholic church being built in Barcelona in Spain.' He lifts his arms above his head and sweeps them sideways and around as if confirming exactly how big the place is. 'It was designed by a famous architect, Antoni Gaudi. Now he was a man with big dreams. He began by designing lampposts of all things. Imagine that. What ambition to start off with a lamppost and finish with a Sagrada. He was influenced by Neo-Gothic styles and Art Nouveau, and because he viewed the natural world as perfect, constantly drew inspiration from all its forms, making his buildings innovative and unique. What ambition. What imagination!'

'It does sound pretty marvellous,' Marianna agrees. 'At least you make it sound so. Tell me more.'

Stefan is carried away now. Truda shows no interest in his fanciful ideas about architecture and art and so this is a conversation that's been a long time overdue. 'The building was started about fifty years ago but remains unfinished, although work still goes on, slowly by all accounts. Gaudi dreamt that his church would be the most famous building in the world. Imagine having even the tiniest input into the interior of a place like that?' He laughs, carried away with his thoughts. 'Just imagine one of my famous bees carved high on the altar and my grandchildren's children pointing, "Ooh look, there's one of Great Granddad's bees!"'

Marianna, elbows on the table, chin cupped in hands, is mesmerised by the warmth and passion in his voice.

'Anyway,' Stefan brings himself reluctantly back down to earth, 'dreaming is an essential part of life. Well, I think so anyway. Without dreams, life would just be a series of days, one leading to another with no sign of anything better or more exciting on the horizon. Even if we don't realise our dreams, the dreaming keeps us alive.'

'And Truda. Does she have dreams?' Marianna asks.

'She certainly does, she dreams of owning her own bakery. It'll be the most exclusive shop in town – artisan of course. A place where all the sweet soft and crisp confections of the baking world are displayed in fantastical style and she is like the magical cake fairy, dressed accordingly of course, who conjures up wondrous delights with the wave of a wand.'

Marianna's expression changes to astonishment.

'Goodness!' she exclaims.

He leans back and stifles a snigger. 'I'm joking! Of course she doesn't. Truda is a lady who dreams have eluded. She's very practical and serious, my wife. I've often told her she should be more ambitious; maybe let the lighter side of life take over occasionally. Not that I can talk. Stuck in my ways at thirty in my cosy little workshop from the Dark Ages. I think running the stall today will give her a bit of a boost. I've told her it's not enough for her to slave away in her kitchen every day with little contact with the customers who enjoy her baking so much; an anonymous person who provides Stanislaw with the best display in his shop. Still, that's up to Truda. She's stubborn and will decide what course to take when it suits her.'

Stefan glances at his watch. 'We should be going. It's one already and it looks very much as if we're in for a downpour.' The sky in the rectangle above them has turned the colour of pewter. A gusty wind blows from nowhere and topples a straggly plant and its pot. They collect their various purchases from beneath the table, he pays for their drinks and they leave.

*

Drops of rain are already spot-marking the pavement and there are the distinctive signs of a storm in the air as the wind picks up and they walk briskly back towards Szeroka Street. Thunder rumbles in the distance and they break into a run as the skies open and a near horizontal deluge of rain begins to fall. Stefan sidesteps into a covered doorway and pulls her in after him. They squeeze close together but still the rain rebounds from the pavement and soaks them.

'Closer,' Stefan urges, wrapping his arms around her waist.

She has her back to him and can feel his breath on her neck. She closes her eyes, relishing the warmth of his body where it touches hers, and breathes in the musty smell of his sweat. Warm rainwater drips from her hair, runs down her face and neck, spreading across her chest like a map. She glances down at his arms held protectively around her; is desperate to touch them but resists. The air is filled with the smell of ozone and the earthy warmth from the doused ground, and as they cower in the semi-dark, Marianna winces at each blinding flash of lightning followed by a violent clap of thunder. The storm is directly overhead.

He squeezes her gently. 'Are you okay?'

She's unable to speak, but nods an affirmation, then another clap of thunder rips the sky above them. She winces and her hands come up to grip his arms instinctively. They're hard and muscular and covered with soft golden hair.

'It's alright,' he whispers, his lips momentarily touching her neck. 'We're safe here.'

The pelting rain persists as disgruntled traders scramble to reload their remaining goods. Horses stand with their heads down, steam rising from their glistening bodies, and water pours from down pipes into gutters unable to cope with the downpour. Unlikely items – an old pram, pots and pans, china cups and glass dishes – have become water vessels, fabrics are sodden and water drips from everything.

As fast as it arrived the storm is rumbling on its way. The sky brightens and the rain eases to a gentle shower.

The wind drops. It's cooler now and Marianna begins to shiver.

Stefan rubs her arms. 'Let's make a dash for it,' he suggests and together they step out onto the glistening cobbles. 'Quick. Before it starts again.'

A mist of condensation rises from the doused ground and windows previously flung wide in the heat are slammed shut against nature's sudden onslaught. Stefan notices Marianna's dress is stuck to her like a second skin and the vision is imprinted on his mind. 'You need to get that off quickly or you're likely to catch a chill,' he says, his eyes lingering on the fullness of her breasts under the saturated cloth.

'You too,' she says, noting the way the fabric of his shirt clings to his broad chest.

They reach home. The stall has been dismantled and the last of the crowds have scurried away to leave the street eerily quiet. Marianna turns, her hair plastered against her head and face. 'Thank you for a lovely morning,' she grins, glancing at her soaked clothing.

Stefan smiles. 'Likewise. The drowned rat look suits you well. We must do it again. Now go and dry yourself before you catch pneumonia.'

*

Marianna closes the door and leans against it with her eyes closed and heart thumping.

'You're back then?' Stanislaw comes through from the back of the shop carrying a crate of rattling empty bottles.

'Look at the state of you. You're absolutely soaked. Storm caught you out by the looks of it and you're making a great wet patch on my newly mopped floor, young lady. Get those shoes off and run upstairs, Leon's wondering where you are. We finished here over an hour ago. The morning has been a great success and he has some new contacts he'll be keen to tell you about.'

Marianna doesn't respond but hurries upstairs.

'Good grief, you look a sight!' Leon exclaims. 'Where the hell have you been for the last four hours? Didn't you see the storm coming? It's been threatening all morning.'

Marianna drops her soaked shoes in the sink and wraps her dripping hair in a towel. 'I've been browsing. The heat was making me feel queasy so I went for a drink and got chatting. I didn't notice the storm coming. I'm so cold, could you make me a hot drink while I dry myself?' She needs to distance herself from him until she calms down. 'I gather from Stanislaw you've had a successful morning?' she calls back as she leaves the room.

'Yes. Well, if you'd been there you'd know,' Leon sulks.

Marianna collects dry clothes and goes to the bathroom. She strips naked and dries herself briskly, all the while muttering between clenched teeth. He's clearly disinterested in who she may have been chatting with and there's not a word of concern that she's soaked to the skin. Typical. She is glad she didn't stand around all morning watching him perform. Mr Charming, Mr Bloody Perfect. Well, damn him. She presses the towel to her face and starts to cry. Her emotions are in turmoil and she's hungry. Beer on an empty stomach was not a good idea. She blows her nose into the wet towel and flings it into the bath. Her face is blotchy so she runs her hands under the tap and presses her fingers against her eyes. *Come on, Marianna,* she tells herself, *pull yourself together, after all you're supposed to be making the best of it.*

'That's better, you look more like your old self now,' Leon comments when she reappears. 'Here's your drink. Now sit down and hear my news.'

She sits, playing the dutiful wife, but in her mind she's in Stefan's arms on that doorstep in the rain.

Leon paces about as he launches into a dialogue of self-congratulation. 'Amelia and I were top notch today. Played better than ever before and at one point we had well over twenty people clapping along enthusiastically. We played to the crowd, of course, all the old favourites. Amelia looked particularly attractive so the men were reluctant to move on. She's certainly a looker that girl. Nothing but an asset, I'd say.'

He pauses for a moment, clearly distracted by the thought of Amelia. 'Anyway, how many enquiries do you think we got?'

'What?' She doesn't really care. 'I've no idea. Several by the sounds of it.'

'Guess.'

'I don't know, Leon. It could be any number.'

'Well, try. Indulge me.'

'Ten?'

'Don't be ridiculous we were only playing for four hours. Three. We got a booking for a bar mitzvah, but the most promising was from the proprietor of that new restaurant Starcja I told you about. He wants us to do a late-night set twice a week. They're paying a pittance but beggars can't be choosers, so we've agreed to go along this evening to audition. So what d'you think?'

Marianna tries to summon up enthusiasm.

'Well, it's good that you'll be earning some money but I'm not very happy about you being out so often.'

'You'll get used to it. I'm sure you'll find something to do. Perhaps you could write a book.' He sniggers and leans across to pat her hand patronisingly. 'We just need to get you sorted out with some more work.'

'I don't particularly want more work. I'm quite happy working alongside Stanislaw in the shop, although perhaps he could give me a few more hours. Even if he doesn't we'll still have enough to live on after we've paid him the rent.'

'I'll try and talk the old miser into lowering it a bit but it won't be easy. He's got money on the brain. Now come and sit by me and show me what bargains you've found.'

She unwraps the silver pot and displays it on the palm of her hand. 'Isn't it pretty?'

'I suppose so. Not much to show for a four-hour shopping trip.'

'I saw lots of lovely things I liked but was reluctant to spend the money. You should be pleased you've a thrifty wife.'

'I'm very pleased I've a pretty wife. Come here.' He kisses her forehead. 'You've lots of other things I'm pleased you have.'

Marianna's heart sinks.

*

Truda is standing by the sink, elbow deep in washing-up suds when Stefan arrives home, his clothes plastered to him like a second skin.

'You're back then. I was beginning to worry.' She glances at the clock on the wall above her. 'You've usually finished browsing by eleven.'

'I know but I've been dithering over possible purchases and it seems I left my bargaining skills at home today. I ended up with this and a small chair that needs some work but will be worth selling on.' He's already hidden the box for Marianna in his workshop.

Truda wipes her hands on her apron. 'Let's have a look then and you'd better get changed. You're soaked.'

Stefan hands her the chisel wrapped in newspaper and goes to get dried off. Truda looks peeved when he returns and has resumed her chores.

'Are you joking, Stefan. Is that it? A chisel? I've been slaving away in the scorching heat all morning and all you've found is a chisel?'

Stefan refuses to rise to the bait. 'Some days are better than others. That's how it goes.' He changes the subject. 'Did you sell all your baking?'

'Yes.'

'And?'

'That's it. I sold it all.'

She slams around with saucepans. 'Everyone said how good the stall looked. Stanislaw thinks we should do it again. Perhaps you could lend a hand next time. It was hard work on my own. In fact it was two days' hard work.'

Stefan can sense she's on the verge of a tantrum and has no time for it. What he really wants is to sit quietly and relive his conversation with Marianna.

'Of course I'll give you a hand next time. Pass me that cloth and I'll help you clear up.'

# Four

Tomas is lurking around outside Stanislaw's shop with intent. He has had his eye on the property for a while and has it shortlisted for rich pickings, but the fat shopkeeper is usually there and alert. This morning there's no sign of him so he slips inside. There's bread and cake on a table within easy reach and broken biscuits in a metal box, the lid conveniently open. Cheese under a glass dome could be a little trickier to reach. He's going for the biscuits and is about to help himself when the sound of tuneful humming stops him in his tracks.

Marianna pops up from beneath the counter clutching an armful of packets. 'Oh!' she squeals.

Tomas exclaims, taking a step backwards, hands held aloft and eyes wide. 'I weren't touchin, nuffinck. Honest.'

He's only nine years old but streetwise beyond his years. His ill-fitting clothes are worn thin. Baggy sleeves dangle over grimy hands and his trousers are frayed at the hems. His shoes are worn down at the heel and the laces are undone. Thick black hair stands out like dry thatch above his red sticky-out ears and he has the largest, darkest eyes Marianna has ever seen. He looks hungry.

'Hello. Can I help you, young man?'

He turns and makes for the door, but Marianna calls, 'Don't go.' Something about him is familiar. 'I've seen you before.' She leans on the counter to look closer. 'Yes. I remember. It was two weeks ago. You nearly knocked me over in the market.'

He takes a step backwards, removes his cap. Wrings it in his hands, shuffling from side to side. 'No, Miss. Not me. Like I said. I ain't done nuffinck. Not been near no market.' His ears have turned purple.

Marianna comes out from behind the counter and squats beside him. She reaches for his hand but he pulls back out of reach. She tries again and he lets her take his dirty fingers in her own soft hand.

'Would you like something to eat?' she asks quietly.

He nods. Eyes downcast.

She leads him to a chair by the window, catching a whiff of his stale body and dirty hair. Tomas has never seen such a pretty woman and his eyes follow her as she moves around collecting bread, a thin slice of sausage and a bottle of fizzy Oranzada and places them on the table in front of him. It's two days since he last ate.

'I'm Marianna. What's your name?'

'Tomas,' he mumbles, chewing ravenously on the bread.

She waits for him to finish. 'Where are your parents?'

'Dead. Bofe of 'em. Gonners. They was really old.'

'Do you live nearby?'

He points randomly. 'Over there. Wiv me bruvver. He's a drunk. I look after meself.'

She nods. His situation is becoming clearer now that she remembers what happened in the market.

'You do know that if you carry on stealing you'll get into trouble?'

'Can't do nuffinck about that. No choice.'

'There's always a choice, Tomas.'

Silence.

'What if I said I might be able to help you. Pay you for doing a few odd jobs. How d'you feel about that?'

'It'd be alright I s'pose,' he says and shrugs his shoulders. 'Yeah.'

Marianna smiles her sweetest smile. Tomas's eyes widen further. She's treated him like a small, injured bird and he thinks she must be a princess. With an arm around his shoulder she leans down, close to his ear. A cloud of sweet femininity envelops him.

'Then I'll have a word with the wicked shopkeeper.' She grimaces playfully. 'I'll see what he can do. I can't promise anything but I'll do my best.'

He turns to leave.

'You'll come back, won't you?' she asks.

Tomas, reaching the shop door, hesitates for a moment then runs towards her and flings his arms around her legs.

*

Stanislaw has enjoyed a substantial lunch followed by a practically instantaneous snooze. Lately he has realised that being a man of increasing years these little breaks are necessary and give him a chance to mull over new ideas. He is congratulating himself on the decision to employ Marianna when she appears in the doorway.

'Just the person I wanted to see. Now that you've had a chance to familiarise yourself with the stock, I'll show you how to work the till so you can serve the customers when I'm not around. It can be tricky, there's a knack to gaining access without losing the tips of your fingers.' His bandaged thumb is testament to a loss of concentration the previous day.

'Oh, and don't forget, the customer is always right, even when they're wrong. I'm not averse to suggestions either, especially if you come up with any money-saving or money-making ideas, in which case I'll be all ears.'

Marianna judges this is the perfect time to approach him regarding Tomas. She doesn't tell Stanislaw that she caught him about to steal, as in Marianna's ideal world everybody deserves a second chance. Neither does she divulge his filthy state and that of his clothing. She'll deal with that if Stanislaw agrees to her proposal.

'There is something I was going to mention. There was a young boy here earlier. We got chatting and the poor lad is desperate to earn a little money. His parents are dead and he and his brother are finding it tough keeping themselves fed.'

'Who is this boy? Where's he from?'

'He lives over that way.' Marianna gestures vaguely towards the square.'A few streets away, I'm not sure exactly where. He's only nine years old, but he seems astute and intelligent. He's a pleasant-looking lad and seems likeable.'

'And what exactly do you have in mind? Don't forget things aren't looking good money-wise. Now's not the time to increase expenditure.'

'I was thinking maybe we could get him to sweep out front and do a few simple odd jobs. Running errands, that sort of thing.'

'Hmm,' Stanislaw mutters unenthusiastically. 'Would we have enough for him to do?'

Marianna nods, adding, 'I think so and I thought of something else that would keep him occupied. Mrs Cohen gave me the idea.'

Stanislaw's ears prick up. 'Go on.'

'She has such trouble walking nowadays she wondered if we could offer a delivery service. Tomas knows the area well. We could get him a second hand bike, one with a basket, and he could deliver the orders. We could give him a little money and supplement it with a loaf of bread or some sausage perhaps.'

Stanislaw is thinking. He rubs his chin with his thumb and forefinger. 'Hmm. Not a bad idea.' He paces up and down for a while, scratching the back of his head.

'You're not just a pretty face, my lovely. I wish I'd thought of it myself. When can he start?'

*

Leon has joined Amelia downstairs for one of their frequent rehearsal sessions on the day Tomas is transformed. Marianna has asked him to come to the shop after lunch when she knows Leon will be out of the way for a couple of hours and Stanislaw will be busy with afternoon shoppers. She doesn't want him to see Tomas until he's cleaned up so she's used some of her wages to buy him second hand clothes: two pairs of grey flannel shorts, a couple of collarless cotton shirts, a multi-coloured striped woollen pullover, a pair of smart black ankle boots and knee-length grey socks.

Tomas waits outside until Marianna considers the coast is clear. An opportunity presents itself when Stanislaw needs to fetch something from the storeroom. Marianna rushes to the shop door, beckons Tomas over and ushers him in. 'Upstairs quickly now. Second floor. I'll be up in a minute.'

Tomas is up the stairs like greased lightning but hesitates on the landing and looks back at Marianna watching from the stairwell.

'Go on,' she hisses. 'Keep going.'

She hears his clomping footsteps fade and the door to the flat click shut.

Minutes later Stanislaw returns and Marianna makes her getaway. Tomas is standing by the window watching the pigeons feed on the windowsill when she joins him. 'Stinkin' things they are.'

Marianna laughs. 'Listen to the pot calling the kettle black. Come here and sit down. Before we start I want you to listen carefully to what I say.'

Tomas sits down and tucks his hands under his thighs.

'Okay, listen carefully, Tomas. There are a few rules you must stick to if you're to make a success of this…' she pretends to be searching for the right word, …'adventure.'

His eyes widen. 'Rules. What rules?' He's suspicious. Rules mean regulations and obedience.

'Don't worry, it's a very short list. Firstly, you must never be late for work – Stanislaw is a stickler for good timekeeping. Secondly, you must always be clean and smart. He's very fastidious. And last but not least never take anything from the shop without asking. We'll be fair to you as long as you stick to the rules. All I ask is that you don't let yourself down and I feel sure you won't do that.' She pauses. 'Any questions?'

Tomas thinks for a moment. 'What's fastid – id – ious?'

'It means he's very concerned about matters of cleanliness.'

He glances at his dirty knees then looks up at her and grins.

'So. Come on, let's get you sorted out. You can have a bath here today and once a week as long as Leon is out. It's best he doesn't know, he can be a little grumpy at times and neither of us has time for grumpiness I'm sure.'

At this moment in time, Tomas believes that if Marianna asked him to cut off his left ear and feed it to a starving dog he would willingly oblige.

'When did you last have a bath?' she asks, busying herself with towels.

'Can't remember.'

She hands him a square block of soap that smells strongly of disinfectant and a scrappy piece of cloth that serves as a flannel. Steam escapes from under the boiler lid, indicating the water is heated, so she transfers several bucketsful to the bath and tests the temperature with her hand. He looks petrified.

'You'll enjoy it I'm sure. I hope I recognise you when you've finished.' She ruffles his hair. 'And then we'll tackle this mop.'

When she's gone he takes his filthy clothes off, drops them in a pile on the floor, leans over the bath and swishes his hands around for a while before cautiously stepping in. The water just about covers him if he lies flat and pulls in his tummy. He relishes the hot water permeating every pore. Sniffing the large block of greasy soap he wrinkles his nose with disgust then turns it over and over in his hands enjoying the smooth slipperiness. It escapes his grasp time and again as he chases it about in the murky water.

Slathering himself from top to toe he slides back and forth creating a wave, slopping water over the edge of the bath. A grey scum lifts from his body, floats away and clings to the side. Kneeling, he lifts the damp net curtain at the window and makes a pattern on the steamy glass with his forefinger.

Outside, the high walls cast deep shadows and block the sunlight. Pigeons coo on the windowsill. He raps on the glass to frighten them off.

'Go away!'

He bangs harder and they oblige with a panicky escape. Laughing he slips back into the water, sinks below the grimy surface, holds his nose until he runs out of breath then sits up suddenly, gasping for air. He tips his head back to lay the soapy cloth over his face and lies soaking until the water turns cool.

Stepping out into a puddle of water, he wraps himself in a faded brown towel, drapes another over his head, opens the bathroom door and drips his way across the landing to the living room.

'Aha! There you are. Well? How was it?' she asks, lifting the towel from his face.

'Was alright,' he says, but secretly he has enjoyed it very much.

'Good. Now dry yourself quickly and we'll tackle that mop of yours.' She points to his hair with her scissors and makes a snip snip action. Marianna has propped a mirror against a heavy pan on the table. 'If you wouldn't mind sitting here,' she says, positioning a chair so that he can watch her work.

'Now, sir, how would you like your hair cut today?'

He shrugs. 'Dunno. Leave it to you.'

'You might regret that,' Marianna laughs and begins to snip away as if she were a professional. Tomas sits still as a statue watching every move from under long dark lashes.

'You have lovely hair,' Marianna tells him. He peers at her and nibbles at his bottom lip, embarrassed. She stands back. 'There. All done. What d'you think?'

He pretends to appraise her work, turning his head from side to side. 'Yeah. It's alright. You done a good job.'

'I'm pleased you're pleased. Now get dressed and let's see you looking like a new man.'

Tomas's skin has been scrubbed until it glows. His fingernails are clean, his hair glossy and his eyes shining. He likes what he sees.

'I look dandy, I do, Miss.'

Marianna places a hand affectionately on his shoulder. 'Then let's go and introduce you to your new boss.'

*

They ease him into his new probationary position as grocery assistant and Tomas takes to his role like a duck to water. After two weeks Stanislaw and Marianna confirm that he's now a bona fide full-time member of the staff at Stanislaw's grocery store and present him with a fancy handmade certificate. Tomas almost explodes with pride, Marianna sheds a tear and Stanislaw gives himself a pat on the back for yet another inspirational idea.

# Five

Later that day Marianna is stacking goods on a high shelf, standing precariously on the top rung of a wooden ladder that wobbles with the slightest movement, when she is startled by a whistle from behind.

'Anybody serving today?'

She backs down carefully.

'Not your usual time of day for handouts, Feliks.'

'Well, I'm certainly not here to buy anything.'

'So what do you want?'

'I've got a proposition for you.'

'For me?' She faces him across the counter now, her interest aroused.

'It's about my work.'

'Your work?' she repeats.

'Yes. My art,' he says, raising his eyebrows, adding sarcastically, 'you know, that thing nobody believes is actually work.'

'Ah,' she says. 'Okay, I'm with you now. Carry on.'

'The thing is, I need a challenge and I want people's perception of me as an artist to change. My jugs may be magnificent but are they enough? I thought I'd managed to capture their beauty but it seems they have little appeal for others.' He sighs dramatically. Marianna hides a smile and takes a seat by the window. Feliks joins her.

'I need to create a new body of work – something different and exciting. Even, dare I say it, a little risqué.'

'I thought you loved painting portraits… and jugs,' she adds cheekily.

'I do, but my work needs to appeal to a wider audience.'

'Do you have anything in mind?'

Feliks closes his eyes, adopting a dreamlike expression, and brushes his hand across his forehead dramatically. 'I need to explore the female form.'

Marianna raises an eyebrow.

He wags his finger at her. 'I know what you're thinking,' he leans forward conspiratorially, 'and this, darling girl, is where you come in.'

'Really? Where is this line of thought going, Feliks?' she asks suspiciously.

Adopting his most persuasive voice and a variety of expressive hand movements he launches into a list of the reasons why she would make the perfect model.

'Number one. You are very beautiful.' He emphasises the point by drawing a voluptuous figure eight shape in the air with his arms. 'Two. You've an air of innocence about you,' at this point he adopts a coy look, lowering his eyes and placing a finger on his lip, 'and three, you're available.'

Marianna laughs, raising an eyebrow. 'Oh, I'm available, am I? You cheeky devil!'

'Well, I certainly hope so. This is an opportunity you shouldn't miss, young lady. Rest assured this is not an excuse for me to gaze at you for hours, though it would be a pleasure to do so. No. I'm strictly professional and would approach this as if I were painting a vase of flowers, or a bowl of fruit.'

Marianna protests but he carries on.

'I'm not giving up on jugs entirely. I've thought this through long and hard.' He paces about, his ideas a jumble as he gabbles on. 'Oh yes! I can see you now. Not entirely nude, that would be too much, but imagine this. There you are, discreetly holding a vessel of some sort with drapes strategically placed for your modesty. I would paint a series of works depicting everyday objects alongside the human form.' He looks at her intently.

'Go on,' she says but looks doubtful. His explanation is not winning her over.

'Listen to me. I'm serious. Each person is unique. Do you not agree?' He doesn't wait for her to respond. 'And these paintings would be groundbreaking in that they would display the complexity of the human form alongside everyday objects. A cracked jug would represent the fragility of life, for instance.'

Marianna is having trouble keeping a straight face.

'Honestly, Feliks, what are you talking about?'

Feliks places his hand roughly where his heart is.

'Darling girl. You don't know me very well. Not yet. But I assure you I'm most sincere.'

He sinks to the ground on one knee.

'I implore you. Be my muse. My inspiration.'

'Oh, do get up, Feliks,' she laughs, 'if anybody comes in they'll think you're proposing.'

'Think about it.' He puts his hands together as if praying and pleads, 'Please. I need help and you need salvation from a life of packet tea and broken biscuits.' He blows her an exaggerated kiss. 'I must go now. I have canvases to prepare.' He pauses in the doorway and with a final flourish announces, 'Creativity takes courage. Help me be brave, Marianna.' With a final toss of his head he steps out onto the pavement and trips over a loose cobble.

*

Leon's reaction to Feliks' suggestion has been one of total indifference and it incenses Marianna that he's apparently unconcerned about her taking her clothes off in front of another man. This is not, she tells herself, normal behaviour. A little jealousy wouldn't have gone amiss and so, defiant in the face of disinterest, here she is about to embark on a new venture, excited and apprehensive in equal measure. She has arrived at the studio early hoping, to catch a glimpse of Stefan in his workshop, but the door is closed and there's no sound from within. She continues along the dingy corridor and, pushing aside the curtain that serves as a door, enters the studio doubling as Feliks' living and sleeping accommodation. A single-storey, bare-brick extension with a glass roof is attached to the rear of the house where finished paintings are stacked randomly. The walls are covered with charcoal drawings and there's a fine film of black ash on the floor beneath. Shelves are stacked with old books, magazines, newspapers and jars of brushes that have seen better days. There are two large easels, one displaying a half-completed portrait, another placed strategically opposite a low couch covered with faded throws. Piled high in a wooden crate are used rags, stiff with dried paint and rank with the toxic smell of turpentine. An oval occasional table, once an elegant piece of furniture, is heaped with a jumble of open tubes, squeezed into tortured shapes from which fresh paint oozes.

The living area is surprisingly tidy and sparsely furnished with a large bed, a table and a couple of Stanislaw's old armchairs. The only luxury item is a radio given to Feliks in lieu of payment for a portrait. He'd been furious not to receive its monetary value but the radio has proved its worth on numerous occasions whilst entertaining his lady friends.

Feliks is lounging in one of the armchairs when Marianna appears. 'Darling girl,' he exclaims, jumping up to greet her. 'Do come in. Make yourself comfortable.' He puffs up the squashed cushion on his chair. 'I consider it an honour that you've come but we need to get things straight from the start. I think we should treat today as a gentle introduction. I certainly don't expect you to stand naked for hours.' He clears his throat. 'Not yet anyway.'

Marianna wants to make her position clear. 'I won't be able to sit for you more than a couple of times a week but I'm happy to help you out because I'd really like to see you make a success of your art.'

Feliks nods. 'This is all fine with me, darling, now let me get you a drink and we'll have a chat and get to know each other a little better.' He busies himself making a pot of coffee.

Marianna is impressed by the work on display and wanders around the studio flicking through his sketchbooks and studying the work stacked against the walls. Coffee made, Feliks settles himself, his legs draped across the arm of his chair.

'Tell me all about yourself,' Marianna says. 'I've heard other people's opinions but I'd like to hear about Feliks from the horse's mouth, so to speak.'

'Hmm. Now where shall I start?' He taps his fingertips together and closes his eyes.

Marianna suggests, 'The beginning is always a good place.'

Feliks adjusts his position and leans forward enthusiastically, pleased to be talking about himself. 'I've always been an artist. When I was a child, all I wanted to do was draw. Anywhere I could find a blank surface. Decent paper was scarce so I'd use the insides of packets, even the spaces around the edge of a newspaper. The best present I ever got was a set of lead pencils and I used those until they were too short to hold. At school I was frequently caught drawing under my desktop. I remember doing a charcoal drawing of our headmaster once who instantly confiscated it, although there was a strong rumour that it appeared on his living room wall shortly afterwards.'

Marianna is attentive. 'That is quite a compliment. What else did you draw?'

'Oh, all sorts of things. Mother's cooking pans, my father's carpentry tools. I still have those somewhere. Perhaps I should give them to Stefan.' He pauses. 'Funny, I've never thought of doing that before.'

'Sometimes I'd perch myself on a wooden box in Stanislaw's shop and draw the customers as they stood chatting at the counter. I think that's when portraiture became my main passion.'

'Did you ever draw your parents?'

'No, I didn't. Art was a sore subject in our house. Although my mother tried to encourage me my father was dead against it. Said it wasn't manly. Truth be told, she indulged me. Spoilt me, some would say.'

'Really? And how did Stefan feel about that?'

'I came along four years after Stefan. Rather unexpectedly, I gather. My parents were always at loggerheads over something or other so I was something of a surprise. Stefan was a perfect brother from the start and I looked up to him. He would sometimes take the blame for things I'd done and often became the butt of my practical jokes though he didn't seem to mind. We were complete opposites in lots of ways. Whilst I was outgoing and boisterous, he was quiet and reserved. He excelled at school; I was disinterested in anything other than art and frequently bunked off. One day when I didn't turn up they went looking for me and found me lying on my back under a big oak tree in the square, drawing a worm's eye view and detailing every leaf and twig so realistically they looked as if they were being fluttered by the wind.'

'What did your father say about all this?'

'My father? He didn't approve at all and constantly whined on about me being so unlike my brother. I think that's why Mother was on my side, to compensate for his disinterest. Stefan could have resented me for that but he didn't. I think he felt Father was excessively critical. Some say Stefan is a soft touch because of the way he supports me but he's not, he's just caring, even though I know I've let him down on more than one occasion. Despite it all he still has faith in me.'

'Why wouldn't he?' Marianna asks. 'You're very talented.'

'My father often told me that I wouldn't amount to anything. Until his dying day he refused to acknowledge that art was the only career I wanted and it was then, from what Stefan has told me, that he had a change of heart. So now I suppose that's why proving I can be successful is so important.' He sits quietly for a moment then offers her another drink.

Marianna passes him her mug.

Feliks sighs theatrically. 'Trouble is I'm not very good at getting on with it.'

'Why not? You just need a little encouragement and success will surely come your way.'

'Like I said, creativity takes courage and time, with no distractions. I'm too fond of the ladies, that's my problem.'

Marianna waits while Feliks sips at his drink.

'At school, when I was very small, the girls got more attention than the teachers. I'd woo them with unwelcome gifts.'

'Like what?'

'Creepy boys' things like a dead worm in a matchbox for instance, or a collection of woodlice from under the mat inside the front door.'

Marianna makes a face.

'Or a butterfly pinned to a piece of card. All these offerings made once they'd been drawn, of course. I suppose women are my addiction. Well, I don't drink too much, or smoke. I can't afford to.'

'So I take it you haven't found your true love?'

Feliks snorts. 'Good God no! The women I meet are like my artwork. Colourful, but unfinished works in progress,' he laughs. 'I'm too selfish to share my life with anybody, though I suppose there must be a woman out there who'll be able to cope with me and love me warts and all. I'm convinced that when I'm a success and have some money behind me, Miss Right will come along and I'll never look at another woman again. In the meantime?' Feliks winks at Marianna.

'You'll be lucky,' she responds.

He produces a pencil and some paper from the shelf behind him. 'Today's the start of a new phase in my life. We have work to do, young lady. It may not have been said yet but the principle of true art is not to portray but to evoke.'

Marianna laughs and slips out of her clothes.

*

Stefan is chipping away at a section of woodworm on an old table when the sound of laughter reaches him from along the corridor. He pauses for a moment to listen, but there is only silence. Then, suddenly, there it is again. Feliks clearly has company, but something in the lilting quality of the visitor's voice seems familiar. He downs tools and slips into the hallway. The curtain is drawn back and Marianna emerges. Feliks lifts her hand and kisses her knuckles in a show of exaggerated admiration.

'Thank you, darling girl. I knew we would make a great team, so until next time.' He backs away, blowing kisses until he's out of sight.

Stefan's blood runs cold. Too shocked to move he's still there when Marianna turns and comes towards him.

'Hello, Stefan,' Marianna beams

Stefan scowls, his face like thunder. 'Oh, it's you!'

Her smile fades. 'Whatever's wrong?'

He places his hand firmly under her elbow and steers her into the workshop, slamming the door behind them.

'Stefan. What is this?'

'You tell me! I can't believe this of you. You know what he's like; his reputation with women is legendary. You must have noticed that at the party, the way he looked at you, the way he touched you.'

Marianna is speechless and feels a little wobbly. She leans on the workbench for support, one hand to her forehead, disbelieving.

'Am I really hearing this? What's wrong with you?'

Stefan flops down in his chair, glaring.

Marianna is furious. 'Will you just let me explain? Not that I owe you any kind of explanation. What I do is none of your damn business. This outburst can only mean one thing and I can't believe you would think that of me. I'm helping Feliks, that's all, and I've no qualms about doing so. There's nothing untoward about our arrangement. He respects me, which is more than you appear to do. I'm more than insulted, Stefan.'

He's on his feet in an instant.

'Marianna, please. I'm so sorry. I'm such an idiot. I've obviously made a mistake.'

'You're right about that! You have. If my husband doesn't object I've no idea what gives you the right to talk to me like this.'

He shakes his head. 'I have no right, none whatsoever. I'm so sorry. I hope my outburst won't spoil our friendship.'

'What friendship?' she snaps back at him. 'You hardly

know me.' The door slams in his face as she makes her exit.

*

Marianna is furious. How dare he! Who the hell does he think he is! She stomps about the flat recalling the conversation and seething with anger, but at least she'd had the last word and he deserved it. She throws a book at the wall and it crashes to the floor, the spine broken. Men! Collapsing into a chair she covers her face with her hands and begins to cry. Hot angry tears flow freely and slowly, and the blame rests solely with her husband's indifference. If he'd had any misgivings about her being there she never would have agreed to Feliks' request. Her crying turns to great racking sobs. Well, damn you both! After a while she calms a little, sniffs, wipes her eyes and takes a deep breath.

She retrieves the broken book and regrets having damaged it in her fit of pique. It was a stupid thing to do. She loves books and it's become a habit of hers to underline in pencil those sections she particularly likes, marking the pages with slips of red ribbon. She hopes one day she'll be able to write something that will move another person to highlight her words in the same way. She loves the act of writing, the way the pencil glides across the paper, the words transferring from her mind through its tip and onto the page.

She chooses a book from the shelf and, removing a slip of silk, reads one of her favourite quotes.

*I'll spread my wings and I'll learn to fly*
*I'll do what it takes, till I touch the sky*
*But what if I fall?*
*Oh but my darling*
*What if you fly?*

There are times when Marianna is a little afraid of herself, but she flew today and it was liberating.

*

Leon is buzzing with his own brilliance. He and Amelia have written two new songs and they hope tonight's second audition at the café will lead to regular work.

'Well, that went well,' he says, hugging Marianna and kissing the curve of her neck. 'Two new songs in the bag today.'

Marianna doesn't respond.

'Mm, Soup smells good. It's nice to know my wife has slaved over a hot stove just for me.'

'I haven't actually, Leon. If you recall I've been to Feliks' studio.'

'Oh yes. And how did that go? Did he seduce you?' He wiggles his fingers and then fondles her breasts like an adolescent.

'Don't do that, Leon, and don't be ridiculous. We had a long conversation and it was very interesting. He's a complex character underneath that flippant exterior. I think he lacks self-confidence.'

Leon huffs. 'Feliks? Are we talking about the same person?'

'Yes, we are. He needs somebody to steer him in the right direction, he's clearly very talented. Some of his artwork is beautiful and his use of colour is remarkable.'

Leon's eyes have glazed over. 'Jolly good. So when will your first joint masterpiece be on display?'

Marianna can't be bothered with Leon when he's like this. She's learnt that the less she responds to his negative comments the happier she remains.

'Come and sit down. Soup's ready,' she says and they eat for a while in an uncomfortable silence.

'I saw Stefan today,' Marianna says. 'I was thinking it would be nice to spend more time with him and Truda. I could get to know them a little better. How do you feel about us inviting them to supper one evening? Nothing fancy of course. If I'm careful all week I'm sure I'll be able to rustle up something tasty.'

Leon looks at her and then carries on eating.

'Well?' she prompts.

He shrugs. 'Why not? I haven't had much chance to chat to Truda since we got back. We've a lot of catching up to do.'

Marianna grasps the moment. 'Good. I'll invite them for Friday. Is that alright?'

'Not Friday, Amelia and I are hoping it will be our debut at the restaurant if tonight goes well.'

'Saturday then?'

Leon hesitates. 'Okay, Saturday. I'll leave it to you

and hopefully you can show them what a lucky chap I am.'

*

Tomas hands the note to Stefan in time to coincide with his lunch break. It reads: 'Marianna and Leon hope you can join them for an informal evening of food, lively conversation and, hopefully, a smattering of laughter. Saturday at seven.'

On a separate piece of paper she scribbles a quick apology: 'Can we start again? I'm sorry I slammed the door in your face. I may have overreacted. So did you, so I think that makes us even? Please come, Marianna.'

He tucks the invitation in his pocket. Marianna's note is placed in the wooden box marked pending.

# Six

Truda usually brings Stefan's lunch to the workshop. It's a routine they rarely break, but today he turns the sign on the door to closed, turns the key in the lock and makes his way upstairs.

Truda is humming and putting away the pans from the morning's baking session when Stefan appears.

'Oh! You startled me.' She glances at the clock. 'It's only twelve thirty. Is everything alright? I was coming down shortly.'

She plants a kiss lightly on his cheek. It's a sure sign the baking has gone well.

'Everything's fine. I thought I'd save you a trip. I know you've been magicking up some new delights for Stanislaw. How did the baking go? Can I try?'

Truda likes him referring to her baking as magical. She thinks the mixing of ingredients is comparable to that of making spells. Combine them in the right quantities and the result can be just that.

'It went very well thank you. Here, try one of these and see what you think. Sara gave me the idea from one of her mother's recipes. I've tweaked it a bit but I think they've turned out well.'

Stefan nibbles at the pastry, concentrating. 'Absolutely delicious.'

'And they are so simple to make,' Truda elaborates. 'Just mix flour and butter together, add eggs, evaporated milk and vanilla. Then you roll it out and cut them into these lovely knotted shapes and fry them in oil. The recipe says to sprinkle them with cocoa powder, but it's difficult to get hold of and I think the white sugar looks just as good.'

'I'm sure they'll be a great success. Clever girl.'

They chat while she finishes tidying.

'Will you stay and have a bite to eat?' she asks.

Stefan's reply is far from enthusiastic. 'I was hoping to take something back to the workshop. I've almost finished the repair to Michal's sewing table and would like him to have it today.'

She looks a little disappointed.

'I'll stay if you'd like me to,' he adds, eager not to upset her.

Truda removes her apron and tucks stray strands of hair behind her ears. 'No. It's fine.' She hands him a plate of pickled vegetables and bread. 'There's fresh coffee in the pot. I promised Sara I'd take her a sample of the pastries so I might as well go now and have something myself when I get back, although I expect she'll want me to stay for a chat.'

'If you're sure? I'll be able to start on the new frame for the bedroom window later, if I can carry on working.'

Truda is about to leave and Stefan is going to miss his chance. 'Oh! Before you go, I forgot to mention that Leon and Marianna have invited us to supper on Saturday. I said I'd get back to them once I'd spoken to you.'

Truda looks unsure. 'Oh. I don't know, Stefan.' She fiddles nervously with the buttons on her top. 'I'm not sure Marianna likes me very much.'

'Why on earth wouldn't she?' He puts his arms around her waist, tilts her chin. 'You silly old thing, you hardly know each other. It's the perfect opportunity to get together and Leon will be so disappointed if we don't go. I know how well you two get along.'

She laughs. 'Alright then, but if I feel uncomfortable I'll give you a sign and we won't stay too long.'

Stefan is relieved. 'Whatever you want, it'll be fun. Now go and stun Sara with your latest delicacies and while you're there get her to give you the weather forecast for the rest of the week.'

Truda slaps his arm. 'Don't be mean!'

She piles the pastries in a basket, covers them with a cloth, slips on her sturdy outdoor shoes and with a cheerful wave leaves.

Stefan waits until he hears the front door slam, balances the plate of food in one hand, carries the coffee pot in the other and follows.

He hurriedly unlocks the workshop, leaves his lunch on the workbench and is next door just as Marianna arrives for her lunchtime shift. They greet each other as if the previous day's confrontation hasn't happened.

'Thank you for the invitation,' he says cheerily. 'We'd like that very much.'

'Oh! Good,' Marianna responds, trying not to sound too enthusiastic. She busies herself behind the counter.

'Anything we can bring?'

'No. Just yourselves.' She fiddles with the till, looks up and smiles. 'See you at seven on Saturday then.'

Stefan nods. 'Yes. See you at seven.'

Marianna calls to Tomas. 'Mrs Cohen's order is ready when you are.' It's clearly a sign that their conversation is over.

He lifts a hand as he leaves. 'Saturday it is then. I look forward to it.'

'Me too,' she replies and looks away.

Stefan whistles his way through the afternoon. Simon's table is finished in record time.

*

On Friday, Stefan and Truda's visit is uppermost in Marianna's mind and just for once she wants the flat to look immaculate. Leon's slovenly habits grate on her natural inclination towards tidiness, but he thinks nothing of dropping his clothes on the floor and the living room is constantly littered with discarded newspapers, empty mugs and glasses.

'I do wish you'd clear up after yourself,' she'd complained one day when particularly peeved at the state of the flat. 'I'm working too and I wasn't born to wait on you.' Her brow creased with annoyance as she continued, 'I've no intention of becoming your live-in skivvy. The floor is not the place to leave clothes when there's a perfectly functional wardrobe to hang them in.'

'Stroppy today, aren't we?' he comments casually. Leon is oblivious to her requests and employs his usual tactics of flattery and wheedling to distract her. He reminds her that he has other qualities that more than make up for his shortcomings, but he isn't her favourite person at the moment so she refuses to be misled into believing there's anything at all that's good about him.

Rehearsals with Amelia are becoming more frequent and it hasn't escaped her attention that there's little music coming from the floor below during these sessions. There's no point in confronting him; he's a master at deviating from the truth and getting an honest response is unlikely. Neither is there any point in speaking to Amelia. Marianna has only seen the girl a few times since the party and then only in passing on the stairs. Apart from the occasional sound of music when she is practising with Leon or alone, she seems to live a quiet life.

She turns her attention to her plans for the following evening and flicks through various recipes, settling on a simple dish of cabbage leaves stuffed with ground beef, sausage and onions in a rich tomato sauce, the juices of which will be mopped up with a loaf of Truda's fresh crusty bread. She wonders whether anything else is necessary after such a heavy meal, but can't resist adding her favourite pudding made with layers of light crispy wafers, filled with a delicious creamy mousse and topped with chocolate. Her weekly budget will be greatly diminished by the purchase of such relative luxuries but despite this fact, she heads to the shops anyway.

*

The main market square in Krakow is a brisk half-hour walk away. She could shop locally but a change of scenery would be welcome and today she feels the need to immerse herself in the bustle of the town centre. The sight of the huge market square never fails to impress as she turns the corner and negotiates her way through the crowds. Dominating the square is the renaissance Cloth Hall that dates back to the thirteenth century and houses shop units that in better times sold everything from baskets to glassware, textiles, spices, leather goods, day-to-day grocery and greengrocery, bread, pastries, meat and poultry. Business is slower nowadays and the choice of goods depleted, but she still enjoys wandering through the covered walkway and stopping occasionally to pass the time of day with the shopkeepers.

The ornate buildings are impressive. At one end of the square is the Town Hall tower and at the other pretty St Adalbert's church. She has enjoyed many trips to town but there's still much to explore so she heads straight for the secondhand bookshops where she spends an hour browsing before heading off to her favourite café. She chooses a table furthest away from the walkway, orders a drink and settles down to watch the passers-by going about their business. Pigeons peck at the paving under her table, squabbling over tiny crumbs, and she is distracted by their squabbling until a couple coming towards her, but still some distance away, catch her eye. The girl has a mass of auburn hair and has her arm linked tightly to that of the man beside her. They stop as he bends to whisper in her ear and, laughing, she reaches up to kiss him. Leon and Amelia are coming closer. Later she will wonder if she imagined it, but for now she is certain it's them and bending to stay out of sight, reaches into her basket as they pass by. When she looks up they've gone.

*

It's late afternoon by the time she returns to the flat, reaches for the vodka, pours a large shot and downs it in one. An hour later Leon bursts in, mutters a cursory hello, kisses her fleetingly on the cheek and makes straight for the bedroom. He rummages in the wardrobe, removing clothes and throwing them about the bed.

'Be a love,' he calls. 'Make me something to eat, would you. Something quick. We have to be at the café in an hour to set up for this evening.'

Marianna doesn't answer.

Leon's head appears round the door. 'Marianna, did you hear me?'

'Where've you been all afternoon, Leon?' she asks, hands on her hips.

'What d'you mean,' he frowns, 'where have I been?'

'Can't you give me a direct answer, just for once?'

He hesitates and avoids eye contact by sorting about randomly amongst the clothes. 'Well if you must know, I got chatting to Chajim and he asked me to join him for a drink. Why? What's the problem?'

Marianna shakes her head, disbelieving.

'I saw you in town,' she pauses before adding, 'with Amelia.'

Leon looks at her briefly and turns away. 'I don't think you did. Like I said I've been with Chajim. Listen, I haven't got time for this, I'm running late.'

He tries a new tactic, pulls her to him, lays her head on his shoulder and strokes her hair. 'I'm sorry I'm out tonight, lovely. You look as if you need cheering up.' He tries to kiss her but she's furious and pushes him away.

Leon wheedles now. 'What's the matter? You look heavy-eyed. You're certainly not your usual radiant self.'

'It's living with you, Leon; you're such a liar. You can get your own food and don't expect me to wait up!'

*

Damn him! Damn him! How does he always get away with it? Getting an honest answer from Leon is nigh on impossible. His clever strategy to admit nothing, deny nothing, commit to nothing is employed whenever he's in trouble. No comment means there's no argument and therefore nothing can be proved or disproved.

That familiar gesture of Leon with his hands held up – 'I've done nothing. Not guilty!' – is a response she has seen so often. She has a choice: either she can ask Chajim if it's true, inevitably leading to gossip amongst the neighbours, or she can say nothing, which will mean that yet again he's won. It's another nail in the coffin of their marriage, which is looking increasingly fragile.

*

Leon is flat on his back, arms flung out wide when she wakes early the next morning. Propping herself on one elbow she studies his face. Heavy dark brows accentuate his straight nose and angular cheekbones. He's a handsome devil, looks as innocent as a baby when asleep; it's hardly any wonder she fell for him, but is it enough? Leon swept her off her feet with his fascinating stories about life as a musician, and the constant attention he gave her then made her feel special. His 'lovely country lass' he'd called her, and the lure of city life had added to the intoxicating mix that made Leon seem like the perfect man. It was only a matter of time before she realised that his happiness depended very much upon being the centre of attention. If criticised his mood turned sulky and childlike, and communicating with him became nigh on impossible. Her father's misgivings were justified, but by then, it was too late.

*

Although they are expensive, Marianna is going to spend some of her small budget on freshly ground coffee beans and she's already in the shop when Stanislaw appears. He greets her with a cheery, 'Good morning, young lady, you're an early bird today.'

'I am. I've lots to do. Stefan and Truda are coming this evening.'

'Let me open up and I'll be with you in a moment,' he says. Stanislaw is a creature of habit and allows nothing to deviate from his daily routine.

The heavy bolts are stiff and they pull back with difficulty. He switches the sign to open, steps out of the door and looks both ways, gives the doormat a shake and, returning with a broad smile, puts his arm around her shoulder and asks:

'So what can I do for you?'

'I'd like some coffee beans, please.'

'My, my, we are being extravagant,' he chuckles and measures a scoopful of the glossy brown nuggets into his new wall-mounted grinder. The ceramic container is decorated with blue sprigs of flowers and coffee is written in flowing script across the front. Stanislaw positions a paper bag under the polished brass grinder and turns the handle until the aromatic coffee grounds fill the bag, then ties the top with a piece of string and, bowing ceremoniously, hands it to Marianna.

'Madam, your coffee. Anything else?'

'No thanks. That's it. I'm off to Elena's.'

'You have a good evening. It's good to know you youngsters are getting together at last.'

*

Elena's flower stall is tucked into the far corner of the square, just a stone's throw from her home. It's a simple structure consisting of a few metal poles, tarpaulin coverings and rustic wooden benches, but it serves its purpose and when the metal buckets are filled with flowers the stand becomes a virtual floral wall. Boris, her elderly tabby cat, goes everywhere with her and today he's sitting in his usual spot on the corner of the workbench where Elena creates her bouquets. Stripped vegetation is strewn on the floor beside her as she puts together a loose bunch, rotating it as she adds each stem.

Marianna arrives and pats the overweight moggy on the head, then leans over the counter to greet Elena with a peck on the cheek. 'Goodness,' Elena says, 'it's a surprise to see you here. Have you come for a chat?'

Marianna surveys the lovely display. 'I've come for a few flowers, something pretty and natural for the table. Stefan and Truda are coming for supper and I want everything to be perfect.'

Elena selects a few late summer cornflowers, pretty greenery, white roses and spray carnations. She twirls the bunch for Marianna's approval. 'There, I think that's enough.'

'Perfect! You're so clever, Elena. I'll take them. How much do I owe you?'

'For you, my lovely, nothing.' Marianna objects but Elena is adamant. 'Just make sure plenty of passers-by see them. If they ask where you bought them, be sure to tell them where I am.'

Marianna hurries home as she has a lot to do and everything must be perfect. Leon, up and drinking coffee, pulls a grim face at the sight of her. 'Oh dear, I'd hoped to catch you before you went out. Come here and sit down. I've bad news about tonight.'

Marianna's heart sinks.

'I'm sorry but the café have asked us to play again and it's too good an opportunity to miss.'

Marianna puts the flowers on the table and drops onto the sofa next to him. 'Oh, Leon, I've gone to so much bother. I've planned a nice meal and it was all going to be so lovely.'

'Look, there's no need to cancel. Stefan and Truda will still come and you'll have a lovely evening getting to know them. Might be a good thing I'm not here, I'd probably hog the conversation anyway and you know me when I get started. Truda and I can catch up anytime.'

Marianna is unsure. 'I don't know. It won't be the same.'

'I don't want you sitting here all on your own, disappointed. You go ahead. It'll be fine.'

Marianna is relieved her efforts won't be entirely wasted and at least she'll get to spend some time with Stefan. The afternoon is taken up with food preparation and Leon lends a hand much to her astonishment. He feels guilty, she concludes, and so he should.

*

Truda has been feeling unwell all morning. Stefan suggests she rests for a while. He's looking forward to the evening rather more than he should and by six o'clock he's already washed and changed. There's been no sound of movement from Truda. He taps on the bedroom door but there's no reply so he knocks again. 'Truda,' he calls quietly and enters. She stirs as he approaches the bed.

'It's just gone six. We're due at Leon's at seven.'

'Oh, Stefan, I don't think I can go, I feel a little better but I'm still feverish and I've a thumping headache.'

He feels her forehead and cheeks with the back of his hand. 'Hmm. I don't think you have a temperature now. Are you sure you aren't up to it? It's very late to cancel.' Stefan can see the opportunity of spending time with Marianna slipping away.

'Oh, I don't think you should do that, we can't possibly let them down, not now.' She hesitates for a while and then, her mind made up says, 'I think you should go alone. Marianna and Leon will entertain you.'

'I don't like to leave you like this. Are you sure?' He's determined to go but the decision has to come from Truda.

'I'll be fine. I expect I just need a good sleep. All this extra baking lately has rather worn me out.'

'You're right. I said you've been overdoing it, didn't I?'

'I know but I can't afford to turn down the orders. We rely on the money. You know that and I'm probably better here on my own anyway.'

*

There's a short wait before Stanislaw answers the bell. 'Come in, Stefan.' He's surprised to see him alone. 'What's this? No Truda?'

'I'm afraid not. She's not feeling too well today. Just tired I think.' He's in two minds as to whether he should mention her workload but decides against it.

'Go on up then. You're in for an interesting evening.'

Stefan is puzzled. 'Really? Why's that?'

'You'll see.' Stanislaw waves his arm upwards and scuttles back to his meal.

Stefan races upstairs, pauses for a moment before he taps at the door. Inside the flat Marianna breathes deeply, sets her expression to one of calm confidence and opens the door.

'Hi, Stefan,' she says breezily and looks beyond him.

'No Truda?' she asks.

'It's just me I'm afraid. I'm so sorry it's such late notice but Truda isn't coming. She's not feeling too well. We hoped she'd perk up by this evening but she has a slight fever and a headache. She sends her apologies.'

He hands her a small brown parcel. 'This is for you.'

'Thank you. You'd better come in.'

He is embarrassed and thrusts his hands into his pockets.

'Oh dear, this is a little awkward,' Marianna says. 'Leon isn't here either. He had a last-minute offer of work at the restaurant and couldn't refuse so it looks like it's just the two of us.'

'Not awkward at all,' he says and actually looks pleased. 'I'm sure we'll have a perfectly lovely evening.'

'Yes. I'm sure we will. Can I get you a drink? Vodka? It's Stanislaw's best. He sold me a bottle at a special price. Apparently.' She laughs again, nervously. Now she definitely needs a drink.

'Vodka would be great,' he says.

Stefan compliments her on the flat. 'You've given the place a new look. Very nice. Flowers from Elena?'

'Yes. Aren't they lovely?' She pours the vodka. Passes Stefan a glass. 'Well, here's to our somewhat depleted get-together.'

'To us,' Stefan says. And they chink glasses. 'Dinner smells good. What are we having?'

'Stuffed cabbage leaves,' she waves a fork around like a magician's wand, 'Marianna style. And I've made my favourite pudding as this evening was the perfect excuse.'

She has laid the table simply with one of her mother's embroidered cloths and some pretty crockery she found whilst sorting out Stanislaw's storeroom. Elena's flowers complete the look. A large lampstand with a pink shade casts a warm glow. Later she'll light candles in quaint pewter holders.

'More vodka?' she asks, noticing that like hers his glass is already empty.

'Please.'

'Right. The meal is ready so we might as well eat now.'

She indicates the seat opposite and places a large steaming dish in the centre of the table. Its deliciously rich aroma fills the room. She has cut thick slices of Truda's bread and displayed them neatly on a wooden board with a bowl of yellow margarine.

'This is delicious, Marianna. You're clearly an excellent cook. Truda would have enjoyed it very much.' He takes another mouthful and points his fork at the parcel. 'Why don't you open your gift?'

She unties the ribbon and opens out the brown paper wrapping to reveal a notebook. Stefan watches her closely as she turns the book over and fans the pages slowly, imagining them filled with her own words.

'I found it at the fair that day we were caught in the storm,' he says. 'I was browsing through a pile of old books and it caught my eye. I thought you might like it for your writing.'

The spine is a little slack, the inside pages faintly lined and the edges faded to soft yellow but it has character. 'It's beautiful. I love the cover. Do you know what type of birds they are? They've been beautifully painted.'

'I'm not sure. Some kind of small parrot perhaps. Or lovebirds?' His forearm brushes against her hand as he turns to the inside cover. Marianna notices the muscular taut strength of his forearms and how fine hairs lie flat against his skin.

The name Camille Dubois, 14, Rue Visconti, St Germainé-des-Prés Paris, August 1914 is written in faded black ink and Marianna is instantly intrigued. 'I wonder who she was and why she never used it. I think the war started around that time. I expect there's an interesting story there somewhere.'

Stefan leans back and, raising his glass, takes a swig of vodka.

She continues, 'We'll never know but at last the book will be put to good use. I promise you that.'

He nods approvingly, knowing it to be true. 'You've some interesting objects there,' he says, pointing to the shelf behind her.

'You think so? Well, I like them. Some are a little odd but they all hold personal memories.'

'Which one do you treasure most?'

'Oh, I couldn't choose a favourite, but I think this is the most interesting.' Marianna reaches back and removes what appears to be a lump of metal. She passes it to Stefan. It's a lock plate, bent along one edge, with two smooth edges and the other jagged and worn. The keyhole is blocked with rust and there are two hexagonal nuts on opposite corners. It's very heavy for its size and aged to a green patina with rust patches the colour of autumn leaves. Some areas are rough to the touch and others smooth as a pebble.

Stefan reaches across and takes the lock from her. 'So now we have a book and a lock,' he says, 'both with untold stories. I can imagine this keeping the secret contents of an old wooden chest safe from prying eyes.' He turns it over in his hands, studying it closely. 'Where did you find it?'

'On a beach on the Hel Peninsula.'

'Really?' he asks, surprised. 'And what were you doing there?'

'My mother and I went to visit my aunt when she was ill.'

'I'm sorry to hear that. Tell me about it,' he asks gently. 'If you want to.'

'Shall we have dessert first?' she suggests.

'No. Leave it a while. I'd like to hear the story first.'

Marianna refills their glasses.

'My mother's eldest sister, Aunt Beata, lived in the small fishing village of Hel, about three hours by train from Danzig.'

'Not sure I'd want to live in a place called Hel,' he interrupts.

'Yes, it's an odd name, isn't it?' She sips her drink and then continues. 'Aunt Beata married a German engineer. If I remember rightly his name was Gunter. Her family was against the marriage but she was determined to go through with it. She lost touch with everyone after that, but when she became ill Gunter contacted my mother. It seems my aunt was desperate to see her again so Father convinced her she should go and take me with her. I was twelve at the time so for me it was a great adventure. The first and last time I ever saw the sea.'

'It's a very long journey, isn't it?' he asks.

'Yes, it seemed to go on forever. I remember we spent all day travelling on one train after another until we arrived late at night.'

'How long did you stay?'

'For three weeks until my aunt passed away.'

'That must have been difficult.'

'Yes it was. Particularly for my mother. I think the significance was a little lost on me. Being away from home was exciting and I treated it as a holiday.'

'What on earth did you do all day?'

'My mother insisted I spend time away from the cottage and the gloomy atmosphere, so I'd take myself off and inevitably make my way to the seafront. I loved the ozone smell of drying, sludge-coloured seaweed and the shrieks of hungry gulls as they dived and fought over tiny scraps of fish thrown overboard from the fishing boats.' She pauses, reminiscing. 'And the sound of the ropes clanking against masts as the wind urged them out to sea. They were colourful with their brightly painted hulls emblazoned with lovely, affectionate names like The Happy Fisher, Wildcard, Serenity, Allsorts and my favourite, Wind Gypsy. Happy boats on their way to fish.'

'How do you remember the names after so long?'

'I wrote them down in my diary. I love to read those pages even now.'

Stefan is fascinated. 'You're taking me there,' he smiles. 'Tell me more.'

'There were sad boats too. Those were the ones that lay like huge dead animals caught in the suffocating mud of the harbour at low tide. I'd sit, legs dangling over the harbour wall, and eavesdrop on the fishermen's casual chat as they mended their nets, aired their oilskins and puffed at their pipes. I didn't understand a lot of what they said, it was sailors' talk, but there were tales of storms they'd survived and giant fish they'd caught and my imagination ran riot.'

'Did you go there every day?'

'Most days, yes. Beyond the harbour to the east was a grassy common surrounded by dense and ancient trees. I never went there. Mother told me not to, although I was very tempted.'

'Did you mind being alone so much?' Stefan empties his glass again and Marianna reaches out automatically to refill it. 'You were very young after all.'

'No, I was happy to be alone. I've always enjoyed my own company and in any case there were few children in the village so I had no choice.' She tucks a loose strand of hair behind her ear before continuing, 'Sometimes, I'd walk in the opposite direction. Beyond the harbour wall was a pebbly beach with wooden breakwaters. I'd stay for hours leaning against the warm wood with my face to the sun, sifting the tiny multi-coloured shingles through my fingers, shuffling their glossy smoothness into little heaps and treading them down with my bare feet. There was never anybody around, apart from a lady with a yappy little dog who walked by at the same time every day. She never spoke.'

'The place clearly left a huge impression.'

'It certainly did. I grew to love the place. I'd stare out at the vast expanse of water imagining how far it was to the next land. Even when I'm in Hel I'm in heaven, I'd repeat to myself over and over.'

'So where did you find the lock?'

'The beach became sandier further along and stretched far into the distance. I found all sorts of strange objects there on the tide line. I'd collect them in a small flowery cotton bag with a drawstring that my aunt gave me. Walking along the water's edge one day, deliberately dragging my toes through the wet sand, I stubbed my toe. I'd found the lock. Who did it belong to, I wondered, and what had it kept hidden? So many questions. So many possible answers.'

Stefan, one elbow on the table, chin cupped in hand is looking at Marianna as if she's found a key to something of his own that has never been unlocked. 'And you still have it after all this time.'

'Later that day when I got back to the cottage, my aunt had passed away. I kept the lock because to me it represented all the mysteries of life about which I knew so little.'

Stefan is quiet.

'I'm sorry,' she says, embarrassed. 'That was a rather long explanation.'

He reaches across the table and takes her hand in his.

'There's nothing to apologise for. I've never been to the coast, well, only in my imagination and I enjoyed hearing about the lock.'

'I've had a yearning to go back ever since but don't suppose I ever will. I once wrote about a cottage on a clifftop. It's pure fantasy of course.' She laughs and pulls her hand away, although reluctant to break the mood. 'You know. Silly girls' stuff.'

'I'd like to read it. If you don't mind of course.'

'We'll see. Now how about that dessert?'

The *andrut* is a great success and Marianna promises to plate up a slice for Truda. They savour its sweet deliciousness in a comfortable silence until Marianna says, 'I had a very interesting chat with Feliks the other day.'

'Oh. When was that?'

'The day we met in the corridor, when I'd been to his studio. The day you lost your temper.'

'And you yours, as I recall.'

'We were as bad as each other.'

They pause, each remembering with embarrassment how they behaved.

'He's an interesting character your brother. You two seem close and yet often at loggerheads.'

'Feliks was a handful as a youngster but he valued my opinion, took the advice I gave, and my mother came to rely on my stabilising influence. His relationship with our father was always volatile. They just didn't see eye to eye. I felt Father was unreasonably harsh so I tried hard to compensate. Home life when Feliks was in his teens was sometimes unbearable. The constant arguing over his future, his obstinacy that he was an artist and that's all he ever would be caused endless friction. Father wasn't going to give an inch on that subject.'

'That must have been frustrating for Feliks.'

'I'm sure it was, but he was petulant and immature and because he was unable to discuss it in a reasonable way they always ended up arguing and so became distant and resentful towards each other. Mother would implore my father to go easy on Feliks and this just seemed to exacerbate the situation. He thought she spoiled him.'

'It must have been hard to live in that atmosphere.'

'It was. Mealtimes became insufferable with Feliks pushing his meal around the plate sulking and Father bullish, refusing to sit at the same table, Mother tearful and unable to cope with it all. Things came to a head after a wealthy businessman offered Feliks a lucrative commission to paint his family's portraits. He saw this as his chance to prove himself and went to see Father at the workshop full of hope, but he refused to loan Feliks the money he needed to buy canvas and paints and bitter words were exchanged. Feliks had gone to Warsaw to find work when Father was taken ill. My father was filled with remorse and made me promise I'd do everything I could to help realise Feliks' ambition and make up for the wrong he'd done him. Within days he was dead and they never saw each other again.'

'That is so sad, Stefan. And did you never feel any resentment that your mother favoured him over you, or that your father burdened you so unfairly with making things right?'

'No. Never. Do you think I should have?'

She shakes her head. 'No. I think it just proves what a wonderful brother you are.'

They move from the table to the sofa and talk for another hour, enjoying the last of Stanislaw's special coffee. It is dark outside now and the room, lit only by candlelight, has an air of expectancy. The sexual tension between them is palpable.

'Perhaps you should go now,' she suggests. 'Truda will wonder where you are.'

'I suppose I should.' He taps the chair arms nervously as their eyes lock and they look at each other for a little too long.

He pats the chair again, agitated.

'Right. I'd better be off. It's a little late and Leon will be back soon, no doubt.'

They walk slowly to the door. She opens it and stands aside to let him through.

'Thank you, Marianna, it's been lovely. I wish every evening could be like this.' Leaning towards her he hesitates for a brief moment, touches her cheek with his thumb and then kisses her mouth.

'So do I,' she responds.

*

She's been lying in bed thinking about Stefan for hours, going over every detail of the evening, when the sound of Leon's key in the lock disturbs her thoughts. She turns on her side, draws her knees up to her chest and curls into a ball. He creeps about undressing and slips into bed beside her, sliding his arm around her waist.

'Marianna. Are you awake?'

She squeezes her eyes tight shut and pretends to be asleep.

# Seven

Stanislaw has commented more than once that Tomas's professional approach to the most menial of tasks is impressive and the boy, not wishing to find himself back on the streets, is keen to cultivate this opinion. Orders for deliveries have increased and he loads his basket enthusiastically with as many items as he can cram in. His customers, at least those with a little cash to spare, are more than pleased with the obliging service he provides with his cheery 'No problem' when asked to perform an extra favour. He's happy to sweep or scrub a front step, polish a pair of boots, run small errands, anything he can easily fit in whilst on his round and that, more importantly, earns him a little extra money.

The close relationship he's formed with Marianna has transformed him. It's her birthday soon and he's saving to buy her a gift. Each day he takes the coins he's earned and hides them beneath a broken floorboard under his bed. Money isn't the only thing he hides from his brother Eryk. Today, Stanislaw has given Tomas some leftover sausage he intends to keep for himself, but first he must smuggle it past Eryk.

Eryk's temper has become more explosive lately and it doesn't take much to set him off. Tomas is afraid of him and hates it when he grabs him with his grimy fingers and clammy palms – thrusts his bulbous-eyed face into his. It makes his flesh creep. He doesn't understand why Eryk is like he is. He knows little about his brother but refrains from asking, judging it wiser to stay quiet.

Eryk's problems began when he ran away to sea. He approached this adventure with youthful enthusiasm and bore with stoicism the pain of having a tattoo, an anchor and rope design, scratched onto his pale forearm. He hated everything from the hard physical work to the forced camaraderie with men old enough to be his father, and his unrealistic romantic ideas were shattered by the harsh realities of life on deck in all weathers. The fearsome winds, salt water and sun reddened his youthful complexion and chapped his hands so badly that the skin around broken fingernails split, forming painful cracks.

Eryk has never spoken about his time at sea, but has the scars to remind him just how hard it was. The other crewmembers laughed at him when he whined about his wounds. 'That's nothing, lad,' they'd tell him. 'Mere scratches they are. Look at the state of us. There's not one of us doesn't get off this ship without a bit missing here or there.'

Years later and back on dry land drinking became an integral part of his life, and as the years passed the habit spiralled out of control and Eryk became an alcoholic. Fine, red, spider-like veins now mark his stubbly face like a delicate map. His mouth is slack, his lips full and fleshy, and his pimpled belly, hard and round like that of a pregnant woman, bursts from his open shirt.

As usual, by the time Tomas reaches home Eryk is in the depths of a drunken sleep. Casting a fearful glance in his brother's direction he removes his shoes and creeps upstairs to savour the fatty sausage in the safety of his room.

*

Since the episode with the pigeons, Stanislaw has forbidden Marianna to feed them on the windowsill. Occasionally, she and Tomas take a bag of crumbs to the cemetery where they sit on a bench and scatter the unusable leftovers of Truda's baking to the 'poor and hungry' as Tomas calls the birds.

The cemetery extends over a sizeable piece of land behind an imposing brick wall with a pair of impressive iron entrance gates. It's a hidden city of granite headstones that once promised remembrance but are now overgrown and neglected. The sounds of the outside world are eerily silenced. It's a place of sanctuary, somewhere to sit in quiet contemplation. Marianna has never suggested he do so but Tomas instinctively removes his cap whenever they enter. They scatter the breadcrumbs and pigeons flock round them in a flapping cloud of grey, pecking greedily at the ground.

'I don't understand why people would want to get rid of pigeons,' Tomas states. 'They don't bovver nobody.'

'Bother, Tomas. Not bovver.' Marianna has been trying to improve his pronunciation but it's an uphill struggle.

'Stanislaw hates 'em. Calls 'em dirty buggers.'

Marianna laughs and gives him an affectionate squeeze. 'You're right. They are quite dirty and they can spread disease so it's best not to touch them.'

'I used to be dirty but you touched me.' He recently lost a front tooth, so his smile has become even more endearing. 'My brother says pigeons are rats with feathers.'

'I'd like to meet your brother.'

'You wouldn't. He's 'orrible.' Tomas shrugs his shoulders and looks away. 'He's 'orrible to me anyway.'

Marianna decides not to pursue this line of conversation. If Tomas wants to elaborate he must do so in his own time.

'Why do they cock their heads from side to side?' he asks, cocking his own head to scrutinise them.

'Perhaps they're wondering why we don't fly.'

'I can fly,' Tomas says, pulling the back of his jacket up over his shoulders, extending his arms wide and running in wheeling circles. 'See.'

'Not exactly,' says Marianna. 'Your feet are still on the ground.' He sits next to her, a little closer this time. Puffing.

'Well, they don't seem to fly much neither… they just walk around. Why do they all look the same?'

'Because they are. They're called urban pigeons because they live in town.'

'What are the others called? Country pigeons?'

'No, they're called wood pigeons. They're much fatter and they make a different sound.'

'My brother says you can eat them.'

'You can. Not urban ones, but lots of people eat wood pigeons. They make a very tasty pie.'

'I hope they're good an' dead before they go in the pie!' He clasps his hand over his mouth to stop himself laughing and looks at Marianna out of the corner of his eye to check that she's found him funny. She has and they both giggle for a while.

'You won't know this fact,' she tells him, 'but in the war they used pigeons to take messages back and forth. They were very brave. They could fly high so were difficult to spot.'

Tomas's eyes widen. 'Did they ever get shot down by a machine gun?'

'Yes and thousands died. Some of them made dozens of trips and were considered to be pigeon heroes. Others got medals for their bravery. They saved many, many lives by carrying vital messages.'

'So pigeons aren't all bad then.'

'I don't think so. No.'

Tomas is quiet for a while, digesting the information. He leans forward to inspect the motley birds at their feet. 'I wonder if there are any heroes here.' He looks at her hopefully.

'I don't think so. The war was quite a while ago.'

'Why don't we ever see baby pigeons?' he asks.

Marianna considers for a while. 'Because when they're small they're so ugly,' she contorts her face into the worst one possible, 'they stay in their nests until they're all feathered up like their parents.'

'They're quite intrestin' really,' Tomas concludes and adds, 'You know an awful lot about pigeons, don't you?'

'I've liked pigeons since I was a very small girl. I had a favourite one called Petronella when I lived at home.'

Tomas wrinkles his nose. 'Petronella! That's a stupid name for a pigeon. Daft!'

Marianna continues, 'She was pure white with grey tips on her wings and a tinge of pink round her neck like a ruff.'

'What's a ruff?'

'Like a collar, but frilly. She would wait for me on the garden path and I would feed her crumbs, while the other pigeons stayed in the trees until she'd finished eating. It was as though she were a princess and they could only come down when she'd had her fill.'

'So now it's Princess Petronella the Pigeon.' He laughs hysterically, rocking back and forth and swinging his legs. 'I bet even you can't make up a story about that,' he dares her.

'I bet I can,' she replies. 'I think it's time we were heading back to the shop. I don't know about you, but I could do with a drink.'

Marianna enters into the challenge of the pigeon story with relish and days later hands him the finished article.

*Petronella looked around dismissively at the other pigeons. She knew her collar of feathers was more beautiful than theirs and she had delusions of grandeur. 'I'm like a princess compared to them,' she cooed conceitedly, her head bobbing from side to side.*

*Her mother humoured her. 'Sometimes things become possible if you want them enough.' Sighing, she added, 'But be warned, being a princess isn't all it's cracked up to be.'*

*'I WILL be a princess,' Petronella sulked. 'I don't care what you say. I was born to be special. I feel it in my heart.' She wanted it so badly that each night, perched precariously in her uncomfortable nest of snaggy twigs she would repeat over and over to herself, 'I will be a princess.'*

*One morning she awoke surrounded by a nest of golden threads, soft green moss and downy feathers. All around pink ribbons hung from the trees. She wove them into her wavy purple, blue and green iridescent hair. Her wings had transformed into slender arms and her skin was porcelain white. Just like a princess. Her dreams had come true. She was thrilled and stood to show herself off to the other birds. But all was not well. A heavy grey skirt of feathers encircled her waist and stuck out behind her, stiff and unwieldy, her legs thick and red, rigid beneath. 'What have I done?' she squawked, appalled by her bizarre appearance. Her ugly feet became caught in the threads. With no wings to flap, she toppled backwards, the fragile nest collapsing beneath her. Her long hair streamed behind her, the pink ribbons unravelling and floating away as she fell. Flightless. Like a stone.*

*Her mother, pecking around for food, discovered Petronella's body in the overgrown garden. Her pretty head lay limp and twisted to one side. Her pink eyes, still open, registered nothing but surprise.* No bird soars too high, *her mother thought with sadness,* if it flies with its own wings. *And she carried on pecking.*

At the bottom of the page she sets him a task:

*Tomas. There's a moral to this story. See if you can work it out.*

*Elena has offered to help if you need a hand reading it.*

# Eight

'It's a shame I have to work on your birthday,' Leon remarks as they sit reading one evening. Marianna says nothing. Since Stefan kissed her a week ago she has thought of little else.

'Are you listening?' Leon asks sarcastically. 'You seem a bit preoccupied these days.'

'Never mind, it can't be helped,' she mutters. 'Work has to come first I suppose.' *And Amelia a close second I wouldn't be surprised,* she thinks resentfully.

'You could come along to the restaurant for the evening?'

'What, on my own? Sit there like a spare part watching you and Amelia perform. I don't think so.'

'There's no need to be churlish,' he says, and returns to his reading. But Leon is feeling a little guilty and comes up with a suggestion. 'Why don't you invite Stanislaw and Elena? I'll pay for a meal. Stefan and Truda may like to come. I don't know. Ask who you like, it'll make up for last week's disappointment.'

It was far from disappointing, she reflects; in fact it

was the best night she'd had since arriving in Kazimierz.

Leon seems pleased with his idea. 'I'm sure they'd look after you. It being your birthday and all.'

He's hit a nerve now. 'It's a pity you don't do that. Me being your wife and all, as you put it.'

Leon turns on her. 'Don't start, Marianna.'

She's about to respond.

'I said don't!'

She's determined to have her say on the subject and turns on him angrily. 'I haven't said a word all these weeks when you've been rehearsing for days on end. Now you're at the restaurant two or three nights a week I'm beginning to feel very un-married. Very alone and neglected.'

Leon shakes his newspaper, crosses his legs and turns a page. 'I'm not listening to this. You're being irrational. Hysterical even. I'm working as hard as I can to earn a living and all you can do is criticise. At least I have a job, unlike a lot of our neighbours. I may not have a full week's work but it's better than nothing, so instead of whingeing, perhaps you should be a little more grateful.' He shakes his paper again, harder this time.

'I don't whinge, Leon, and don't be unkind. I hardly ever complain, I'm just trying to make you understand how I feel. For goodness sake, we've only been married a short while and it's like we've been married for fifty years. You spend more time with Amelia rehearsing and it makes me sad.'

'Yes. Well, it's not all about you.'

'You just don't want to see my point of view,' she accuses him. 'Okay book a table at the damn restaurant and I'll invite people whose company I enjoy.'

Marianna storms into the bedroom, slams the door and sits fuming on the edge of the bed, hating him with every fibre of her body.

*

Stanislaw and Elena are delighted they're invited for the meal. Feliks wants to bring a 'friend' but Marianna says no, not unless he's willing to pay for her meal.

'We can't afford to spend money on your casual girlfriends, Feliks; I expect you'll have someone new next week. I hope you aren't offended.'

He isn't, so is coming on his own.

She ponders the best way of extending the invitation to Stefan and Truda. Should she approach him when he's in the workshop? It would give her a good excuse to see him alone, but she decides to ask Truda instead, who she hasn't seen since she was ill.

*

Tomas is browsing the stalls at the Saturday bric-a-brac fair, looking for a gift for Marianna. He's asked Elena to come with him.

'Just in case anyone sees me that I used to nick stuff from,' he explains in his best matter-of-fact voice.

'Of course I'll come with you. It'll be my pleasure. Anybody starts trouble I'll tell them I'm your grandmother.'

Tomas likes the idea of this but is convinced that nobody will recognise him now that he bears little resemblance to the dirty urchin who used to plague the stallholders.

'We'll have to start early,' she tells him, 'or all the best bargains will be gone.'

Saturday morning arrives with a drizzle of rain. Tomas thinks this is a good thing. Fewer visitors, lower prices. He's never bought anybody a present before. In truth he's never paid for anything either and so today will be a new experience. They browse one side of the street, then the other. Nothing catches their eye and Tomas is beginning to feel despondent when a new cart arrives. Everything is jumbled together. There are toys with books, old tools with china, bits of metalwork with clothing and so on, but Tomas spots an ornately cut glass scent bottle with its stopper missing. He gives it to Elena to hold while he ferrets around and there it is, a top in the shape of a pinecone. It fits snuggly with a pleasant chink.

He inspects the bottle carefully and assures Elena that it'll clean up a treat.

'Just like me,' he laughs.

They negotiate with the seller but he wants more than Tomas can afford.

'I'll give you the difference,' Elena offers, 'and you can pay me back when you've done more errands.'

Tomas beams. What a grandmother she's turning out to be.

The bottle is roughly wrapped in a piece of newspaper. Tomas was never this pleased before, even when he'd managed to pinch a silver-plated pocket watch from a distracted bystander, but today he's learnt a valuable lesson. There's far more satisfaction in paying for something with money hard-earned.

Elena has been lucky too. She's bought Marianna a fountain pen. Not new of course, but it looks elegant lying on its satin pillow inside a battered red leather box. The seller has assured her it's in good working order, and it has a very attractive appearance too with its gold and black Egyptian key border and an arrow-shaped clip.

They are two very satisfied customers when they drop into Stanislaw's for a drink and a pastry.

'Let's see what you've got then,' Stanislaw bellows with one arm round Elena's waist and the other on Tomas's shoulder.

Elena puts a finger to her lips. Winks at Tomas. Shakes her head. 'You'll see soon enough.'

*

On Thursday evening Tomas smuggles the scent bottle into Marianna's flat, tucking it under his arm and clamping it flat against his side. Adopting his best casual swagger does nothing to detract from his rather strange gait.

'Have you hurt your arm, Tomas?' Marianna asks, concerned as he lurches across the room towards the bathroom.

'Nah. It's just a bit stiff, that's all. Too much carrying,' he adds.

'As long as you're alright.'

'Yeah. Hot bath will sort it out.'

Once safely out of sight he unwraps the bottle and stands it on the windowsill while he fills the bath. He lowers himself into the water and then, removing the stopper and balancing it on the edge, swishes the bottle about between his legs, filling it with soapy water and emptying it from above his head. He likes the sound of the water glug-glugging its way out and falling back into the bath and repeats the action many times. Screwing the corner of his flannel into a point he squeezes the fabric in and down, twisting at the same time to clean the sides. He panics a little when it appears to have stuck, but it's alright. It comes out. He soaps up the bottle and rubs it until the grime has come off, gives the stopper the same careful treatment, puts the two together and nods to himself with satisfaction.

Once dressed, he adopts the stiff-arm look once again and bids Marianna a hasty goodbye. She's a little disconcerted by this unusual behaviour. He never leaves without indulging in a mug of hot chocolate.

*

Back home Tomas's sleeping brother Eryk is slouched in a chair, his legs splayed out in front of him. His trousers are undone at the fly and a wet patch has spread down his leg towards his knees. With his head slumped back and his mouth wide open he's snoring and dribbling like an old man. Tomas looks at him with disgust. He removes his shoes and creeps upstairs, checking for sounds from below. Cupping the bottle in the palm of his hand he kneels by the bed and unfolds a piece of brown paper Elena has given him.

'What've you got there, you thieving little bastard?'

Tomas gasps as Eryk lurches towards him, red-faced, eyes bloodshot and bulging. He puts out a hand to stop him but he's too slow.

'No! That's mine! It's a present for Marianna. Leave it!'

'A present! What you gotta give 'er a present for? Pathetic little goody goody you've become. Still thieving though I bet.' Eryk smells of stale beer and urine. His breath is putrid.

'I didn't steal it!'

Eryk aims a fist at Tomas's head. He ducks and Eryk loses his balance, staggers forwards onto the bed. They grapple and Eryk loses his grip. The bottle falls to the ground and it spins across the floor, stopping just short of the wall. Tomas makes a lunge for it, grabs it and curls his fingers tightly around it. Despite Eryk's drunken state he reaches the door and blocks Tomas's exit, hurling verbal abuse at him all the while. Tomas darts and ducks this way and that, squeezing between Eryk's legs, and is out of the room in a flash, clutching the bottle as if his life depends on it. Heading for the stairs he is gripped from behind. Eryk has hold of his jacket collar as he aims another blow. This time he makes contact with Tomas's right eye, but he's swaying dangerously near the top of the stairs. He aims another blow. Tomas avoids it but there's a sickening thud as Eryk, unbalanced, tumbles downstairs and lies in a heap at the bottom.

Tomas flees to his room and waits. An eerie silence fills the house. There's no sound to indicate that Eryk is moving, but he waits a little longer and then opens the bedroom door and creeps downstairs. He peeps round the open door to the living room and is shocked that Eryk is back in his chair as if nothing has happened. Tomas returns to his room, jams a chair under the door handle and lies fully clothed on the bed rigid with fear for what may be in store. He stays like this for hours and it's still dark when he decides he must get out before Eryk wakes. With the gift in one hand and his shoes in the other he hurriedly leaves.

*

Tomas is sleeping, slumped sideways, in the shop doorway when Stanislaw opens up next morning. He shakes the boy's shoulder gently and Tomas stirs. He has an ugly red mark across one side of his face, his eye is swollen and blood has dried and congealed in clots above his eyebrow and across the bridge of his nose. He begins to cry.

'Good God, boy!' Stanislaw exclaims. 'What's happened to you? What on earth are you doing here at this time?'

'It's me bruvver. He hit me. He was drunk. He tried to steal the present. I hate 'im.' Tomas collapses and heaving sobs shake his body.

'Come on, boy. Get up and let's get you inside. It's disgraceful, a grown man hitting a young boy like that. You'll be alright. Come on in and calm down, you've had a nasty shock.' Stanislaw helps Tomas to his feet. 'We need to get that face of yours cleaned up, young man. Sit here and I'll get a cold cloth for your eye then I'll see if Marianna's up. She'll have a gentle touch.'

Marianna comes to the door bleary-eyed.

'You'd better come down. Tomas is in a bad way.'

Her hands fly to her face. 'Oh no! What's happened?'

'Brother trouble. He's beaten him up a bit. Poor mite has a swollen eye. He needs some attention. Sorry to wake you.'

'It's alright.' She wraps the belt of her gown around her middle and hurriedly ties a knot. 'I was just dozing. I'll come now.'

He is indeed a sorry sight.

'Oh, you poor lamb,' Marianna cries, hugging him close. 'How could he! The monster!'

It's a long time since Tomas has been held in an affectionate embrace and the suppressed emotion that surfaces gives rise to a fresh outburst of crying.

Marianna prepares a bowl of soapy water and with a soft cloth gently removes the dried blood from his face. He squirms and squeals a lot but with gentle persuasion he's cleaned up. The damage is less severe than at first appeared. His eye will be black for a few days but apart from a couple of scratches on his forehead he's unmarked.

Stanislaw has been busying himself making hot chocolate for all three of them. Tomas abandons all worries about his street credibility and sits on Marianna's lap, indulging in the comfort of the rich drink and the softness of her body.

'Tell us what happened,' she urges him gently.

Tomas retells the story, deliberately leaving out details about the bottle, but Stanislaw can tell he's holding back.

'So what was all this about? What was Eryk trying to take from you? Must have been something worth having.'

This is not how he intended to give Marianna her gift, but he reaches into his jacket pocket and thrusts the parcel towards her. 'Happy birthday,' he whispers. 'Might as well open it now.'

It's the prettiest scent bottle she's ever seen. 'Oh. It's beautiful.' She draws him in once again. 'And you are one very special boy.'

Stanislaw clears his throat. 'Er yes. Happy birthday. I hadn't forgotten but what with all the upset and so on.'

*

The situation with Eryk has caused a deal of worry for Marianna and Stanislaw.

'There's no way he can go back. Not after this,' she says, pacing about. 'I'd be happy to let him sleep at the flat. I could make up a bed in the living room but Leon will hate the idea, I know that without asking him.' She bites her lip, pondering over the alternatives.

Stanislaw slaps his thigh. 'Well, there's only one thing for it. He must stay here. The storeroom has a small window. I could take out a few shelves and he could make the space his own, barring a few dozen jars of pickles and some boxes of candles,' he chuckles.

Tomas, exhausted, has fallen asleep in the chair. Stanislaw breaks the news to him when he wakes and there are more tears.

'I'll – I'll make it up to you,' he stutters, mid sob. 'But what about my brother? He's bound to come looking for me.'

Stanislaw thinks this unlikely. 'Don't you worry about him. If he does he'll have me to deal with and he'd regret that.' He balls his fists and moves his arms like a boxer. Tomas laughs. 'That's better. Come on. Let's go and take a look at your new home.'

# Nine

Leon is lying on his back, spread-eagled across the bed when she returns. 'Aren't you coming back to bed?' he asks hopefully.

'It's my birthday, not yours,' she mumbles back.

'Is it?'

'It is. Thanks for remembering.' The sight of him fills her with a brewing discontent as she selects clothes from the wardrobe, dresses and leaves, slamming the door behind her. He might have made an effort to get up but still, Tomas's thoughtful gift has more than made up for it so there's no point in allowing Leon to spoil the day. She unwraps the little bottle, turns it around lovingly in her hands and places it on the shelf with her other precious things.

Leon's not in when she returns at lunchtime and he's left no note, so she has no idea where he is and despite her intentions to the contrary becomes more upset as the day slips by.

It's late afternoon when he reappears. 'Sorry I'm so late,' he breezes. 'Had a few things to sort out.' He plants a kiss on her cheek as he thrusts an extravagant bunch of flowers into her hands. 'Anything to eat?'

'There's plenty of bread and some of last night's meal if you're desperate. We'll be eating tonight so I haven't bothered.'

'You'll be eating, you mean. I'll be working my butt off.'

'Like I said, there's plenty of bread.'

Leon is about to respond but the look on her face suggests he does otherwise.

'Help yourself. I'm off to have a bath. And thanks for the flowers. Very thoughtful,' she says sarcastically.

She fills a vase with water and plonks them in unceremoniously.

*

A spiral staircase from the pavement leads down to the basement restaurant where Marianna, Stanislaw and Elena are directed to a large oval table in one corner. The walls are painted a deep red and are covered with dozens of paintings crammed closely together. Inviting archways and cosy nooks, lit by candlelight, create an intimate atmosphere perfect for die-hard romantics. *How ironic,* Marianna thinks.

Leon and Amelia are setting up their music stands and raising his hand, he saunters over with Amelia shadowing his every move. She looks extremely elegant in her all-black performance clothes, her red hair piled high in a mass of curls.

'Sorry you've been stuffed into this corner,' Leon says but doesn't sound particularly concerned. 'It's my fault I expect as I left it too late to get the table up front and the manager wouldn't swap them. He says it's reserved for important guests.'

The comment cuts Marianna like a knife.

'Anyway, about the meal,' he continues, 'you can order what you like, within reason. I've arranged for a bit of a deal on the prices in return for our performance tonight.'

Stanislaw rubs his hands together. 'Even better now I know you're paying, son.'

'Only the food,' Leon adds hastily. 'You'll need to pay for your own drinks, I'm not made of money.'

As an afterthought he adds, 'And, Stanislaw, make sure my wife has a jolly evening. She's been a bit down in the dumps lately.'

Marianna is speechless and watches open-mouthed as he takes Amelia by the arm and leads her away.

The rest of the party arrives and there's much bobbing up and down as they reach across the table to greet each other.

Stanislaw sits to her left and she saves the place on her right for Feliks. Truda will be next to him which will place Stefan between his wife and Elena. More importantly, he'll be directly opposite her.

Everyone is impatient to give Marianna her gifts and once settled Feliks is determined to be the first. He presents her with an accomplished pencil portrait of herself and there's no doubt it's a beautifully sensitive piece of work.

'I'm a poor starving artist so I'm afraid it's the best I can do.' Everyone groans with exaggerated sympathy. Feliks sinks his head onto his folded arms in mock tragedy and they all laugh. The drawing is passed around the table and Stefan looks at it admiringly, glancing occasionally at Marianna opposite as if comparing the likeness.

'Come on, Stefan.' Feliks raps on the table. 'Move it on, I want to hear from the others how brilliant it is.'

Stefan passes it to Elena and transfers his gaze to the real thing. Truda is watching him and lays her hand over his possessively.

'Open ours next,' Stanislaw and Elena say in unison.

'How lucky am I to have you all here this evening,' she says, looking round the table.

'Too right you are,' Feliks adds emphatically. 'I had a hot date, but here I am and anyway, how could I not be here for this lovely woman's special day?' He squeezes her shoulders.

Stefan fiddles with his cutlery and shifts in his chair. He hates himself for it, but he's finding it hard to conceal his jealousy.

Marianna loves the pen. 'Now I'll have to write something worthwhile and do this justice.' She blows them both a kiss.

The waiter comes to take their order but Stefan waves him away politely with instructions to return a little later.

Truda reaches into her bag and passes Marianna a small but weighty parcel. 'We hope you like it. Stefan seemed to think you would.' She smiles half-heartedly.

Marianna's precious key lock has been expertly mounted on a wooden plaque and framed by a border of carved seashells. She beams. 'Goodness me! This is lovely.'

Stefan looks pleased.

'I love it! Thank you. And you too, Truda.' Truda nods and says, 'You're welcome,' but sounds a long way from meaning it.

There's a buzz in the restaurant as the music begins and much discussion ensues over what to choose from the somewhat limited menu.

'Don't forget! Go steady on the drinks,' Stanislaw jokes, 'I'm paying for those.' Conversation flows amidst much laughter and Marianna notes with pleasure that Truda has dropped her guard and is chatting amicably.

Marianna is enjoying her view of Stefan. When they engage in conversation the rest of the diners and the music seem to fade to a background hum. Her pulse is racing and it's not the vodka. Her head is spinning and it's not the heat. She's having a lovely evening but deep inside she wishes the rest of her guests would disappear. Just for a while. Occasionally she'll catch him looking at her but he averts his gaze quickly.

There's a sudden burst of applause as Leon and Amelia take a bow at the end of their first set. He has an arm around her waist and she's looking up at him adoringly. Marianna's suspicions are confirmed. She's known it all along of course; there's a lot more to this friendship than meets the eye, but with a sinking feeling she realises that she just doesn't care.

*

Leon and Amelia rejoin them at the table and Marianna shows him her presents. She hopes he realises his lack of effort compares poorly to the kind generosity and consideration the others have given to her gifts. She gets no pleasure from feeling like this and in any case Leon seems oblivious to everything except Amelia, who is lurking around like a small child waiting for her parent to finish speaking. Marianna almost feels sorry for the girl.

It's nearing the end of the evening and Feliks has been uncharacteristically quiet.

'Everything alright?' Marianna asks.

'Yes. I'm fine. I've just been thinking a lot and I'm wondering if I could exhibit my work here. People seem genuinely interested in the paintings and I notice there are a few sold labels, which surprises me in the current climate.'

'I think that's an excellent idea. Why don't you approach the owner? See what he thinks.'

'I will. What's more I've an idea for some new work, but I need to think it through first before I approach my model.' He winks.

Stefan has been watching them like a hawk. He's desperate to move her attention away from Feliks and interrupts abruptly. 'I was very interested to hear about your writing the other evening. I'd love to read the seaside piece you mentioned.'

'Really? Well, if you like I could give it to Tomas. He'll drop it in,' Marianna replies.

'Why not bring it yourself? I could read it while I'm having my lunch and perhaps you could have a coffee with Truda. What d'you think, Truda? It would give you two a chance to have a chat.'

'Oh! Well, yes, I suppose so,' Truda replies, somewhat taken aback.

'So tomorrow lunchtime then?' Stefan insists. It sounds more like an instruction than a request.

Stanislaw stands and taps his glass. 'Quiet, everybody. I'd like to propose a happy birthday toast to the lovely Marianna.' They raise their glasses.

'Happy birthday!'

Stanislaw continues, 'It's been a thoroughly enjoyable evening not least because Leon is paying the bill.' He laughs at his own joke but the others look a little embarrassed. He's drunk rather too much and his face, now very pink, is testament to that. But he hasn't finished. 'And now,' he clears his throat, 'I'd like to surprise this lovely lady on my left.' Elena looks puzzled.

'I'd like to ask,' he's temporarily forgotten her name, 'I'd like to ask this fairest flower if she'll do me the honour of being my wife.'

He hands her a small blue box. It's not a diamond or anything like that,' he says apologetically, but Elena squeals with delight anyway and throws herself round his neck, smothering him with kisses and declares, 'I thought you'd never ask!'

Leon reappears, Amelia in tow. 'What's this? What's all the excitement about?'

Stanislaw slaps his back. 'Well, son, I'd like to introduce you to your soon-to-be stepmother.'

Leon laughs. 'In that case, Elena, I think commiserations are more in order if you're prepared to take on this old sod!'

'That's no way to talk to your father,' she scolds.

Leon nods towards his father. 'And it seems you deserve each other,' he says, ducking out of reach of her playful slap. 'When's the wedding?'

'As soon as possible,' Stanislaw says. 'It'll be a small affair, all expense spared,' and he laughs as if it's the funniest thing he's ever said.

*

Marianna and Leon are tired. It's been a long evening so they skip their usual late-night drink and go straight to bed. Marianna watches as Leon unbuttons his shirt. His thick dark hair curling on his forehead, strong shoulders and muscular arms give him the look of a Greek athlete. As newlyweds, their enthusiasm for each other in the bedroom was boundless, but their lovemaking has become less frequent in the last few weeks, although Marianna hasn't minded in the least. She suspects he's probably satisfying this need with Amelia. Her mind is distracted with thoughts of Stefan and all she wants is to be left alone.

'We were pretty impressive tonight, don't you think?'

'You played very well if that's what you mean.' In fact, she'd spent little time listening, being more intent on admiring the way Stefan's hair caught on his collar when he turned his head and the way the candlelight cast a shadow under his angular jaw and caught the light in his eyes.

Marianna would scream inwardly at any minor shows of affection he made towards Truda. The pain like an imaginary chisel chipping away at her insides, the pulse at her temples thumping like hammer blows. Sometimes she could feel his eyes on her but they would shift swiftly to Feliks or Stanislaw when she glanced in his direction and leave her wondering if she'd imagined it.

'Is that all you've got to say?'

'Well, I could say that you and Amelia seem like the perfect pairing but no doubt you'd deny it.'

He laughs cruelly.'God, are you jealous? I didn't know you cared. Let's just say our instruments are finely tuned.' He laughs again, removes his trousers and flings them aside.

He's already semi-erect when he slides into bed beside her, draws her down to his level, takes her chin in his hand, rubs his thumb across her mouth, parts her lips roughly and replaces it with his tongue. As she turns her head to the side he slobbers his way across her cheek and neck and bites her earlobe.

She pulls away, annoyed. 'Don't, Leon. You know I don't like that.'

'You are a frigid one tonight. What's eating you?'

She doesn't answer but turns away unenthusiastically when he searches for her mouth again.

'There's no point you acting the little miss coy, young lady,' he sneers, spreading her legs and hurting her thighs. His hands go to her crotch, probing and rubbing her, his stiffness hard and bruising against her thigh. She wonders that she ever found his lovemaking exciting as he slides his hands beneath her buttocks and, pulling her towards him, thrusts with all his strength. His heaving body judders to a climax almost immediately and with one final push it's over and he collapses onto her, damp with sweat. He grunts and rolls onto his back, breathing heavily.

'That's better,' he sighs. 'How was it for you?'

She turns away, curls herself into a tight ball and pulls the sheet around her chin with clenched fists as tears roll down her cheek and soak the pillow.

# Ten

Marianna is looking for her cottage-on-a-cliff top piece of writing. She's not sure if she should be showing him and wonders if Stefan's interest is born only from politeness. However, she tells herself, when you're trying to improve your writing the views of an impartial reader are always valuable and his interest is certainly a refreshing change to Leon's indifference.

If she thinks too much about the state of their marriage, she may well despair. Less than a year and already the cracks are beginning to show. She resolves to write to her mother and ask her advice as soon as she plucks up the courage to put pen to paper. In the meantime, she hopes that a little time spent with Truda will improve their relationship. She has seen little of her since she started work in the shop. Truda brings her baking before the shop opens so she has time to arrange the display undisturbed and this early start guarantees that their paths don't cross. They met briefly one day in the market square and exchanged pleasantries, but Truda was in a rush and hurried off, leaving Marianna with the distinct feeling she'd been snubbed.

*

Stefan, alone in the workshop, is feeling the heat. His forehead drips with perspiration and his clammy hands are struggling to cope with the delicate carving on Mr Cohen's furniture. Particles of wood dust fill the still air and the overpowering scent of pine sap makes him nauseous.

He downs tools and relaxes in his rocking chair. The rhythmic movement is calming, and before long his head droops sideways and his eyes close.

He is asleep when Marianna puts her head round the workshop door. She watches him for a while, absorbing every detail of his face. His forehead is beaded with sweat and the front of his hair damp. She maps every line from his forehead to the corners of his eyes down past his nose and around to his lips, now slightly parted as his breath escapes, long and slow. His jaw is covered with light stubble and she can see the steady pulse in the vein on his neck where his shirt gapes to one side. His muscular hands and forearms lie relaxed on his lap. She longs to reach out and touch him, wake him so that she can speak with him, but he looks so peaceful she decides against it and looks around for somewhere to leave her writing. There's nowhere that seems quite right so she carefully places it on his lap, slipping one corner under his hand.

*

Marianna makes her way upstairs.

'Hi. Come on in,' Truda says cheerfully.

Marianna decides not to mention Stefan is asleep. Truda is bound to be annoyed.

'What a dreadfully hot day,' Marianna says, mopping her brow. 'I hope for your sake you haven't had to bake.'

'Not today, thank goodness. I need a bit of a rest. Coffee?'

'Thank you.'

Truda indicates a chair for Marianna to sit and retrieves the already stewed brew from the stove. 'So how's it going with the shop?'

'Oh, very well I think. I'm pleased to have something to do and earn a little money, which helps with the rent and so on. Leon is doing well at the restaurant, although he's out for at least three nights of the week.'

'And you don't mind?' Truda queries.

'Yes, I do a little. But it's the way it is with musicians.'

'Oh, I wouldn't put up with that.' Truda replies, and from the stubborn expression she adopts it's clearly true.

Marianna asks about Amelia. 'Has Leon known her for a long time? I mean, I know he knew her before but he hasn't told me anything about her, apart from her being a good musician.'

'He's told you nothing? Well, I'm surprised about that. They were a couple before Leon went to Tarnow and everyone assumed they would get married and from what she's told me, she thought so too. But that wasn't to be. Obviously.' She gives Marianna a look that says 'thanks to you' and adds, 'She was heartbroken when he left. Poor girl.'

Marianna is shocked by this revelation and can't help feeling Truda seems a little heartbroken herself that the pair didn't get together. She's unsure how to respond so changes the subject.

'Feliks is very talented, isn't he?'

'Feliks? Well, yes I suppose he is,' Truda agrees begrudgingly, 'if only he would apply himself and spend less time philandering. I hear you've agreed to model for him.'

'Did he tell you?'

'No. Stefan did. He seemed to think it was a bad idea for some reason. Seemed quite put out about you getting involved like that, but a lot of people would think it a strange thing for a married woman to do. Don't you agree?'

Marianna is determined to play it down and smiles. 'Not at all, it's all very innocent. Leon is perfectly happy about it.' She's surprised at her ability to lie so easily. 'I find it quite liberating and spending time in Feliks' company is enjoyable.'

Truda sniffs and adopts a superior voice. 'I wouldn't stoop to those levels if you paid me. Still, if it works I'm sure he'll be grateful. He does need a break and it would put a stop to his never-ending borrowing. I wouldn't mind so much if he ever paid it back. Stefan never complains, he's his brother after all, but I get very resentful sometimes.'

Marianna is forming the opinion that Truda is often resentful and, unable to come up with a suitable response, searches for a new topic of conversation. 'It's wonderful news about Elena and Stanislaw, isn't it?'

Truda's face brightens a little. 'Yes it is. They've become very fond of each other and are meant to be together I think. Just like Stefan and me. I always knew we'd marry and have a family. We hope to anyway.'

'Oh. Are you planning to start a family?'

Truda sighs. Purses her lips. 'I hope so, but it's not always straightforward. Did you know I've had two miscarriages?'

'No I didn't. I'm sorry to hear that.'

'Well, I have. We've had a particularly hard time of it and unfortunately the second one was shortly after my mother died, so it may have been the stress of that, who knows. The doctors have no idea what the problem is and say we should just keep trying. We will of course and hopefully it'll be third time lucky, but time is slipping by and at my age I'm already considered old for childbearing. Still, I'm lucky to have such a caring husband. Stefan is wonderful about it.' She stares wistfully towards the window and repeats, 'I'm so lucky.'

Marianna chooses to ignore the reference to Stefan and says, 'I'm sorry about your mother. You must miss her terribly.'

'I do of course. We were more like sisters since my father died in the war. It had been just the two of us for a long time.'

Marianna is surprised Truda is sharing so much personal information and feels she should reciprocate.

'Leon and I have no plans to start a family. Not for a while anyway. We have to get used to each other first.'

They sip their coffee in silence until Marianna asks, 'I was wondering if I could have the recipe for those lovely sugar-dusted pastries you make for the shop. I like cooking, but I'm not a baker like you. Still, it would be fun to have a go at making some myself.'

'They are simple to make, but of course if you need the recipe I'll write it out for you and drop it in sometime.'

It hasn't been the most successful meeting and although they came together in a small way at the end, Marianna leaves with the distinct feeling that she and her neighbour have parted on barely better terms than they were before.

*

Back at the flat Marianna is restless, wondering if Stefan has found her writing and annoyed that she didn't call in after seeing Truda. The conversation about starting a family has added to her frustration and the thought of Stefan and Truda making love fills her with agonising jealousy. She chastises herself for following this ridiculous line of thought and determines to put her energy to better use.

It's time to write to her parents so she gathers her pen and some writing paper, makes herself comfortable and begins.

*Dearest Mother and Father,*
*I hope this finds you in the best of health. I'm sure you expected to hear from me sooner but time has passed so quickly, what with everything being so new so I hope you'll forgive me. Stanislaw organised a lovely party for us the day we arrived. It was a lively affair with dancing and the neighbours were very welcoming. We have a nice little flat on the top floor, with a great view over rooftops all the way into the heart of town. Amelia, who is Leon's musician friend, lives on the floor below. She's very quiet and I have seen little of her, although she spends a lot of time rehearsing with Leon. Stefan and Truda gave us a beautiful little chest as a wedding gift. He's a very talented carpenter so we are very lucky to have something so unique and special. The little embroidered cloth you gave me fits its top perfectly. On Saturdays the whole of Krakow seems to descend on our little quarter for the bric-a-brac fair. You would enjoy browsing the stalls. I have a feeling that life here is being less affected by the awful situation than perhaps where you are. I hope you are both managing. We are very lucky I think. A lot of people have far less than we do. Many have no job at all but those who do can still afford fancy ingredients. We get by, but absolutely nothing is wasted. I manage to scrounge a few crusts of Truda's bread to feed the pigeons. Krakow is a very elegant town. The wonderful buildings would impress you and there are many beautiful churches. It would be lovely if you could visit one day. I would love to show you around. Stanislaw is a kind and mostly jovial man. Father would enjoy his company. As father-in-laws go I think I've struck gold. I work in his shop four days*

*a week serving and taking orders. The customers always want to chat which is nice for me as Leon is out a lot during the day practising and then hard at work again in the evenings, playing in a local restaurant. Truda, who has been a friend of Leon's since they were young, was a little offhand to start with but I think we are better friends now, although truth to tell we have little in common as she's a town girl through and through. I so miss the tranquil countryside and open skies, although I suppose home is here now. It doesn't seem like it. Not yet anyway.*

*I must mention Tomas. I think of him as my adopted son. Silly girl, I hear you say, but I hope I've rescued him from an unsavoury future of begging, stealing and possibly worse. He's a darling boy and totally transformed. Stanislaw has been wonderful with him too. I think he thinks of him as a surrogate grandson. He now lives at the shop (I'll tell you the story of why another time) and helps out with deliveries and other small tasks. He and I have some very interesting conversations, usually whilst sat feeding the pigeons in the local cemetery. I was telling him about Petronella a while ago. How is she by the way? Still first in the pecking order I bet.*

*Now here's a bit of news you may find quite shocking, so I hope you are sitting down. I'm an artist's model! (Spare time only and unpaid). What d'you think of that? Mother, I expect you're telling Father already with that worried frown of yours. Well, don't fret, it's all perfectly innocent. Stefan's brother Feliks is an artist. A very good one at that and I have become his 'muse'. He's working on some new ideas he hopes will make his fortune, although a decent living would be a start. He is excellent company and good fun. Like I said, it's all very innocent so don't go worrying your head about it. Oh. I forgot to tell you. Stanislaw and Elena (his long-time friend) are going to be married. It is something happy to look forward to. I had a lovely evening on my birthday. Twenty-three already! Leon was working, but Stefan and Truda etc. were there and we had a lovely evening.*

*I think that's all my news for now. I'll write again soon. I promise.*
*Much love.*
*Marianna*

*PS 'This is written with my very elegant pen that was a birthday gift from Stanislaw and Elena. Oh and one more thing. Remember the old lock I found all those years ago on the beach at Hel? It's now beautifully mounted and surrounded with a framework of Stefan's exquisite carving.*
*PPS Leon sends his regards.*

She has failed miserably to do what she set out to do and confide in her mother, and as for 'Leon sends his regards' that makes her laugh out loud. He hasn't mentioned her parents since the day they left Zalipie. Hopefully her mother will read between the lines and, if she asks, Marianna will tell all, but for now she'll keep her problems to herself.

*

When Stefan wakes the envelope has dropped to the floor, but he recognises Marianna's writing and is about to open it when he hears a noise. He swiftly closes the door and makes himself comfortable in his rocking chair with one foot pushing rhythmically against the bench. He loosens the sealed flap and removes the contents. He unfolds the sheets of paper. She has written a short note: 'Don't feel obliged to read this. I won't be offended if you don't, although if you can find the time I would really value your opinion.'

*A Headful of Dreams*

*The granite cottage stands on a rocky clifftop surrounded by cushions of cropped grass studded with pink sea thrift. The occasional cry of a seabird breaks the silence and a gently babbling stream finds its way between the boulders from somewhere inland.*

*A rose-covered porch conceals a heavy oak door leading to a flagstone entrance. Relish the peace as the latch clicks shut and stand for a moment immersed in the silence within. The smoky whiff of a burnt-out fire lingers in the air and logs are piled on the hearth ready for the next. Odd pieces of furniture sit comfortably and at ease with each other. A coffee table with books piled haphazardly on its surface and a deep ceramic bowl filled with shells and pieces of driftwood sits in front of a worn sofa with big soft cushions and colourful throws. From the comfort of a deep window seat is an uninterrupted view to the cliffs and sea below and westwards to where sunset will mark the end of another perfect day. Upstairs a large airy room is home to a bed with crisp white linen and pillows soft as summer clouds. The open casement windows allow the breeze to rhythmically whisper the curtains gently back and forth and the relentless pounding of the waves in the bay below is the only sound that intrudes into this meditative space. Outside is a pretty private garden filled with foxgloves, bluebells, primroses and wild garlic. An ancient apple tree is saved from collapse by a sturdy wooden stake. The silence is broken, but only by the clucking of hens and the twittering of birds as they play hide and seek in the hedgerow.*

It's exactly how he imagined she would write and Stefan is transported to a place he has long dreamt about. He reads it again and imagines himself there.

*

Truda's irritated voice brings him back to reality.

'Stefan, are you staying down there all night? The stew is getting spoilt.'

He's on his feet in an instant, hurriedly replaces the story and the note in its envelope and slips it under a pile of paperwork. He is, to all intents and purposes, standing at the bench contemplating the piece of work before him when Truda pushes the door open.

'What's keeping you? It's way past closing time. Do hurry up.'

Tutting, she retraces her steps, muttering all the time about inconsideration. She's in a petulant mood and Stefan is late. These are two facts that are bound to spark a row.

'For goodness' sake, you know what time we eat. It's so annoying when I've made an effort to cook a meal and you just turn up when you feel like it.'

'Don't start, Truda. I lost track of time, that's all. Hardly a hanging offence.'

'It's just plain rude. Talk about take me for granted.'

'I'm not taking you for granted. Don't talk rubbish. What's got into you this evening? What's sparked this off? Get it out in the open, Truda, and let's not spoil the entire evening.'

'It was Marianna's fault if you must know.'

'Marianna? What's she got to do with it?'

'It was when she came up for a coffee the other day. She started talking about families and having babies and it just got me riled, that's all.'

'And you've been brooding about it all this time? That's hardly her fault. I expect some busybody has told her about the miscarriages. Like Sara, for instance. Bloody gossip. I don't know why you enjoy her company so much. Not only is she a gossip, she's a total bore. I'd have thought you would want more stimulating company, what with spending so much time on your own.'

'Sara is none of those things and no, Marianna didn't know. But she asked me if we were going to start a family and it upset me so I told her myself.'

Truda crosses her arms and stands tapping her foot.

'I'd quite like to know the answer to that question too.'

'The answer to what question?' Stefa. is irritated now.

'When we're going to start a family. It takes two to have a baby, you know. You don't seem all that interested in our love life lately. Why's that? I'm always the dutiful wife. I never refuse you.'

Stefan prepares himself for the usual onslaught of personal insults and name-calling. He raises a hand.

'Stop! Please. I've heard all this a hundred times. You know how I feel about the subject. Until our relationship is on better terms I don't want to bring a child into a dysfunctional marriage. Now drop it, will you.'

'Dysfunctional!' Truda screams at him. 'That's a new one.'

'Alright, I'm sorry. What I mean is less than perfect.'

He's making the situation worse and knows it. 'I know it's been hard for you since the miscarriages but you don't make it easy for me. Making love to a woman who's only doing it for the sake of procreation isn't exactly a turn-on.'

Truda wheedles now. 'Please don't be unkind, Stefan. You know losing those babies was a huge blow. I need you to make more of a fuss of me, be more attentive. I don't feel attractive anymore.'

'I do my best,' Stefan mutters, 'in the circumstances. Let's not argue anymore. Let's try and enjoy each other's company this evening and who knows what will happen.'

The evening passes reasonably amicably. Bedtime comes. Stefan holds her close and says the things she wants to hear. Truda lies like a shop manikin, cold and unresponsive. Stefan makes love to her but it's Marianna he's thinking about.

*

When Marianna pops into the workshop the next morning she's disconcerted to see Stefan rocking back and forth, leant forwards with his head in his hands.

'Are you alright?' she asks, feeling awkward.

'Far from it,' he says, leaning back.

'I'm sorry to hear that. Is there anything I can do to help?'

He doesn't answer but sits for a while considering his response before his face creases into a wide smile. 'Yes. There most certainly is. You can keep me company for a while.'

Marianna thinks his smile the most beautiful she's ever seen and his mouth the one she wants to kiss more than any other. She thrusts her shaking hands into her pockets afraid of the effect his physical presence has on her.

'I've got something to show you,' he says.

The box from the bric-a-brac fair has been varnished and the rusty hinges replaced with brass ones. Inside the wood grain glows, deep and rich, the colour of a ripe conker.

'That's quite remarkable. What a difference. I must pay you something for the time you've spent repairing it.'

'You'll do no such thing, it was my pleasure.' His fingers touch hers as he hands her the box.

She doesn't move away as he whispers, 'Close your eyes.'

She does and he kisses her lips, so lightly she can barely believe it's happened.

'This isn't right,' she says.

'I know,' he replies. And kisses her again.

# Eleven

Feliks has been mulling over the idea of exhibiting at the restaurant and has produced half a dozen preparatory sketches that he hopes will excite the manager into allowing him wall space.

Little persuasion is needed. 'This is exciting work, Feliks,' he says, examining each one closely with a discerning eye. 'We could certainly do with some fresh work. Some of these paintings have been here for months.'

In his mind's eye Feliks can already see red sold labels attached to each piece. 'Do you charge for the wall space?' he asks.

'No, but I take a small commission on any works sold,' he replies.

'How small?' Feliks asks.

'Just ten per cent of the sale price. I think that's fair.'

Feliks agrees that it is and shakes the manager's hand.

'Oh, just one more thing, Feliks. I don't want anything too racy. Nobody wants to sit with a row of tits in their face when they're eating.' The manager guffaws and slaps Feliks on the back.

'There's no need to worry on that score,' Feliks assures him. 'My model is a beautiful woman and I'm sure your customers will be drawn to her looks rather than her appendages.'

'When will the work be ready?'

Feliks hasn't mentioned that so far he doesn't have any.

'I'm working on six paintings,' he bluffs. 'They'll be ready in about four weeks' time, maybe less. I can't say for sure. I won't exhibit anything less than my most accomplished pieces, so bear with me if they're a little late.'

Feliks leaves the restaurant and strides home feeling elated. First stop Stanislaw's. Marianna has been so supportive she must be the first to know.

She's behind the counter serving when he bursts through the door beaming from ear to ear. She raises a finger to indicate 'just a moment'. As soon as the customer leaves he sweeps her up and swings her round.

'We've done it! I'm in.'

She clings on, squealing as he goes faster and faster.

'Stop, Feliks, I'm dizzy. Please stop!'

He does but they sway about a bit, dizzy.

'Oh, Feliks, what fantastic news. I'm so pleased.'

'It's my big chance, Marianna, but there's a lot to do. I need to spend some time planning and then we can start on the actual paintings. How about next week?'

'That's fine with me,' she says. 'Gosh this is exciting.'

Compared to the conflicting emotions she's struggled with since kissing Stefan, this is something Marianna can be positive about.

Feliks pecks her cheek. 'Okay. I'm off. I've got serious work to do.' Marianna's faith in him has been rewarded and only good things can happen from now on.

*

The days pass and Marianna's concentration is under severe pressure. Leon has noticed how withdrawn she is and is annoyed that the meal she's cooked has clearly been thrown together at the last minute.

'Getting a bit slapdash, are we?' he grumbles.

Normally comments like this would rile her and he'd receive a sharp response. These days he never says anything nice to her, except when he wants her. 'If you say nice things,' she told him one day when she was particularly disgruntled and he was being particularly grovelling, 'you should mean them or they're worthless.'

She's in a state of anaesthesia where he's concerned and has developed Leon antibodies. He can do and say what he likes. She's not bothered. With her mind so preoccupied she's been making mistakes in the shop, overcharging and short-changing customers while she keeps one eye fixed on the door in the hope she'll catch a glimpse of Stefan as he passes by. He's been calling into the shop more often, buying random items he doesn't need, spending time chatting about mundane day-to-day things that usually wouldn't interest him. Any excuse will do, as long as he gets to see her.

*

Feliks has started work on his paintings for the restaurant and is working like a demon. She's astonished at the intensity with which he works, mixing, applying and smoothing, scraping and reapplying the paint until he's happy with the result. The silence in the studio is broken only by the sound of brushes on canvas and the swish of his wide-sleeved artist's smock as he expresses himself in paint. Feliks smokes a cigarette as he paints; it's the only time he does. 'It helps me concentrate,' he says when Marianna expresses surprise. A thin plume of smoke curls slowly in the air as the cigarette gradually burns down and ash drops to the floor.

He loves to describe what colours he's using and reads the names to her as he chooses and mixes. Rose Madder, Prussian Blue, Burnt Sienna, Alizarin Crimson, Terre Verte; there's a touch of alchemy in the names. She relishes being in the studio with him, it's like inhabiting another world. Modelling for Feliks allows her the luxury of being alone with her thoughts for hours on end with the added bonus that Stefan is only a few yards away in the workshop. Popping her head round the door to spend a few minutes with him before returning to the flat is equivalent to a bee finding the nectar that will quench its thirst and see it through to the next day. She has seen Stefan almost every day and delights in the relaxed relationship developing between the brothers as they spend more time in each other's company. Marianna was coy when he first appeared, unsure about him seeing her naked, but now she's comfortable in his presence. They talk a lot, the three of them contributing equally to discussions about which is better, town or country, what makes a man a real man (Feliks has all the answers to this one) and the worrying and ever-increasing hardship that rural Poland is enduring.

Feliks has never seen his brother more visibly happy than when he's in Marianna's company. *Good luck to them,* he thinks. Truda certainly won't hear about it from him; they've never hit it off and as far as he's concerned, Leon is a womanising egotistical bastard who doesn't deserve her. For two weeks Marianna spends as much time as she can at the studio, but Leon hardly notices and he's seldom at the flat when she arrives home.

*

Some weeks after Marianna wrote to her parents she's pleased to receive an envelope in her mother's spidery writing. Tucking it into her apron pocket she intends to read it later when Leon is at the restaurant.

'We've got an extra shift tonight,' he tells her, 'so don't wait up. It's going to be a late one.'

Marianna is indifferent to his frequent and prolonged absences. They give her the opportunity to invite Tomas for something to eat and the boy's company, always entertaining, is enjoyable.

She's helping him improve his reading and writing and he's proving to be the perfect student, always on time and eager to learn. After they've eaten, Marianna clears the table and he pores over his exercise books, working studiously for an hour. Marianna helps him every time he gets stuck on a word and each evening he goes away just a little closer to being literate.

To round off the evening they curl up on the sofa and she tells him stories of her childhood. Tomas has never been out of town and is enthralled by her description of the countryside and village life. When she asks him to reciprocate he replies, 'Ain't got no stories, Miss, ain't had no childhood.' She hugs him and makes hot chocolate, which they sit and sip in the half-light. He leaves at nine o'clock and is tucked up in bed in his sleep cupboard, as he calls it, within minutes.

*

Alone in the flat at last, she retrieves the letter from her pocket, curls up on the sofa and reads.

*Dear Marianna,*
*We were so happy to receive your letter. Your father and I were beginning to wonder if you'd actually arrived! It was good to hear that Stanislaw is a kind man and that your neighbours made you so welcome with a lovely party, which sounded fun. You are very lucky to start off with a flat of your own and I'm sure you've made it very comfortable. It sounds as though Truda is a little jealous of you, my darling. It's always difficult for a woman who has become used to being the centre of attention to take*

*to somebody new. Especially somebody as lovely as you. I can hear you now, telling me to stop it. But you are my daughter so it's only natural that I should think so. Stefan sounds very talented. You seem to have a good rapport with him at least, although it seems you have become very fond of Tomas. He sounds like a real character. Tell him Petronella is still pecking away, although I have to tell you that pigeon numbers have depleted somewhat since a fox moved into the village. So far so good, for Petronella.*

*Well! I must say your father and I were a little shocked about the modelling but then we are old-fashioned. If you tell us it's all above board we will have to get used to the idea. I told the girls in the village and they were all of a giggle.*

*I don't have very much news from Zalipie. We are both well, although your father works far too hard and is always tired. We consider ourselves lucky to have so many hens as their eggs have become currency and we swap them with our neighbours for other food items. The shops in Tarnow will accept them in payment for other goods and this keeps us going. The weather has been good and already we are harvesting early crops. We'll be alright so please don't worry about us.*

*We couldn't help noticing that you didn't mention Leon. Reading between the lines, we can't help wondering if things are all they should be. Am I right? A mother always knows these things and you sounded a little despondent. Dare I say this next bit? I'm not sure but I will anyway. Stefan seems to feature in your life quite often. Is this a good thing? I only ask out of concern and we only ever have your best interests at heart.*

*I expect you are thinking what fusspots we are, but if you ever need to come home, for a little holiday, or even longer, you will be more than welcome. This will always be your home and we miss you very much.*

*I think that's enough for today. It would be lovely to hear your up-to-date news if you've time to write. We are keen to know how the paintings are coming along.*

*Much love from us. Always.*

*Mother and Father xxx*

Marianna reads it again, pours herself a large glass of vodka, and takes herself off to bed.

*

She is woken by the sound of Leon stumbling around the room and lies still, holding her breath. He throws himself on the bed, breathing heavily and occasionally belching. The smell of alcohol and a distinctly familiar perfume permeates his whole being. She recognises that sickly sweet scent; he smells of Amelia.

She clenches her fists as his arm reaches across and shakes her. 'You awake?' he slurs. She doesn't respond.

He shakes her again, harder this time. 'Wake up, you bitch. I said wake up!'

Marianna turns on him. 'How dare you! Get your hands off me! You're drunk and you stink!'

'I've had a couple of drinks. What's wrong with that? A man has to get his pleasure somewhere.'

Marianna sits up and confronts him. 'I suspect you've had more than just a few drinks. Haven't you? Where have you actually been, Leon?'

He laughs. Pulls her down on top of him, searching for her mouth. His rancid saliva wets her face as he grasps the back of her neck and in the struggle to keep her still, bites her lip.

'Get off me!'

He laughs again. 'Come on, you know you want it.'

She struggles to free herself but he's strong even in his inebriated state. He pushes her onto her front, pressing her face into the pillow and pins her arms wide. Her jaw feels as if it will break and she tries to scream as he pushes her legs apart with his knee.

'Come on, girl, loosen up and I'll show you what pleasure is.'

He's too strong for her as he thrusts into her, time and time again, pulsing her body against the bed. He grabs the back of her hair and pulls her head up.

'Scream if you like it,' he spits out between gritted teeth. She struggles and bucks against him as he lets go of her hands, but she manages to reach back and grab his crotch just as he rises up to dismount her. She squeezes with all her might, digging her nails in. He groans in pain and pulls away from her, clutching his crotch. She scrambles from the bed, grabs her dressing gown and makes her escape. Shaking, she leans against the table for support, that precious place between her legs violated and dripping with his vile seed and the metallic taste of blood in her mouth. She wipes it away with the back of a trembling hand and realises with devastating clarity that their marriage is a sham.

*

Marianna has spent a sleepless night on the sofa. Leon is still asleep and snoring like a pig. His body odour is still on her and the thought of him fills her with revulsion. She scrubs herself until her skin glows, creeps into the bedroom, collects some clean clothes, dresses in the kitchen and is working in the shop by the time he wakes. With any luck she won't have to see or speak to him until the evening.

She can barely look Stanislaw in the eye. If he knew what a disgusting creep his son was he'd be horrified. She moves about the shop like a zombie. Stanislaw glancing at her from time to time asks, 'What's happened to your lip?' and moves in for a closer look.

'Oh, it's nothing. I slipped in the bathroom and hit my mouth on the edge of the sink,' she mumbles, turning away.

But Stanislaw isn't convinced. Something isn't right; she looks desperately tired and on the verge of tears, is unusually quiet and is seemingly unable to engage with the customers in her usual friendly way. He's afraid to ask what's wrong because he has a sneaky suspicion that Leon may be the cause.

*

There's nothing quite like anger for galvanising action, as a result of which Marianna has spent the day manically cleaning and tidying. She's been juggling words in her head all day, practising her speech for when he gets home.

The ironing awaits and she relishes the thought of all that hissing steam and heat. It will match her mood. She drags a weighty blanket from the cupboard and spreads it across the table. The smell of a thousand scorchings rises from the thick grey fabric, and pieces of burnt fibre detach from its fraying edges, landing like wingless insects on her cream top. Irritated, she brushes them off, smooths the cloth over the tabletop and pushes it into position beside the only socket in the room.

Resting in a battered cardboard box the iron lies waiting like a skulking creature, its stiff striped cord tail wound tightly around its waist. A gift from Stanislaw and Elena, the new electrical appliance is easier to use but she reminisces about the homely ritual of using her mother's heavy iron heated on the kitchen stove and used with a thick cloth wrapped around its handle. Ironing at home was a relaxing and satisfying task, contentedly carried out in a room filled with the rich aroma of some delicious stewy dish or the smell of baking bread.

Sighing, she separates Leon's shirts from the pile of fresh laundry heaped in a basket, flings them to one side, muttering 'Bastard' every so often under her breath and sorts the remaining items into order, ranging from flat and easy to small and awkward.

She plugs the iron into the wall socket and stands hands on hips, waiting for the magic of electricity to happen. Agitated, she pushes the window open and peers out into the street but there is still no sign of him. Where the hell is he?

Sheets, the first to feel the extent of her anger, are shaken, stretched and folded into rectangles. She fills a jug at the tap and flicks a handful of water drops onto each surface, stacking them to allow the moisture to permeate. She tests the heat of the iron tentatively with her forefinger and starts to press down and across with broad sweeping strokes. A cloud of hot vaporised freshness rises up and she leans back quickly out of its line of fire. The more she recalls the previous night the angrier she becomes.

Damp hair sticks to her forehead and her face becomes flushed as the creased pile is transformed into smooth layers of crisp linen. Flat items finished, she slows the action to smooth each frilled edge or awkward seam on her own clothes and carefully arranges them on hangers hooked onto the curtain wire at the open window. Leon's creased shirts are dumped back in the basket. He can do his own ironing in future.

Ironing finished, she unplugs the appliance and slumps into a chair, smoothing her hair back from her sweating face. Her back aches and her head throbs. The iron quietly clicks and ticks as it cools. She stuffs it back into its box, refolds the blanket and shoves them in the cupboard just as the door slams.

She turns her back to him, busying herself at the sink. Leon has been working on his strategy and he's carrying a huge bunch of Elena's best blooms and sidles up to her, kissing the back of her neck.

'Forgive me,' he says in a childlike voice. 'I'm a swine and I know it. I don't know what came over me.'

Marianna closes her eyes and sighs. She might have known. Clever, manipulating Leon. She turns to face him.

'It's no good, Leon. A roomful of flowers can't make up for what you did to me.' She pushes him aside. 'You behaved like an uncouth pig. I hate you, Leon.'

He follows her, tugging at her arm. 'Please, Marianna. Forgive me.' He's ridiculous now as he gets down on one knee. 'I'll make it up to you. I really will.'

Marianna looks down at him and grins patronisingly.

'Really? Are you capable of that, do you think? And how exactly will you do that, by sleeping with Amelia twice a week instead of four times, or five, or however many times you inflict your loathsome self on her?'

Leon feigns shocked disbelief. 'Amelia is nothing to me. Nothing. We are musicians together, that's all.'

'Rubbish! I'm not stupid, Leon. I could smell her on you and I've seen the way you behave when she's around you. You're obsessed with her and she with you. Well, she's welcome if that's the sort of treatment you give her.'

He grovels again. 'Okay. I admit I spend too much time with her. I'll stop. I know it's wrong. I love only you. You are the one. Please, Marianna. Give me another chance.'

She has no intention of giving him another chance, but she has to live somewhere and there's no alternative short of returning to Zalipie.

'You'd better make an effort, Leon. And don't think for one moment that you'll be coming anywhere near me until you do. I may be a country girl but I have feelings and self-respect. One more episode like that and I'll be gone.' Her planned speech hasn't gone quite as well as she'd hoped and yet again Leon's wheedling appears to have prevailed.

# Twelve

The following Monday the sky is clear and the day is already uncomfortably hot. 'Another sweltering day,' Stanislaw grumbles as Tomas appears spruced up and ready for work. He has taken to his new routine with ease and now spends even more time in the shopkeeper's company. Stanislaw makes Tomas laugh and the boy repays him by responding to Stanislaw's beck and call without question.

Eryk has so far failed to appear since the incident with the bottle, as a result of which Tomas is more relaxed.

'Only one delivery this morning,' Stanislaw informs him. 'I swear Mrs Cohen only buys this much cheese in order to have you visit. Lucky for you she can afford it. She's practically the only customer who can.'

He ruffles Tomas's hair.

The shop bell jingles and Lidka breezes in. She's barely recognisable from her previous dowdy self. Her mousy features are less plain now that she's gained some weight and perfected the art of smiling. Previously lank, her hair has been styled into a neat bob and frames her face flatteringly. Rumours abound that she has a crush on

Feliks, although as far as he's concerned they're just friends. Lidka has other ideas, however, and as part of her strategy to win him over has become proficient in the art of mixing paint, cleaning brushes and keeping the studio spick and span. Feliks likes the idea of having an assistant and they have a mutually convenient arrangement that means Lidka calls in once or twice a week. She's very happy to comment on the work in progress and has become his chief critic. Lidka has a surprisingly expert eye, and as her comments often prove valid he accepts her advice with good grace. His initial reaction to her obvious affection for him was one of amusement, but lately he's started to look forward to her visits and the once-steady flow of female company to the studio has slowed to an occasional dalliance.

'Good morning, young lady,' Stanislaw beams. 'You look very fetching in that outfit if you don't mind me saying so. Going somewhere special?'

Lidka is flattered and grows another inch. 'Father made it for me. Isn't it elegant? And in answer to your question, yes, I've an appointment at the Town Hall. They need somebody to do filing, cataloguing, that sort of thing, so I'm putting myself forward as a trainee clerk. Quite a step up for me, don't you think, after working in that awful abattoir for so long.'

'Indeed it would be a great improvement. I hope you get the job,' Stanislaw says.

'I do hope so. I know of at least fifteen other people who are going along today. There's such a shortage of jobs it would be quite something if I get it.'

'You certainly look the part I must say' Stanislaw responds.

'Thank you. Mother says that if it stays hot like this all day I'm going to suffer in this little suit.'

Stanislaw can't help but smile. *Like mother, like daughter,* he thinks.

'So what can I get you?'

'I've just popped in for a loaf of Truda's seeded bread. Mother won't venture out in this heat.'

'Good luck with the job,' Stanislaw says as she tucks the wrapped loaf under her arm and struts out onto Szeroka Street. He scratches his head and shakes it in disbelief. Who'd have thought a single tango could so transform a person.

'Do I know her?' Tomas asks. 'I sort of recognise her but I'm not sure.'

'You certainly do. But she's not who she used to be.'

Lidka turns left and left again and enters the door to the studio, unaware that her mother is watching.

*

Michal's expert skills are being put to good use as he cuts a pattern for a pair of gentleman's trousers. The scissors glide through the worsted with a satisfying 'sssssst'. Wire-framed glasses are perched precariously on the tip of his slender nose and his tongue repeatedly rubs the edge of his neat pencil moustache in concentration. One slip now and the valuable fabric will be wasted.

Sara bursts through the door and stomps across the room. 'I told you! I've seen her going into his place again and I'll wager she's up to no good.'

Michal looks up and the scissors slip. 'God damn you!' he swears and drops into the seat beside his sewing machine, hands held high in despair. 'Now look what I've done! This fabric is worth a fortune. I'll have to waste this section now.' His face is like thunder. 'What do you want anyway, woman? It'd better not be another helping of gossip!'

Sara huffs impatiently. 'It's not gossip and you may not wish to hear this. Our daughter is a hussy and that's a fact.'

Michal sighs. 'I've told you before for God's sake! You are talking rubbish, woman. She's a grown woman, Sara, and it's time you accepted the fact.'

'No matter, you may be on her side but I can't have her carrying on like this, it's shocking behaviour. All this tarting herself up, like some brazen wench! And then visiting his flat alone! There's clearly something going on, she looks as guilty as hell whenever his name's mentioned.' She pats a stray hair back into the tight bun at the nape of her sweating neck and blinks agitatedly. 'It's a disgrace, that's what it is.' Her cheeks flush maroon and her thin lips purse.

Michal sighs impatiently. 'You are being ridiculous!' He inspects the damaged fabric, sighs again and turns to face her. 'They're young. Let them enjoy life.'

'There's enjoying and then there's... well. You know...' Sara insists.

'You don't actually know that but what of it anyway?' Michal is increasingly annoyed.

'What will the neighbours say? That's what worries me,' Sara says, anxious for their reputation.

'Bugger the neighbours. As long as she's happy.' Michal fiddles with a tray of cotton reels, averting his eyes from her disapproving gaze.

Sara stands within inches of his face, wagging her finger. 'Mark my words that daughter of ours is setting herself up for heartache. "Mother," she said to me yesterday, "he's the only man for me." "Well, Lidka," I said to her, "he seems wholly unsuitable and I can't see him sticking with you in a million years."'

'That was a cruel thing to say, Sara. She is your daughter!'

Sara looks momentarily sheepish.

Michal waves his scissors at her, his expression determined. 'I'd keep opinions like that to yourself if I were you.'

Sara's neck stiffens and she points a finger in his face. 'I blame the tango. That's what started it.'

'Tango! Good grief, what are you talking about?'

'Yes. That's right. The tango. The dance of the Devil, I'd say. At the party! All that leg-to-leg touching and eye-to-eye contact and,' she pauses, 'other stuff.' But Sara hasn't finished. 'He's only after one thing and when he gets it, he'll be off.'

'I've never heard such nonsense. You're being ridiculous and even if it's true, I reckon he'd be a lucky man to have our Lidka.'

'Oh, you think so, do you? Have you no morals?'

'Morals? I have, of course I have, but I think it's about time you let Lidka get on with her life and stopped trying to control her.' He turns away.

Sara, huffing, opens the door to leave. 'There's no point discussing it with you, Michal Krawczyk, I'm going to Truda's for tea. She'll know what's going on and I'm sure she'll agree with me.'

Over his shoulder Michal declares, 'There's only one thing the pair of you will brew, and that's trouble. Now get out of here before you cause any more damage.' He screws the damaged fabric into a ball and throws it down in disgust.

Sara frowns. 'Well, don't say I didn't tell you when she comes home broken-hearted.'

Michal moves to his workbench and prepares to sew a pocket. He threads the needle on his machine, throws her a scornful look and turns the handle as fast as his arthritic hands will allow.

# Thirteen

The Saturday bric-a-brac fair has become a regular feature in the calendar for both Stanislaw and Truda, who has now become proficient at selling her own products. Feliks puts in an occasional appearance though his enthusiasm has visibly waned now that Lidka is a regular feature in his life. The small amount he earns from the drawings is earmarked for a very important payment. He's had a troubled conscience since the day he stole money from Stefan's workshop, but Truda is in charge of their finances, squirrelling money away in a locked tin and only dishing it out for essential purchases, so he's concluded that somewhere along the line communication between the two of them has allowed the short payment to go unnoticed. He could just forget it of course, but he owes his brother some loyalty and is determined to repay the money.

There's been talk of closing Elena's stall and selling flowers from Stanislaw's. 'It makes sense to consolidate,' Stanislaw's words, not hers, 'and think of the money you'll save on rent. Your regular customers are sure to support the new venture and in doing so attract new customers for the shop. It is, without doubt,' Stanislaw assures her, 'the best way forward.'

Leon and Amelia's music is sorely missed, as they now have a regular lunchtime slot at the restaurant which is always busy on Saturday, so with everybody occupied Marianna and Stefan are free to wander the stalls. Most weeks they find themselves in their usual coffee haunt comparing purchases and swapping stories about missed bargains. For Marianna the time spent with Stefan is the highlight of her week and it's over all too quickly.

There is, at last, respite from the intense heat of high summer, and Marianna and Tomas's trips to the cemetery have become less frequent. When they do find time to visit they take advantage of windy days to blow the cobwebs away, breathe in some fresh air and wander amongst the graves and tombs, relishing the sound of the wind in the trees and kicking up the crisp autumn leaves that pile in every corner. Tomas continues to test Marianna's knowledge with a different question for every minute they spend in their alternative world in the middle of town.

In the flat above the workshop, Truda spends an increasing number of hours baking. Her relationship with Stefan is no better and an underlying feeling of resentment and disappointment hangs over them like an invisible cloud. The baby question is unresolved, stifling their conversations and erasing laughter. It's an unfulfilled, obsessive desire on her part, a lack of enthusiasm on his. Stalemate.

Next door, Leon and Marianna cohabit, with underlying distrust on her part. Leon has made an effort to be more thoughtful, less critical, but she is used to being alone and prefers it that way so the less they see of each other the better. It's not satisfactory, Marianna thinks wistfully, but it'll have to do.

# Fourteen

Marianna has tidied the flat, had a late lunch and is getting ready to go out. Leon took himself off to town an hour earlier on some unspecified trip.

'Perhaps we could meet and have a drink,' she'd suggested in an attempt at reconciliation but Leon looked unenthusiastic. 'Let's not plan anything, I don't know if I'll have time.'

Halfway to town she twists her ankle on the cobbles and the heel of her shoe comes off. Damn! She examines the broken shoe but it's clear her trip will have to be curtailed and she limps back home. Stanislaw is surprised to see her back so soon. 'You too? Leon has only been back a short while. Seems like you both had wasted trips. What happened to your shoe?'

'Blasted heel came off,' she says, holding it up for him to see.

'Give it here. I'll soon pop that back on for you. Give me the other one. I'll check that out too.'

Barefoot, Marianna makes her way upstairs. She's just passed the first-floor landing when she stops dead in her tracks. The sound of laughter is coming from Amelia's flat. She recognises Leon's deep throaty chuckle and her stomach churns. She grips the banister, her ears straining to hear every sound. Retracing her steps she sits on the stairs outside Amelia's door. It's quiet for a while. A draft wafts the smell of cigarette smoke and ground coffee up the stairwell from below and Stanislaw's muffled voice can be heard chatting to a customer. She wonders if her ears are playing tricks on her and thinks she must have been mistaken but no, there it is again. The distinctive sound of Amelia's giggle and Leon's gravelly voice urging her on. Amelia groans and Leon grunts as their breathing becomes faster and faster until, just as Marianna thinks she can bear it no longer, they meet in one climactic gasp and it's done. Her head sinks onto her knees. She's known it all along of course. Her knuckles turn white as she grips the strap of her bag and squeezes her eyes shut against the image in her head. She is frozen to the spot until she hears soft whispered terms of endearment from Leon and tears from Amelia, and the reality of his infidelity hits home. She rushes upstairs, breathless and panicking. There's only one way out of this. Back at the flat she grabs a battered brown suitcase from the top of the wardrobe, flings it on the bed and shoves items of clothing in haphazardly, pressing them down to fit more in. There's no time to lose. Looking around frantically her eyes alight on the red lacquer box on Stefan's chest. She wraps it in a scarf along with Tomas's scent bottle and the framed lock and stuffs them into her bag. She can't be here when Leon returns; she must get away and give herself time to work out how she can extricate herself from this meaningless marriage. Her final act is to scribble a hasty note on a piece of scrap paper.

*Have left for Zalipie. Father is unwell.*

*Don't know how long I'll be gone.*

*Couldn't wait.*

*Bus leaves in an hour.*

She grabs her winter coat from the wardrobe and struggles, in her panic, to put it on. Downstairs she stays out of sight until Stanislaw has his back turned then slips noiselessly out of the door. She should turn right to town but instinctively turns left and immediately left again.

Stefan looks up, surprised to see her standing in the doorway. 'What's this?' he says, and glances at her case, concerned.

Her face is pale. He notices her hands trembling as she wipes a tear from her cheek. 'I'm leaving,' she stutters. 'My father is ill.' The lie has to be followed through.

'I'm sorry to hear that,' he says, moving closer to her. 'How long will you be gone?' She shrugs.

Stefan looks puzzled. 'Do you have to go in such a hurry?'

She nods. She can't bear to look at him. He's a step away from her now.

'Is there something else? You look terrible,' he says.

She drops her head and doesn't answer.

'Tell me, Marianna. What is it?'

She shakes her head. 'I can't.'

'Why not? What's wrong? Please. I can't let you go like this.'

'I have to. It's for the best.'

'Best for who? Not for me. You must know that.' He touches her cheek. 'Please don't go,' he pleads, pulling her towards him. She leans against his shoulder. He pushes the door shut behind her, cups her face in his hands and kisses her tenderly. She's intoxicated by the sweetness of his breath, the softness of his mouth, and returns the kiss passionately.

'Take your coat off,' he whispers. She slips her arms free and he takes it from her. She relishes the agonising perfect slowness as his hands cradle her head, her silky fragrant hair held between his fingers. He kisses her again and her insides turn to liquid as their tongues meet. Unbuttoning her blouse he slides it gently over her shoulder kissing the hollow place at the base of her neck. He can feel her pulse surging as he slowly slides his lips across her shoulder – tasting her, biting her tenderly. Her head rolls back and she meets his gaze as he strokes her cheek with the back of his hand. She takes it in hers and kisses each fingertip. He claims her mouth again, hungry for her.

As Marianna undoes his leather apron the earthy smell of freshly worked wood lingers on his clothes beneath. She pulls his shirt loose, slides her hands up and around his back. His muscles tense with the feel of her flesh against his. Sweeping tools and paperwork aside, he lifts her onto the workbench.

'Pull up your skirt,' he says, his breath coming faster, and she does. He slides her silk panties to the floor and gently spreads her legs as she undoes the button on his trousers and sets him free. They are gasping and desperate with desire as he reaches up and touches her full, open mouth and she draws his thumb in, sucking everything from him as he groans in the sheer bliss of her.

He looks at her with an intensity she returns and he enters her, filling her entire being with his love. It is everything they imagined it would be and more, as they watch each other until they drown.

*

She's unaware of her surroundings as she half walks, half runs the distance from home to the town centre. Her head is bursting with conflicting emotions and she can't think straight. She has no choice but to escape and give herself time to think. Twice she steps into the road to avoid dawdling pedestrians and twice she comes close to being run down by a passing cart.

The bus to Tarnow is ready to leave as Marianna weaves her way blindly through the crowds and arrives just in time to purchase a ticket. She finds a space and spreads her belongings over the adjoining seat. The engine starts with a disconcerting rattle and she's on her way. It starts to rain as the bus pulls away and rivulets of water flow down the window. There are hours of journey ahead in which to relive their goodbye and tears fill her eyes as she imagines Stefan's face looking back at hers in the reflection.

The bus travels through the centre of Krakow with its impressive historic landmarks, but Marianna takes no notice and they pass by in a blur. It travels onwards through utilitarian industrial areas where queues of hopeful job seekers line the pavements and others cling on precariously to the back of trams as they cross the city in search of employment. A few imported cars, the privilege of the wealthy, crawl behind horse-drawn carts. A few kilometres on and the bus enters a scene more akin to the Middle Ages. Run down cottages replace urban sprawl and cobbled streets disappear to be replaced by dirt roads.

It's early evening when the bus arrives in Tarnow and Marianna sets out to walk the dusty road to Zalipie. It's a long uncomfortable walk and her heavy bags become increasingly cumbersome. A passing farmworker offers her a ride on his cart and she gratefully accepts. The village is in total darkness when she arrives and the silence is a little disconcerting after the noise and bustle of city life.

Although shocked by her revelations, not once do her parents say we told you so. They are sympathetic, worried and pleased to see her in equal measure. She pours her heart out, tells them everything she can but spares them the sordid details. A couple of weeks in the country will do her the world of good, her mother assures her. Her father is less restrained and voices his concern. 'He was a bad egg from the start. Self-obsessed he certainly was. He doesn't deserve you, my girl.'

Marianna's bedroom is small and tucked under the eaves of the house with a tiny window looking out over the garden. It's been the same since she was a child with its bright white walls, wooden bed and chest of drawers decorated with the same colourful pattern of flowers and swags of leaves.

The emotional turmoil of the day and the uncomfortable journey has drained her of energy and she needs to rest. Undressing with the strength of an invalid she slides beneath the soft quilted cover, lays her head on the feather pillow and sleeps until the midday sun fills the room with shafts of golden light. Marianna lies motionless, listening to the pigeons cooing in the oak tree outside her window, its twigs scratching against the glass as the wind sways them back and forth.

She relives the day that descended into an emotional rollercoaster. Hearing the crude truth of her husband's infidelity sticks like a knife in her belly. She despises Leon but also her own lack of courage and wishes she had stayed to confront him. Most of all she hates herself for using her dear father as the excuse for leaving. It was a cowardly departure, made worse by the fact that she had no word of goodbye for Stanislaw or Tomas.

But it is Stefan that dominates her thoughts. The memory of their lovemaking is still vivid as she relives their passionate encounter over and over again. The agony of her indecision as he begged her not to go; her uncontrollable crying; his desperate clinging until the moment she finally dragged herself away and left without a backward glance. All these things whirl around in her mind like a tornado of regrets and confusion.

The homely smell of baking bread lures her to the kitchen. 'Ah, my darling. There you are.' Marianna's mother, Olga comes towards her and envelops her in her arms. 'You've had a good long sleep. Do you feel rested?'

Marianna nods and kisses her mother affectionately.

Olga pulls out a chair. 'Come and eat something. There's fresh bread and some of this year's honey. Our bees excelled themselves thanks to the wonderful weather.'

The honey is smooth and a rich golden colour with the subtle scent of dried flowers. Marianna slathers it on warm thick slices of bread.

'Mmm,' she sighs. 'I'd forgotten how delicious this is. Our bees never let us down, do they.'

They indulge themselves in this most delicious of combinations, drink copious amounts of coffee and talk for a while.

The room is awash with brightly coloured painted designs and Olga points out her new artwork.

'It looks lovely,' Marianna tells her. 'Have you been taking lessons from Ania?'

Olga laughs. 'How did you guess? She's an excellent teacher, don't you think? You should call and say hello when you feel like it. It will do you good to chat with her.'

'I will, Ma. But not yet.'

Olga clears away the dishes. 'Now then, young lady, it's a beautiful day. I think you should go for a walk. It will blow away the cobwebs.'

'I'd quite like to stay around the house this morning. Perhaps I'll go for a walk later.'

The wooden house is long and low with a red-tiled roof and two small attic windows. The garden boundaries, unmarked, make it difficult to tell where the land of one property ends and another begins. Nearest to the house is the vegetable plot, and although it's late in the season, round-headed cabbage, smooth orange pumpkins and pungent onions await harvesting. The dark rich earth is piled roughly where potatoes once grew, their decomposing leaves and stems piled into mushy heaps nearby. In summer the garden poured forth a potpourri of scents from sweet lilac and heady roses, lemon thyme and wild honeysuckle. Now, in autumn, the musty smell of decaying vegetation lingers in the damp air.

Marianna's shoes are soon wet with the morning dew as she wanders around the plot recalling how she and her mother spent precious time sowing and nurturing their plants together, Marianna chatting all the while.

'Shush,' her mother would say, a finger to her lips. 'Listen. Do you know what bird that is?' Once identified they would carry on working, mother digging and weeding whilst Marianna poked around in the soil gathering worms in a pot. They were at one with the earth and each other as year after year they reaped the rewards of their hard work.

A row of sunflowers, their drooping heads gone to seed and veiled with gossamer spiders' webs, border the path that leads to the orchard and its ageing fruit trees. A shower of dewdrops wets her hair as she twists an apple from its branch and she smiles as she recalls how her mother would climb a rickety ladder to reach the biggest fruit, while she waited below to gather them in her skirt.

'Here comes another!' Mother would shout, and 'This one's a whopper, look out!'

Marianna would hold her skirt wide, peering upwards, squinting in the bright light. Occasionally she would catch one, but more often would scramble about gathering up those she'd missed and giggling as she tried to keep up with the falling missiles. Yelping if one hit her hard on the head.

Beneath the trees a dilapidated chicken coop still houses a dozen hens who peck around in the dirt beneath, their feathers ruffling in the breeze. She had loved looking after the hens.

'If you look after them well, they will reward us with lots of lovely eggs,' Mother insisted, and Marianna had taken her responsibilities seriously – refreshing their bedding and water, scattering grain and vegetable scraps. She loved to see them running at the sight of her carrying their food bucket, but best of all was collecting the eggs.

'Go gently,' she was encouraged as she ran from one nesting site to another, brushing the straw aside eagerly in her search for eggs. Later they would dip toasted bread into the porcelain shells and savour the silky golden yolk.

The hives are silent now that winter is just around the corner, but she can still imagine the sound of gentle humming that came from within as she watched the bees work endlessly throughout the warm summer days. They fascinated Marianna and she loved to see her father dressed in his protective clothing collecting the honey.

'You can watch but don't go too close,' Mother would advise. 'Just let them get on with their work and we'll have golden honey for our tea.' Marianna would sit on the grass, watching from a safe distance, and thread daisies into chains for them both to wear.

Little has changed since those golden days of her childhood. There's the same jumbled mix of cultivation and wilderness, especially along the far boundary of the garden where the remnants of last summer's wild flowers remain. The shattered umbrella-like umbels of hogweed and brown, spiky seed heads of teasels provide a valuable source of food for the wild birds that fill the garden with joyous song.

She gazes at the view beyond, to ploughed fields and wooded copses, the open sky and distant hills and wonders why she ever wanted to leave.

*

It's late afternoon and, as predicted, the wind has increased and reached gale force.

'I'm not sure you should go out in this,' Olga remarks.

But Marianna is determined. 'Well, if you insist, but do be careful and don't go too far. There's a storm threatening,' Olga warns again.

'Don't worry I'll be fine. You know how I love a windy day. I promise I won't be long.' She wants to be alone and is prepared to take a somewhat calculated risk so she sets off at a brisk pace. The sun is a watery yellow in a glassy sky and grey storm clouds race intermittently overhead as the wind swirls around her and one moment she's in dark shadow, the next bright sunshine. She passes a farmer heading home after a day in the fields and a young girl slapping her heavy stick on the road in front of her as she herds her geese back to their yard and safety.

Blown leaves gather in flocks and take flight on the updraft like starlings rising into the late afternoon light. It's exhilarating and she smiles as each gust grows, gathering in intensity until it reaches its crescendo. She laughs as her coat is flapped around her uncontrollably.

Trees creak, their heavy branches labouring with the effort of staying joined to the mother trunk. The wind sweeps upwards over the valley floor, rippling the late summer crops like liquid silver. The tallest trees sway alarmingly as the wind catches them with its full force, turning them into bronze sails, their huge trunks visibly flexing as the clouds race overhead, like a speeded-up film.

She reaches up, arms outstretched to counterbalance the feeling of unsteadiness. This is the moment and the right place. Despite those warning voices in her head, she takes a chance. Striding forward she stands directly beneath the tallest tree with twigs and falling leaves landing on her like dry rain. She laughs and moves closer, leaning against the trunk, trusting its immense size to stay upright. She can feel the life within its warm spongy bark and, experiencing a moment of complete euphoria, whoops into the wind. A sudden crash of thunder breaks the spell. Great drops of cold rain fall and she makes a run for home.

The storm passes but a strong wind persists all night, rattling the windows and causing the trees outside to creak ominously. Marianna has a restless night. Tomorrow she must send word to Stanislaw and Tomas. A letter to Stefan will take longer. Leon can wait.

*

She is woken next morning by the persistent crowing of the neighbour's ageing cockerel. Leaving the snug warmth of her bed, she pushes the lace curtain aside, opens the window, leans out and takes a deep breath of fresh country air. There's an autumnal chill in the air despite the sun having risen above the distant hills. The squawking that accompanies a newly laid egg can be heard from the chicken house, accompanied by gentle contented clucking from those yet to lay.

Now is the perfect opportunity to write to the men in her life. She creeps around the house gathering paper and pen, makes coffee and takes it back to her room. A pile of crumpled pages lies at her feet as one beginning after another is written and discarded. She rests on the bed for a while gathering her thoughts.

*Darling Stefan,*
*I have no idea how to start this letter, or indeed whether I should be writing it at all. Those words that will tell you how I feel should come easily, but in reality the floor around me is littered with rejected beginnings although my head is full to overflowing with the things I need to say. For my actions on the day I left, I should be ashamed and I hope you will forgive me. Since the day I met you my heart has been filled with longing. I can think of nothing but you. You are there when I wake, you stay with me throughout every day and you're the last thing I see before I close my eyes to sleep. There's not the smallest space in my heart for anyone else.*

*I composed a beautiful letter to you in the sleepless, endless hours of the night, but now that I come to write it's all gone. Often as I lie awake, I wonder if you ever think about that day. I need you like parched earth needs the summer rain. I miss your beautiful sensitive hands and your eyes. I feel joined to you by an invisible thread of desire. Am I imagining this?*

*My marriage to Leon was a mistake, my acceptance of his proposal a rash decision. I know that, now that I've met you, and I have no idea how I can ever be happy with him again. I think it is too late for reconciliation. You've brought me joy like no other man, but we both have responsibilities and so, when I return to Kazimierz, I must learn how to live close to you and yet stay apart. It will be like slowly dying. Whatever happens, I will always love you.*
*Marianna*

It's mid-morning by the time she's satisfied with what she's written. Reading it one last time she folds it neatly, seals the envelope and slips it inside another addressed Private and Confidential, The Proprietor of The Workshop, 9 Szeroka Street, Kazimierz. It's done and she lies back for a while to clear her head then, taking a clean sheet of paper, refills her pen and writes:

*My dearest Stanislaw,*
*How will you ever forgive me for leaving so suddenly and without saying goodbye? Please believe that I had no choice and I will probably stay here for a while. I don't know how much Leon has told you. Probably nothing knowing him and I don't feel it's my place to say unkind things about your son so I hope you'll understand if I don't go into detail in this letter. It's funny to recall we were married in March, a lucky month for brides superstitiously. Not in my case sadly. Rest assured I'll return as soon as I can. My mother and father were so pleased to see me that their welcome was only marred by my sadness at leaving you both in such a thoughtless manner. I hope that you are able to cope in the shop without me for a while. I'm sure Tomas will be a great help.*
*Please don't worry about me.*
*Much love*
*Marianna*

Tomas's note is shorter but just as heartfelt.

*Dear Tomas,*
*I'm relying on you to be a man beyond your years for a little while. You will in effect become Stanislaw's assistant manager while I'm gone. It'll be good for you to take more responsibility. I feel you are ready for it. So good luck, darling boy. Do your best and I'll see you soon.*
*Love as always*
*Marianna x*

*

The garden has always been Marianna's favourite space, and in need of some fresh air she slips on her coat and steps outside. Beyond the orchard is her father's workshop. She pushes the creaking door and it opens to a dark interior with a low beamed ceiling. It smells earthy, of damp drying logs and the sweet scent of newly cut wood. The floor and surrounding surfaces are littered with wood chips, flung randomly from an axe and left to lie where they land. Spiders' webs, like the flimsiest of fabric, quiver in the darkest corners and a million specks of dust take to the air as a draught disturbs the stillness.

Garden tools hang in a row along one wall. Spades and forks, hoes and rakes, sieves and trowels and above them, on a high shelf, sit tins and jars containing weed killers, lime, fish blood and bone meal, ant killer and mouse traps, scraps of string and wire ties. Pea sticks and beanpoles are tied in bundles and stacked ready for use in the year to come.

Work overalls hang limp on wooden pegs, their fibres

stained with the sap of pine logs, harvested from the forest that borders his land. She remembers the sound of trees bending and snapping, branches ripping and crashing to the ground, the victims of their need for a supply of logs to warm them through the long winter months.

Marianna gazes round at the treasure trove of hacksaws, bow saws, axes, sledgehammers, hatchets, wedges and clamps. The two-man crosscut saw that required so much strength has long been relegated to a shelf, its rusted teeth no longer employed to gnash their way through heavy branches. A lethal new chainsaw, carrying an unpleasant whiff of petrol, has taken its place.

Under the workbench unrecognisable broken machinery parts are piled haphazardly. A brown hen scratches the floor around them, her beady eyes alert for tasty woodlice, while another sits ruffling her wings in a dirt bowl, murmuring contentedly.

As a child she would sit on a felled log and watch her father with pride as he swung his hatchet with ease, turning the piles of heavy logs into kindling, and eagerly awaiting her chance to help stack the pieces in a pile against the wall. She would listen, in awe of his knowledge as he educated her in the ways of wood. 'Stack this way. Leave a space between to speed the drying. Knock the logs together. If dry, they'll ring loud and hard. If damp, there'll be a dull thud. Always use soft wood for kindling and hard wood for the hottest fires.'

Was there anything he didn't know? And what a coincidence that the two men she loved most should be so knowledgeable and skilled in the ways of wood.

He has left his pipe and a tin of flaked tobacco on the workbench. She lifts the lid and breathes in the familiar smell. How contented she'd been, playing outside on the grass while he laboured away inside.

Marianna pushes through brambles and overgrown vegetation to the rear of the building where, protected under a heavy tarpaulin cover, she finds what she came looking for.

The bicycle is covered in dust and cobwebs but is perfectly usable. Tarnow is a long uncomfortable walk from the village, but she estimates that if she cycles, she can post her letters, call into the café where she met Leon and be home again by lunchtime. She brushes dust from the bike, dresses, stuffs a chunk of bread into her pocket, leaves a note for her mother and sets off for town.

As she passes through the village she notices the cottages are more decorated than they used to be. It's become a tradition that the ladies of the village paint the bare surfaces in and around their homes with brightly coloured floral designs and it's one of the things she loves about Zalipie. Even in the midst of a freezing winter the colourful decorations lift the spirits.

Ania, Marianna's friend since childhood, is standing by her cottage door. She's an artist and has painted every spare surface inside as well as outside her house. She's never without a brush in her hands and she raises a paint-spattered arm as Marianna comes into sight. 'Marianna! You're back!'

'Good morning,' Marianna waves to her friend, wobbling dangerously and skidding to a halt.

'How lovely to see you. How is married life? How is Leon?' Ania asks, enthusiastic for Marianna's news.

Marianna has no desire to discuss Leon. 'Oh, he's fine. But listen, Ania, I can't stop now as I need to get some letters to Tarnow. I'll catch up with you later. Tomorrow perhaps?'

'I look forward to it,' Ania replies.

Marianna pedals on until she reaches the edge of the village. With the letters safely tucked in her pocket and her enthusiasm for cycling revived she picks up speed. The wind tangles her hair and the bike jolts and swerves on the rough road as she swerves in an attempt to avoid the ruts. Her skirt slides over her knees and, exhilarated, she lets the pedals go and freewheels joyfully downhill, her coat flapping like giant crows' wings and a trail of dust filling the air in her wake.

Half an hour later she props her bike against the wall outside the post office, straightens her clothes and attempts to smooth her tousled hair.

The postmaster has worked here for as long as she can remember and he greets her enthusiastically, his arms held wide for an embrace.

'It's good to see you, Marianna.'

'And you, Ernst.'

Ernst has a voluminous beard and a bald head, small pince-nez glasses and an enormous nose.

'I've two very personal messages to send, Ernst. I know I can trust you with them. I wonder if I need to send them by telegram. Perhaps there's a fast post that will do as well?'

'Leave them with me, I'll make sure they go in the most expedient but speedy manner.'

'Thank you, Ernst. You are very kind and efficient.'

Ernst loves to hear this. His eyebrows raise with delight. 'I've a letter for you too. It arrived this morning.'

The scrawling writing is immediately recognisable but it can wait.

Marianna enters the café with a mixture of emotions. This is where her whirlwind romance with Leon began. Johan, the owner, greets her enthusiastically and they share a jug of coffee while he updates her with the local news. She says little about Leon but concentrates on describing life in Kazimierz, her work in the shop and her new career as a life model. This amuses him greatly.

'You! A model. Goodness, you've become bold.'

It's good to catch up with the news but Leon's letter is burning a hole in her pocket. She's impatient to read what the rat has to say so makes her excuses and leaves.

*

Back home, lying on her bed, she takes a deep breath, 'Here goes,' she mutters.

*Dear Marianna,*
*I know why you left. I found your handkerchief on the stairs outside Amelia's flat and put two and two together. It's the only explanation for such a hasty departure. I realise I've overstepped the mark and I can hear you*

*saying 'that's something of an understatement'.*

*The truth is, I should never have married you. Our marriage had its high points but I think we both know that the saying 'marry in haste, repent at leisure' applies pretty well to our situation. I've made a lousy husband. I think I may have been flattered by your unflinching admiration and the romantic notion of being your 'musician lover'. I can't help feeling you won't be surprised and may even be relieved to hear that Amelia and I are leaving Kazimierz for Warsaw. There'll be better opportunities for work there. Amelia and I are compatible in every way. I should have realised that before I became involved with you. The flat is now free for you to come back to, if you wish. I don't intend to return so have taken the few belongings that were mine. Father knows I'm sending this letter. He is furious and I wonder if our relationship will survive. It's always been precarious. He says I'm a disgrace and a fool in equal measure. Perhaps he's right when he says that I didn't deserve you. I suppose I should apologise for what it's worth, but one has to follow one's heart, don't you agree? Though we did have some good times, didn't we? I've no idea what the future holds for any of us. We can only try to make the best of it.*

*Leon*

Her hand drops to her side, the letter scrunched in her fist. So that's it? She hadn't expected anything more but the tone of the letter is blunt and highlights all Leon's worst traits. Leon is a selfish bastard. It's as simple as that and she's well rid of him.

*

Marianna has settled into a comfortable morning routine helping her mother around the house and garden. Her father works tirelessly in the fields from dawn to dusk and by the time he's eaten the evening meal it's time for him to retire for the night.

'I'm managing,' he replies when she expresses her concern. 'We country folk are resilient to hard work, but rest assured once things get back to normal, I'm going to take life a little easier.'

In the afternoon she usually rides alone to some secluded spot with the intention of writing, but this has proved difficult with her thoughts inevitably returning to Stefan. She is confused as to why he hasn't responded to her impassioned letter and wonders if she misread his feelings. Her head tells her this must be so, but her heart believes otherwise.

Stanislaw has replied and assured her that they're thinking of her and she should take as much time as she needs before returning to Kazimierz. Tomas's own personal note is touching. He's clearly been taking his lessons seriously and manages to write (with Elena's help, she has no doubt) a short message:

*Dear Mary Anna Marianna,*
*I'm sorry you had to go away but I'm doin what you said. Stan has been kind an'all. He gives me more cake now an I fink I'm gettin fat. How is Petrin Patron… that pigion.*

*You know. The royall one. I carnt wate to see you.*
*Tomas x*

*

Ania has invited Marianna to join her for coffee on numerous occasions, but she isn't ready to answer questions about Leon and so far has managed to avoid meeting her. In the idyllic days of their youth the pair would roam the woods and fields nearby, gather flowers from the meadows and picnic on chunks of home-made bread, smeared with berries gathered by grubby hands from the hedgerows. Their small group of friends would meet at the pond on the edge of the village, act out their fantasy adventures and swim in the clear waters overhung with weeping willows. Today she's decided it's time to revisit, and the wooden pontoon will be the perfect spot to write whilst dangling her feet in the cool water.

Cycling along the track that leads to the willow pond everything seems smaller, more closed in than she remembers. The wispy trees that once lined the banks have trebled in size, their foliage dense and hanging like lengths of loosely plaited hair. In her childhood days the banks were smooth and slippery, providing an earthy slide by which to enter the water. Now they are covered in wild flowers and grasses, creating a lush haven for wildlife. The pontoon, fashioned from a random assortment of planks, has begun to disintegrate, and she leans warily on the broken rail reminiscing about swinging on the willow branches and dive-bombing the water, now still and covered in patches of waterweed.

It's a warm day and the lure of a solitary dip appeals. She removes her shoes and unbuttons the front of her dress, slips her arms free and wriggles it effortlessly to the ground, leaving her petticoat on. Bees and insects take flight as she pushes through the dense foliage to sit at the pond edge. The water is dark and satin smooth. The fallen leaves of the willow float about on the glassy surface and spin in circles like tiny unmanned boats. A startled fish plops at the surface and agitated water boatmen dart away as she tests the water with her toe. Slimy green weed strokes her ankles and she levers herself forward, stretches her arms out and glides into the pond with trepidation. The water gushes over her back and shoulders with a whoosh. Taking a deep breath she sinks below the surface. There's little to see; the bottom is flat and featureless save for a few water snails searching for food, but she stays submerged for as long as her breath lasts, then surfaces. Gasping, she slicks the water from her face and hair, smooth as sealskin. Her petticoat sticks to every curve of her body as she flips herself over to lie floating on her back with her arms spread wide. The water laps at her face, and with her ears submerged the world above is silenced, the sound of her breathing hollow and distant. The sky above is peppered with clouds that can be interpreted as strange distorted creatures. There's a dog with wings and a horse galloping, its legs forever lengthening as the cloud changes. A whale with a huge eye where a blue patch has formed slowly morphs into a shoal of smaller fish as the cloud breaks up and scatters.

The swim has both calmed and exhilarated her and she is comforted by the womb-like environment. The water holds no fear for her, but in reality she's drowning in the depth of her feelings for a man she knows she can never have.

Warmed by the midday sun, the pontoon is the perfect place to dry off. Marianna folds her dress and, using it as a pillow, lies down on the rough planks, water running from her body and dripping through the cracks back to the pond below with a rhythmic plop. A gentle breeze picks up and wafts the willow branches backwards and forwards, agitating the surface of the water with a swishing motion. The grass is full of the sound of buzzing insects and a lone frog croaks sleepily from his hiding place amongst the rushes.

Marianna is enjoying that blissful state halfway between awake and asleep when the sound of somebody approaching along the gravel path disturbs her and, sitting up, she sees Ania cycling towards her.

'Hi!' Ania waves enthusiastically as she approaches. 'So I've found you! I saw you come in this direction and guessed where you were going. I've brought a drink and some pastries. Would you like some?'

Marianna pats the space beside her. 'Of course' she says, 'come and join me. It's blissfully quiet here, but goodness how it's changed. I hadn't intended to swim but couldn't resist. I'd forgotten how enjoyable a solitary swim could be. There's something quite spiritual about being enveloped by water, it's as if something higher than yourself is keeping you buoyant.'

'I know,' Ania replies. 'I often come. I love it here.' She retrieves her basket from the handlebars and dumps her bike unceremoniously on the path. She hugs Marianna and sits cross-legged beside her. Ania is a free spirit. An artist. Colour is her joy and creativity her expression. At age ten she decorated the entrance to her parents' house and hasn't stopped painting since. She's a unique artist and her work is everywhere in the shape of bouquets and swags of flowers painted in all the hues of the rainbow. She's a real talent and has become well known in the local area. The friends became inseparable from an early age, and with similar personalities and values have been close ever since.

'Kindred spirits, that's what they are,' Marianna's mother would say. With no siblings of their own the girls went everywhere together until the day Leon arrived. Ania happily accepted that a new phase had begun in Marianna's life, although their parting when she left for Kazimierz was emotional.

'Enjoy your life,' Ania urged as Marianna sobbed into her shoulder, 'and relish every second of it. True friends never lose each other, we're bound to meet again.'

Marianna had been the least brave of the pair. 'I know all this but I'm sad because I'll miss you so much.' With a heavy heart she'd waved goodbye and sworn they would never lose touch.

'So now that I've got you alone I want to hear all the news. What's Kazimierz like, how's your handsome husband and have you found any work yet? I can't believe you've been back all this time and we haven't had time to talk. So come on, Marianna, spill the beans.'

Marianna concentrates on eating and gazes into the distance to avoid Ania's questioning stare.

'Marianna? Is something wrong? It's not like you to hold back.'

The afternoon light is fading and Marianna has become chilled by the time she's related all that's happened since her arrival in Kazimierz. Ania has listened attentively and puts her arm around her friend as Marianna rests her head on her shoulder. Her uncensored confessions have been a truly emotional outpouring.

'You poor lamb,' Ania says, squeezing her arm affectionately. 'Who would have thought things would turn out to be so traumatic and disappointing.'

Marianna sighs theatrically, lifts her head and declares, 'There's only one thing that can lift my spirits right now.'

'Tell me what it is and I'll do my absolute best to make sure you get it.'

'Oh, I don't know. It'd be asking a lot.'

Ania takes both Marianna's hands in her own. 'Tell me now. What is it?'

Marianna looks at Ania seriously for a moment and then, her mouth curling into a mischievous smile, says, 'I don't suppose there's any more of those pastries?'

'Why of course, why didn't I think of that?' Ania cries and rummages in her bag.

They devour the last of the pastries as if they're the first they've ever eaten. 'You're quite right,' Ania states emphatically, licking the last of the sticky sugary crumbs from her fingers. 'These are the answer to everything.'

'Not quite everything.'

'True. There's still the problem of what you're going to do about your romance with Stefan.'

'What!' Marianna exclaims. 'What romance? The whole situation is a positive nightmare!'

Ania adopts an exaggerated sorrowful expression and Marianna starts to laugh. Ania joins in.

'Stop!' Marianna says. 'Don't! It's not funny!' but collapses in a fit of hysteria.

They're rolling around on the pontoon now, unable to stop. Marianna stands up to catch her breath. 'Stop! I can't stand it. I'm going in,' she yells, 'to get away from you.' Like a silver dart she dives from the edge of the pontoon, causing a wake of water to swamp the bank and the leaves from the willow trees to bob about in the sudden disturbance.

'No you won't,' cries Ania, undressing at lightning speed. She strips naked and is about to jump in when Marianna shrieks.

'Shoes! You're still wearing your shoes!'

*

They're sitting in Ania's cottage later that afternoon, their wet clothing drying on a line above the cooking range when Marianna comments, 'I see you haven't put your paintbrush down since I last saw you.'

Ania shakes her head. 'I can't. There's absolutely no point in trying. I'll go to my grave clutching a pot of paint. The way I see it is why leave a boring space blank when you can cover it with flowers?'

'True,' Marianna agrees, 'but this obsession with painting everything seems to have become a little out of hand.'

Ania doesn't take offence because it's not the first time it's been said, and it's certainly true that it's become impossible for her to leave anything untouched. The frames of pictures, the bed head, crockery and cutlery, the kitchen bucket and even the mop are covered in glorious multi-coloured flowers.

'I really don't mind what people think. It's better to be absolutely ridiculous than absolutely boring and anyway I've just started showing some of the ladies in the village how to do it. They repay me with eggs and vegetables, which is kind, so we're all happy. They'll have to go some, mind you, to keep up with me.'

'I know I joke about it, but the house looks truly amazing, Ania. One day, in the distant future, when we're all dead and gone, it'll be a museum unlike any other and people from around the world will come and wonder at your unique home. With your inspiration, the whole village will soon be like a giant painted canvas.'

Ania laughs. 'I'm not sure about that but it certainly brightens the place up.'

'Feliks would be fascinated, although he's a traditional painter and your work is fresh and unique, folksy I suppose you'd call it. He would appreciate the passion that goes into creating it.'

'I like the sound of Feliks,' Ania comments. 'He sounds like a man after my own heart. As for you becoming his model, I'm quite bowled over by the idea.' Marianna pouts and strikes a pose in her petticoat. Ania does the same and they collapse laughing.

*

They meet as often as possible over the next weeks and Marianna confides to Ania that it's her conscience that troubles her the most.

'I know you aren't particularly religious,' Ania says one afternoon, 'but do you think you'd find it helpful to visit the chapel? Not the church here, the little chapel outside the village. It's still open and you could sit quietly without distraction.'

Inwardly Marianna winces. She doesn't 'do' chapels. Outwardly she smiles and, unwilling to offend, agrees that perhaps it would be a good idea to have some quiet time in the place where the locals have worshipped for over one hundred years.

*

Very little light enters the shuttered windows and despite her reluctance to be there an unexpected feeling of calm surrounds her. She lowers herself noiselessly into one of the austere wooden seats and sits upright like a child waiting for chastisement, with her hands clasped tensely on her lap. The only sound is the birds chattering in the trees outside.

The red-tiled floor and brown walls, the colours of misery, give the space a sombre, claustrophobic atmosphere. An ancient fan, humming quietly, is full of dead flies and other insects sucked from the atmosphere of religious piety. There's a wooden altar covered in a faded cloth displaying a random selection of figurines and a crudely carved wooden crucifix next to a garish Madonna with rosy cheeks and chipped fingers. Curiously facing away from them is a ceramic kneeling angel, her faded eyes looking heavenward. Above the altar is a black and white photo of the Pope, turned sepia with age, its corners curling and adorned with an oversized set of wooden rosary beads and oppressive metal cross. A cheap faded print of Jesus is tacked to the wall beside it.

Despite her cynicism the chapel fills her with an inner calm. Her shoulders relax as her mind stills and she stays far longer than intended.

# Fifteen

The day Marianna returns to Kazimierz you could light a room with the smile on Tomas's face. It's been weeks since her untimely departure for Zalipie, and her sudden reappearance is as unexpected as her departure.

Stanislaw greets her with open arms. 'It's so good to see you, Marianna. We've missed you.'

'And I've missed you too,' she replies, hugging him back. 'I'm sorry I left in such a hurry.' Stanislaw holds her at arm's length.

'I don't know what to say about Leon,' he says. 'Words fail me. He may be my son but I must tell you that I'm ashamed of him. He's always been wilful and selfish, and the way I feel at the moment I won't be the only one who won't be sorry if he doesn't show his face in Kazimierz ever again.' He purses his lips and shakes his head from side to side. 'And that's an awful thing for a father to admit.' He slumps into a chair, pulls a rag from his pocket, wipes his eyes and continues, 'I've put up with a lot from him over the years, not that I want to go into all that now.

I'm just glad my dear wife isn't here to see it. She doted on the boy and would be so disappointed.'

Marianna has no words of comfort.

Stanislaw looks at Tomas who has been listening with his mouth agape and places a hand affectionately on his head. 'The boy and I were worried you wouldn't return, but here you are and that's all that matters.'

Tomas has been draped around Marianna's waist gazing up at her doe-eyed with a huge grin on his face. Stanislaw recovers quickly from his outburst and chuckles. 'I've never known him so quiet as he's been for the past few weeks, but look at the transformation in him already.'

'How have you managed while I've been gone?' she asks. 'I feel bad that I let you down.'

'Elena has been lending a hand but sales have been very slow. Still, it's not all bad news.'

'Oh. You have good news?' she asks.

'We've set the date for our wedding in two weeks time. It'll be a simple affair, but no doubt we'll eat and drink well that day.' Patting his stomach he adds, 'We're banking on you joining us.'

'I wouldn't miss it for the world,' she says.

'Well, go on up and I'll give you a hand with this luggage. The flat is as you left it. Leon has taken his belongings so the place is yours now.'

*

A cursory glance towards Amelia's door is the only thought she gives to the events that led to the dramatic change in her life. Her time spent in Zalipie has cleared her mind and she has returned with a spring in her step, full of determination to make life in Kazimierz work.

Alone in the flat she wanders to the window. It's late afternoon and there are few people about as the last of the daylight fades. A sudden gust of wind sends scraps of paper hurtling along the gutter as the familiar figure of Tomas comes into view, pedalling as fast as he can against the unexpected gust. A dilapidated cart rumbles over the cobbles and somewhere in the distance a dog barks repeatedly. Pigeons coo on the windowsill. Nothing has changed, but this is a fresh start and she must make the best of it.

*

Tomas is out of the door like greased lightning the moment he gets a chance and arrives at the workshop just as Stefan is closing for the day.

'She's back!'

'What? Who is?' Stefan asks wearily, his mind elsewhere.

'Who d'ya fink!' He points towards the shop.

'Whoa. Slow down, young man. Now tell me calmly.'

'It's Marianna. I thought you'd like to know. You know, like to know that she's back!'

Stefan's heart is racing but he maintains a calm exterior. 'Is she now? And when did this happen?'

'Fifteen minutes ago. So are you gonna come and talk to her?'

'I think we should let her get settled in before we descend on her, don't you?'

'S'pose so. Just thought you'd like to know. That's all.'

"That was considerate of you. So you're spreading the news, are you?'

'Nah. Just tellin' you. Nobody else. See ya then.'

And with that he turns on his heel and races back to the shop to deliver his last order of the day while it's still light. He's nervous of the dark alleyways and shadowy corners and prefers to be back at the shop with the door closed securely behind him by the time night falls.

Today old Mrs Cohen keeps him longer than usual and he pedals back to Szeroka Street as if the Devil himself is in pursuit, hoists the bike up the kerb and wheels it into the shop puffing and blowing like a steam engine. 'I'm back!' he announces triumphantly as though he's overcome some kind of challenge. Stanislaw and Marianna are expected to respond enthusiastically and whilst they think it highly amusing they fulfil their role with gusto. 'So you are!' they chorus. 'Well done!' Stanislaw slaps him on the back. 'I think a hot drink and a slice of apple cake are just what this young man needs.'

'I tell you what,' says Tomas a few minutes later when his mouth is full of cake, 'it's dark out there. I ain't gonna do no more late runs till spring comes back.'

Stanislaw reassures him. 'One more tomorrow and

then you're done for a while, son. I'm not happy about you riding about after dark any more than you are.'

A shadowy figure watching from the opposite side of the street has gone unnoticed. He watches until Stanislaw has locked up for the night, takes a long drag on the soggy remains of his roll-up cigarette, flicks it to the floor, extinguishes it with a twist of his boot and slopes off into the night.

*

Stefan loses track of time as he sits on the bottom stair, his mind in a whirl and his hands shaking uncontrollably. He clasps them tightly together in an effort to calm himself. She's back! He's thought about this moment every day since receiving her letter. She's been gone for six long weeks and the days have seemed endless and empty. Leon's departure with Amelia astounded him, as despite her sweet demeanour and musical prowess, she appeared to offer little else. What exactly was the attraction? He has no idea but concludes they deserve each other. His unsent reply to Marianna's letter lies creased from a thousand re-readings and is hidden under a pile of old orders. Now that she's here he must decide what to do. Perhaps he'll show her the letter, perhaps he won't. He's desperate to see her, but knows he must wait. He doesn't want to arouse suspicion with Truda who will surely notice the change in his mood.

She's calling him with that tone in her voice he finds so irritating. 'Stefan! How much longer are you going to be?'

He sighs. 'Coming,' he calls back. Eating is the last thing he wants to do and a row is the last thing he needs. Almost immediately she calls again and, sighing wearily, he makes his way upstairs prepared for another evening of fake contentment. It's going to be a long night, but there's one ray of light. She's back.

*

Truda looks tired. She's lost weight and this accentuates her angular shoulders and the slack flesh on her neck. Her chest and arms are like an adolescent's and comparisons with Marianna's voluptuous curves are inevitable. He tries to be kind and make her happy, but her relentless nagging wears him down. The moment she sets eyes on him she starts. 'Why are you so late? Have you finished those two repair jobs yet? I hope so. They've been waiting long enough.'

Stefan sighs. 'I'm not a machine, Truda, I'm a craftsman and I refuse to rush jobs. People come to me because they know I'll do a good job.'

'No, they come to you because they think you're cheap,' she spits back at him, her face taut with resentment.

'I consider my prices fair. In any case, money isn't everything.'

'No. But it helps.' Her mouth pinches into a thin line, her tone bitter.

'I've explained all this a thousand times and I'm not going over it again,' he replies.

Truda tuts, her bony fingers like a bird's claws agitating with the knot in her apron strings. 'It's a good job my baking's so popular or goodness knows where we'd be.' She undoes the apron and flings it over the back of his chair. She's been quick to enlist his help since he lost interest in browsing the stalls on a Saturday morning, but he resents being relegated to the position of dog's body; feels like a duck out of water with an apron on, wrapping pastries and making small talk with customers. 'We've no money, so there's little point in you looking for things to buy,' she bullies when he suggests he might have a wander. 'You'd just as well make yourself useful.'

Stefan does his utmost to avoid arguments. He knows that if he gives vent to his true feelings he'll say something best left unsaid. The baby problem has remained unresolved and the more determined she is to become pregnant the more reticent he is about starting a family. If he's totally honest, it's not the baby he doesn't want, it's the certainty that having one would inevitably lead to a lifetime of commitment to a woman he's becoming less able to love as the weeks and months go by.

They eat their meal in silence and afterwards Stefan, feeling increasingly agitated, makes an excuse to return to the workshop for an hour to 'finish something off'. Tonight he needs to put as much space between them as possible.

Truda has gone to bed by the time he returns but is still awake and reading. She watches him over the top of her book as he undresses. 'Have you nothing to say?' she asks when the silence has become unbearable.

He looks at her for a moment before responding. 'No, Truda, absolutely nothing.'

She closes her book and turns on her side.

Stefan lies awake until he hears the sound of the clock in the square strike three and he finally falls into a shallow, restless sleep. The last thought he has is that Marianna is just the width of a wall away.

*

Stanislaw has thoughtfully left Marianna a hunk of rye bread, cheese and pickled cucumber, a jug of milk and a small packet of coffee. She draws the curtains to block out the darkening sky, fills the kettle, spoons some coffee into a jug, kicks off her shoes and sits waiting for the water to heat. The bread and cheese are delicious and her energy returns with every mouthful. She pours a mug of coffee and, cupping it in both hands, closes her eyes and inhales the rich aroma. There's a light tap at the door and Tomas peeps into the room.

'Come in if you dddaaaaare,' Marianna jests, adopting a spooky tone. He smiles and runs across to join her at the table.

'Ah, now let me see. I've a couple of little gifts for you. If you're interested in gifts, of course.'

'I ain't never had no gifts.' He is wide-eyed now.

'Okay. Well, here you are. You'll like this and you don't have to share it with anyone. You have my permission.'

Tomas opens the brown bag and removes a large glass jar. The lid is covered in a soft fabric cap tied on with thin string. A handwritten label reads, 'This Honey Belongs to Tomas.' 'Wow!' he exclaims. 'I love 'unny. And it's all for me?'

'It is and it was made especially for you by my parents' honeybees. They collected nectar from the flowers in our garden. Believe me, it's like no other honey you'll ever taste.'

Tomas opens the jar and sticks his nose in, sniffing deeply and inelegantly. 'Cor, yeah. That's real smelly. In a good way though. Fanks. Fanks a lot.'

Olga has knitted Tomas some extra thick socks and a pair of gloves. 'My mother was very worried about your feet and hands getting cold in the winter,' Marianna explains. He tries them on and parades around the room clasping and unclasping his fingers, waving his hands back and forth as if testing the gloves' insulating properties.

'Yeah, they're right warm they are. Fanks, Marianna's mum.' His grin widens. 'I'll start wearin' 'em straight away.' He leaves the gloves on as he sits down next to her.

They talk animatedly for a while until Tomas goes quiet and looks thoughtful.

'What's up?' Marianna asks him.

'Nuffing. Just thinkin'.'

'Sounds mysterious. About what?' she asks.

'Jus' that I told the doc about you being back.'

The doc?' She's puzzled. 'Who is the doc?'

'Stefan, of course.'

'Why d'you call him that? He's not a doctor.'

'Yes he is, it says so in the window,' he says confidently.

'Does it?'

'Yeah. Says he's a doctor of chairs.'

She laughs and ruffles his hair. 'Oh, I see! So it does, and what did the doc say to that?'

'Not much. He went a bit white and said that maybe we should let you get settled in.'

'I'm sure he's right about that. I'm very tired and intend to have a long sleep, after I've had a nice hot bath, so I think you should run along and enjoy your supper with Stanislaw. I'll see you tomorrow morning.'

The bathroom is freezing cold, but Marianna lingers in the water for as long as the heat allows. Her face is blotched red and her toes and fingers have started to wrinkle from the prolonged exposure. It's time to get out. She wraps herself in a large towel and winds another, turban-like, round her head. Back in the flat, she opens the stove door, allowing the warmth from within to escape, and rubs her hair vigorously until it dries. She pours herself a glass of vodka, and the intoxicating drink warms her stomach and makes her feel sleepy. It's time for bed. The last thought she has before drifting into sleep is that Stefan is just the width of a wall away.

# Sixteen

Keen to get back to normality Marianna is ready for work early the next morning and arrives before Stanislaw.

She's reacquainting herself with the unpredictable workings of the till when the shop bell rings. Struggling with the bolts she opens the door and comes face to face with Truda weighed down by a basket of bread.

'Oh!' Truda can't disguise her surprise. 'I didn't expect to see you.'

'I didn't expect to be here,' Marianna retorts.

Truda has no idea what to say as they stand facing each other, so Marianna takes control. 'Come in, Truda. Stanislaw isn't around yet but I'll give you a hand with this and please don't feel uncomfortable. I think it's best if we don't mention Leon. I know he is your friend but there's little good in what I have to say about him and I expect you know what's happened anyway.'

Truda looks relieved. 'You're right about that, but I must tell you I'm shocked he could do such a thing. It's not like him at all.'

Marianna wonders if they are talking about the same Leon but politely responds, 'I'd rather not comment further so let's leave it at that.'

Truda smiles. 'Thank you for helping me. I've more baking to do this morning so I'm a bit pushed for time,' and with that they set about displaying the freshly baked goods in harmonious silence.

Throughout the morning Marianna works with one eye on the door, and every hour that passes without sight of Stefan, she becomes more agitated. Surely he'll call in. But what will she say if he does? And what will she do if he doesn't?

*

Later that day Mrs Cohen has sent a note to the shop with a list of extra items for Tomas to deliver and he isn't happy about it as he understood they'd all agreed that deliveries after dark were to stop.

Stanislaw is apologetic. 'I'm sorry, Tomas. I promise this is the very last one and I expect she'll make it worth your while.'

Tomas glances out of the window at the fading light. 'You did promise,' he says.

'I know I did,' says Stanislaw, patting Tomas on the back reassuringly. 'This will be the last time. Now give me a few minutes to fill your basket and you can go right away.'

*

Mrs Cohen has become fond of Tomas, enjoys his company and loves to extend his visit with a tempting drink of hot chocolate. 'It's getting chilly out there these evenings. This'll keep you warm,' she says, fussing round him.

Tomas drinks as fast as he considers polite, but by the time he leaves it's already dark and there are few people on the streets. He's making good progress when the bike suddenly wobbles and he hits the kerb with a thump. He dismounts to inspect the damage, but it's difficult to see in the dark so he squeezes the tyre between his fingers. It's flat. He looks around for help but there's nobody about. There's only one thing for it: he'll have to push.

At the top of Szeroka Street he stops to catch his breath. The shop is in sight so he relaxes a little. But Eryk has been waiting in the shadows and as Tomas approaches he moves further into the darkness, tips his cap down low over his face and allows the boy to pass before silently falling into step behind him. He lunges forward and grabs Tomas round the neck with one hand. The other covers his mouth before he has a chance to cry out. Tomas tries to wriggle free but Eryk is strong and forces him into a narrow alleyway. He slams him face first against the wall between two trash bins. Tomas doubles over, winded. Eryk pulls a long piece of rag from his trouser pocket, forces it into Tomas's mouth, parting his jaws, and winds it round the back of his head. His eyes are wide with fear as Eryk ties a tight knot and the veins on Tomas's neck stand out as he struggles to escape.

'I'll give you something to squeal about, you little toe rag,' Eryk sneers, tying Tomas's wrists tightly with a piece of cord. 'Think you're high and mighty, do ya? Think I'd forgotten about our little run-in? Well, I ain't. I'll teach you to go off and get yourself a fancy job. Let's see if you feel so great when I've finished with ya.' Tomas swings his shoulders back and forth in an attempt to release Eryk's grip but it's no use.

'Still scared of the dark, are we? I've seen you rushing back home with the Devil on yer tail.' Saliva collects in the corner of Eryk's mouth and his lips part in a sneer that reveals nicotine-stained teeth.

Tomas turns his head to avoid the stench of Eryk's sour breath as he drags him away from the bike and frog marches him along the street, darting into doorways when anybody comes near. Dragged along, Tomas stumbles as his knees give way with the effort of keeping up, and all the while Eryk hurls insults and threats in a stream of verbal abuse. They're getting further from the shop with every step, but Tomas recognises where they are.

The great iron gates of the cemetery loom ahead. Beyond lies infinite blackness. 'Know where you are, eh? I thought you could spend some time 'ere on yer own, since you like it so much, you and that prissy madam. Sittin' here swinging yer feet like you got no cares in the world. Not so much fun at night though, is it?'

Beyond the gates the air seems colder and damp. Wings flap in unison as a flock of birds are disturbed and rise up like those displaced by a plough in a field. Tomas hasn't taken much notice of the gravestones before but now in these blackest of surroundings, they resemble huddled sinister beings. There are no sounds save for the wind in the trees from which long curtains of ivy hang, like the tattered sails of a storm-battered ship.

'Scared yet?' Eryk sneers as they reach the seat.

He laughs and pushes Tomas onto the ground, ties his ankles together and lashes his upper arms to the back of the seat. Tomas lets out a muffled, terrified cry.

Eryk chuckles, satisfied that his little plan is working. 'Yeah alright. Stop snivelling. I'll do one thing for ya. Not that it'll do you any good, they're all deaf in 'ere so no point shoutin'.' Untying the gag, he throws it to one side, spits at the ground and strides away.

Tomas is panic-stricken and breathless. The musty smell of decaying leaves fills the air as his boots scuffle them in his struggle to free himself. He starts to cry and trickles of salty tears run down his cheeks. Surrounded by mysterious dark shapes, his imagination runs riot and he stiffens, paralysed with fright. A rustling in the undergrowth becomes an approaching demon, the breeze on his neck the breath of another and a headless statue, its torso scabby with lichens and fungus, yet another, as it stands ready to pounce. He squeezes his eyes shut against the imagined horrors around him.

'Hello,' a small voice whispers, though it's more an exhalation of breath. 'What's your name?'

Tomas doesn't speak.

'Who is he?' says another, smaller voice.

'He won't say.'

'We won't hurt you,' says a third.

Tomas opens his eyes and lifts his head. The three children stand together holding hands. His mouth drops open as he stares at each of them in turn. The children stare back, unsmiling. He is mesmerised by their strange appearance. A stream of grey vapour escapes from their pale lips and their bloodshot eyes peer from the depths of sunken sockets, emphasising the ashen pallor of their complexions. The girl speaks again.

'What are you doing here?'

'Me bruvver grabbed me. Brought me here.'

'Why did he do that?'

'Dunno.' He shrugs. 'Please untie me, my arms hurt,' he pleads.

'We can't,' she says, shaking her limp gossamer hair back and forth across her bony shoulders.

'Please try,' he begs.

She steps forward and reaches for his wrists but he feels nothing and her hands seem to pass through his without touching. 'Told you,' she says, matter of fact. 'We'll stay with you until somebody comes, if you like.'

'I seen you before,' the smallest boy says. 'With a pretty lady.'

'I ain't seen you,' Tomas replies.

'Can't see us in daylight,' the other boy whispers.

Tomas asks, 'Can you find somebody to help me?'

They shake their heads. 'They won't see us. Nobody can.'

'I can,' Tomas says, feeling braver.

'Not for long,' says the girl.

They stay for a while, silently watching over him. Water-stained, lichen-covered headstones stand solid behind them like a group of silent witnesses. Suddenly, and with disturbing ease, the children merge as if one, float away and disappear into the darkness.

*

Stanislaw is waiting to shut up shop but Tomas hasn't returned. 'He's taking his time tonight,' he says for the third time, glancing up at the clock. 'I expect Mrs Cohen is indulging him with a treat. I don't blame her, he's a great kid and she's a lonely old soul. Still, he's very late.'

Marianna feels unsettled. 'I'll hang around down here if you want,' she offers. 'I'll lock up when he's back. Hopefully he won't be much longer.' She spends an hour tidying behind the counter, polishing the brass scales, weighing out and bagging up dried goods. It's gone seven and she's becoming more than a little concerned. Surely he can't still be with Mrs Cohen. She decides they have waited long enough.

*

'No, my dears, he's not here,' Mrs Cohen tells Marianna and Stanislaw, concern written all over her wrinkled face. 'He left about an hour ago. I do hope he's alright.'

Marianna tries to reassure the old lady, although she's increasingly worried herself. Stanislaw suggests they take the shortcut back to the shop, as it's the route Tomas would most likely have taken. Turning into Szeroka Street they come across the abandoned bike.

'It looks as if he had a puncture, but why he didn't come straight back goodness knows,' Stanislaw says. He pushes the bike back to the shop, but there's no sign of the missing boy.

'What are we going to do?' Marianna asks. 'I wonder if he's gone to his brother.'

'Most unlikely,' Stanislaw responds, 'the lad is scared stiff of him.'

'You're right, but I can't think of anywhere else. I think we need to pay Eryk a visit.'

Stanislaw seems reluctant.

'Don't you agree?' Marianna asks.

'I do, but he's a nasty piece of work. I think we need to be careful.'

'We can at least go and find out if he knows anything.'

'I think it would be good to have somebody else along. I'll ask Stefan. Eryk is less likely to be violent if a younger man confronts him.'

Flustered, she replies, 'Isn't there anybody else we could ask?'

'I think he's our best bet. He's a level-headed chap, he'll know what to do,' and he's gone to the workshop before she can object. She's going to have to face Stefan right now and the thought panics her. This is not the ideal situation, but here he is already.

'Marianna.' He stops dead in his tracks as they face each other.

'Stefan,' she stammers. 'How are you?'

'Well. And you?'

'I'm fine, she replies timidly and fiddles with the collar of her blouse. Seeing him again has brought her suppressed feelings to the surface. Her stomach churns and her breath catches in her throat. God help her. How she loves this man.

He pushes his hands deep into his pockets and, reluctant to lose eye contact with her, turns to Stanislaw. 'We'd better get going then.'

Stanislaw is a brisk walker for a man of his stature and strides out in front. 'This way,' he beckons, turning down a narrow alley. The air is cold and their breath evaporates in clouds around them.

Stefan grasps Marianna's elbow as they walk side by side in silence. 'We need to talk,' he says, desperate for her to look at him. But she keeps her head down.

'Not now, Stefan, Stanislaw will hear us. It can wait.'

'Okay, but we must talk soon.' He walks on for a minute and then grabs her arm urgently. 'I can't tell you how much I've thought about seeing you again. There have been times when I thought I would go mad. All these weeks without you have been hell.'

They are breathless now as they talk and try to keep up with Stanislaw. 'I'm not sure I believe that,' Marianna responds icily. 'Did you not receive my letter?'

'Of course I did and it broke my heart.'

'So you didn't feel the need to reply?'

'I did. But I didn't send it. I don't know why, it just seemed wrong.'

'Well, of course it's wrong. We both know that!' she hisses between gritted teeth. 'Now stop.'

'Please, Marianna.' Stefan tries to hold her hand. 'Let me explain.'

She pulls it away. 'Don't. I said not now.' She walks a little faster to put some space between them, catches up with Stanislaw and asks, 'How much further?'

'We're nearly there. I hope I've remembered it right. Only been here once when Tomas collected his things.' They walk on for another hundred yards and he points to a rundown building. 'Yes, we're in the right place, this is it.' He bangs the door several times with his fist and takes a step back. There's complete silence from within so he tries again. A light comes on in the house opposite and the shadow of a curious neighbour is seen hovering at the window. 'Eryk!' he calls and bangs again.

They're about to walk away when a hand pulls aside the grubby net curtain at the downstairs window, pauses for a moment, then lets it drop back into place. From inside comes the sound of shuffling. Eryk opens the door just enough to see them. 'What d'ya want?' he growls.

Marianna steps forward. 'Eryk?'

The door opens a little wider. 'Woss it to you, madam?' Marianna steps back as his foul breath reaches her. His slurred voice indicates Eryk has been drinking.

'We're looking for Tomas. He hasn't returned from his deliveries. Have you seen him? It's terribly late and we're very worried.'

'Ooh, terribly late is it? Worried, are ya? Thas a shame. Yer little errand boy gone missin'?' he sneers. 'No more cosy chats eh?' He pushes his face into hers, sucks in his cheeks and hurls a globule of phlegm to the pavement behind her.

Stefan steps forward and gently moves Marianna away. 'Just tell us where he is, Eryk. He's only a kid. We need to find him.'

Eryk sneers, 'Oh, the carpenter hero speaks up. Brought you along as their bit of muscle, eh?' Eryk's hand comes up, his fist clenched. Stefan reaches out and grabs his wrist so tightly Eryk visibly winces.

'Enough of this nonsense, man. If you know where he is tell us and don't mess with me. You won't come out of it quite so pleased with yourself.'

'Leave go ov me. I ain't saying. I ain't 'urt im. Just givin' 'im a bit of a scare, thas all.' His mouth twists into an evil smirk as he adds, 'But he might as well be dead. Where he is.'

'Just tell us,' Stanislaw growls.

Eryk stumbles about waving his arms. 'Work it out for yerselves.' He lurches backwards and slams the door. They hear a dull thud as he slumps to the floor.

Stefan is puzzling over what Eryk said. 'I've got an idea. He referred to your chats, Marianna. Do you think it could be the cemetery? You've been there lots of times with Tomas. That bit about he might as well be dead.'

Marianna nods. 'I think you could be right. What d'you think, Stanislaw? We've nothing to lose.'

*

Tomas is cold, the tips of his fingers numb. He's stopped trying to free his hands, as his wrists have become sore with the chafing, but at least he can breathe freely without the gag. His brain has been on sensory overload since the children left, and he's become more aware of the wind in the trees and the occasional rustle of a mouse or other small mammal, shuffling around in the blanket of fallen leaves around him. Tomas has no fear of mice, he's seen enough of them in the storeroom at the shop, but he licks his lips, dry with anxiety, and can taste the blood that oozes slowly from a cut above his mouth.

He's becoming accustomed to the dark and constantly scans his surroundings for danger. It's the headstones that frighten him most; they are menacing in their solid stillness, like a crowd that's been paralysed on its way towards him. The path that leads back to the entrance is a narrow, barely visible ribbon of grey, and Tomas strains his eyes in the vain hope that he'll see somebody coming.

A milky white moon shines through the skeletal branches of the trees along the cemetery boundary giving the illusion of a deep band of black lace. Those closer loom over him like deformed limbs, creaking eerily. Occasionally there's an agitated flapping of wings as something disturbs the roosting birds, and fear seizes him, sapping his energy.

*

Stanislaw goes back to the shop in case Tomas returns. 'Somebody needs to be there,' he says. 'You two youngsters can scour the graveyard. I'm too old to be clambering around amongst gravestones.'

When Marianna and Stefan reach the great iron entrance gate it appears to be locked.

'Blast!' Stefan exclaims. He glances up and down the street, judges it's all clear, and before Marianna can stop him, manages to climb halfway up until the bars become wider and there's no foothold for him to reach the top.

'Come down, Stefan!' she urges. 'You'll fall. There's no lock on the gate, I've checked, so it must be open.' Stefan drops the last six feet to the ground and falls awkwardly. 'Oh God. Are you alright?' she cries. But he's already standing.

'I'm fine. Come on, let's push together.' There's a grinding sound and the gate moves slightly then jams. He bends down. 'Look. There's a rock jammed under the bottom. I wouldn't mind betting Eryk had something to do with that.'

They lift the rock away and the great gate creaks open. 'God knows why they build such fortifications round a cemetery. Nobody wants to go in and sure as hell nobody will be coming out,' he says.

'This way,' Marianna takes his arm and leads him forwards. He reaches down and takes her hand in his, forces her to stop for a moment. They're unable to see each other in the dark.

'Marianna,' he whispers, but she squeezes his hand tight.

'No. Not now. Come on. Let's just think about finding Tomas.'

She calls ,'Tomas! Tomas! Are you there?' as they walk deeper into the graveyard. She can just make out the bench and rushes towards it. They don't see Tomas at first, but he's heard them and turns in their direction. The light of the moon shines on his face and Stefan cries out, 'There he is. Thank God!'

Marianna rushes to his side. Tomas starts to cry. 'Why did he do this to me?' She holds him close as Stefan bends low, struggling to undo the ties in the dim light.

'Was it Eryk?' he asks.

Tomas is sobbing uncontrollably but manages to nod.

'Bastard!' Stefan swears. 'He'll pay for this. First thing tomorrow I'll be paying him a visit.'

'Ssssshhhh,' Marianna urges, 'let's just get him home. He's frozen. Poor lamb. Tomas, can you stand?' He nods again. 'Okay. Hold my hand and we'll get you out of here.'

Stefan takes his other hand and they walk together back along the pathway, past the headstones and the creaking trees, Tomas stamping life back into his aching legs.

'The children couldn't help me. They went away,' Tomas mutters to himself.

'The children?' Marianna questions.

'It's nothing,' he replies.

*

There are two police vehicles and a number of officers outside Eryk's house when Stefan arrives next morning.

'What's going on here?' he asks.

'D'you know Eryk Kaminski?' asks a fresh-faced officer.

'I didn't know him exactly but I met him briefly yesterday evening.'

'Then what do you want with him?' The officer looks suspicious.

'I need to speak to him about his brother. Why? What's happened?'

The police officer calls down the hall. 'There's a gentleman here you may wish to speak to, sir. Shall I send him in?'

A gruff voice calls back and 'You'd better go in,' the officer says.

*

Stefan removes his hat and steps over the threshold. A plain-clothes police officer is standing beside Eryk's body.

'Good God!' Stefan exclaims at the sight of Eryk with his legs splayed at peculiar angles, blood congealed on the floor around his head and his eyes wide open in a deathly stare.

'He had one hell of a fall,' says the officer. 'Drunk as a skunk apparently.' He turns to face Stefan now. 'And you are?'

'I'm Stefan Holcer. I've a workshop on Szeroka Street. I was hoping to speak to him about an incident involving his brother.'

The officer looks disinterested. 'Won't be speaking to him now,' he says, stating the obvious. 'Look at this place. Empty bottles everywhere. The whole place reeks of alcohol. He must have been carrying this,' he points to a box on the floor, 'and lost his footing on the stairs. Neighbours heard the crash apparently but couldn't get a response when they knocked so they called us. We don't suspect foul play. It was clearly an accident. The man was an alcoholic by all accounts.'

'What happens next?' Stefan asks.

The officer is matter of fact. 'We'll get him taken away and inform his next of kin.'

'I don't think there are any family members, apart from Tomas,' Stefan informs him. 'He's Eryk's younger brother. He lives and works at Stanislaw Novak's grocery store.'

'Hmm.' The officer puts a finger to his lips. 'That's interesting. The neighbours tell us Eryk's parents lived here until five years ago. Both dead now by all accounts. Said they assumed his wife had left him, as they've seen nothing of her for years. Apparently there were rumours about her and another man. There have been no sightings of his son for months and they assumed he'd gone to be with his mother. Bit of a vagabond by all accounts. Didn't say anything about a brother.'

Stefan is trying to absorb this information. A wife? A son? Tomas is Eryk's son? It's looking increasingly likely. Stefan scans the papers strewn across the floor. There must be something here that will clarify the situation.

'D'you mind if I have a look around?' Stefan asks.

'Can't see why not in the circumstances, but don't remove anything until I give you the say so,' the officer says, tucking his pencil behind his ear and pocketing his notebook.

The contents of the heavy wooden box, a little larger than a shoebox, have been scattered in the fall. The corners are bashed and splintered, the brass hinges broken. A faded black and white photo of an attractive young woman with dark hair and a baby in her arms is pasted inside the lid. The names Eryk, Maja and baby Tomas (aged six months) have been scribbled on the back. Another photo shows a group of young people, linking arms. It has been ripped so that one man's face is missing.

Next to the box lies a barely legible note.

*Eryk,*
*I can't take no more of your drinking. I'm leaving and going with Hugo. He loves me but he doesn't want the kid so I'm leaving him with you. Your mum and dad will take care of him, I know that. Don't come looking.*
*Maja*

Other envelopes contain letters from Eryk to Maja that have been returned. They all bear the same message. He is unfit to be a father and his parents are too old to care for the boy. He can't cope and begs her to come home.

There are photos of Maja and Eryk in happier times. Casual photos of the couple walking arm in arm; sitting at a café table; Maja lying dramatically across Eryk's lap with her head thrown back like a film star and dressed in fancy clothes.

Above the stove is a framed photo of Tomas sat on an elderly gentleman's knee with the lady beside him holding Tomas's hand affectionately. It's clear there's only one explanation. Eryk is Tomas's father and the couple who Tomas believed to be his parents were in fact his grandparents.

This is going to take some explaining and Stefan doesn't relish the task. 'There are a few things here that Tomas might like,' Stefan says to the officer. 'Is there any chance I could take them with me?'

'Best wait until we've finished our investigations, but I don't see why you can't have them. Put them to one side and when we've finished here I'll drop them round to the shop. Novak's grocery store on Szeroka Street, is it?'

'That's right,' Stefan confirms, 'but it may frighten the boy to have a police officer call on him, so will it be alright if I explain to him what's happened? At least it won't be such a shock if he's forewarned.'

The officer nods. 'Of course and you should give him this. It's got the boy's name on it.' He hands Stefan a small package. 'I found this in the chaps' pocket and if you need anything else you can contact me here.' He hands Stefan a card.

'Thank you, Mr Wozniak,' Stefan says. 'You've been very helpful.'

*

It's been an upsetting morning and Stefan is visibly shaken as he describes the awful scene in detail to Stanislaw and Marianna. They discuss the best way to break the news to Tomas, and Marianna insists she'll be the one who will tell him.

'I'll have a nice quiet talk with him. I know how to handle him. It'll be fine.'

Stefan is reluctant to relinquish responsibility but she's made up her mind. 'Don't worry, I'll be very careful what I say.'

'Promise to let me know how he takes it? I gather the police are calling round later this morning. Perhaps speak to him before they arrive.'

'Yes of course and I'll call by later and let you know what happens.'

*

She explains the circumstances of Eryk's death to Tomas as gently as possible, making sure to spare him the horrific details. The fact that Eryk was his father is hard for him to accept.

'But why did he treat me like that if he was my dad?'

'He was clearly broken-hearted when your mother left him. Taking care of a small child, especially after your grandparents passed away, was a huge responsibility and he says himself that he wasn't capable of being a good father. I imagine the drinking didn't help.'

'Why did he drink so much? Was it because he hated me?'

'Nobody could hate you, Tomas. No, I'm sure it was because he was unhappy. Sometimes people drink to forget their worries.'

Tomas looks unsure. 'But they looked happy in the photos, didn't they?'

'They did, but people change for lots of reasons. Nobody knows what life will bring. He must have been very sad when she left.'

'But how could she leave me? Just leave me behind like that?'

'It sounds to me as if Hugo convinced her not to take you.'

'But how could he?'

'I don't know, Tomas, but sometimes when people fall in love they do things or make decisions that are wrong.'

'Then I ain't never gonna fall in love if that's what it does.'

Marianna smiles wryly. 'It's not the same for everyone, Tomas. Being in love can be a wonderful feeling.'

Tomas goes pink. 'I ain't gonna talk about bein' in love no more. S'daft.'

She hugs him to her. 'You'll see. One day. It's not so daft if it's real.'

'But what will happen to me now?' he asks.

'Everything will stay the same as before. You can live here and carry on working in the shop.' She smiles and pats his hand. 'If that's what you want, of course.'

He nods solemnly.

'Don't worry. We're your family now and we'll make sure you're safe.'

Tomas's sniffling subsides and she judges it the right time to give him the package. His name has been scrawled on the wrapping and he opens it slowly, reluctant to reveal the contents. Tomas holds the watch in his hand for a while before rubbing his thumb over the dusty glass. The dial is still readable and on the reverse side is the inscription – always yours, Maja xx. He turns the winding mechanism, adjusts the hands to the correct time and holds it to his ear. A slow smile crosses his face as he hears it tick. The accompanying note reads:

> *Tomas,*
> *I have no way of making amends for the way I treated you. This watch was a gift to me from your mother. Please take care of it. It's the only thing of value I've ever owned. It's not much to show for a man's life but one day it will be yours anyway so I'm giving it to you now. I'm sorry.*
> *Eryk*

He returns the watch to its wrapping and snuggles against Marianna.

'There's one thing I wanted to ask you,' she says.

'What's that?'

'You mentioned something about children when we were leaving the cemetery. What did you mean?'

Tomas thinks for a moment. 'It was nuffinck,' he mutters. 'I fink I must have imagined them.'

*

Stefan has his back to the door and is unaware of Marianna's presence. She's standing silently in the doorway, watching him work, every movement considered as he carves the detail on Mr Cohen's piece of furniture. She adores the back of his head, bent in concentration, the muscles in his arms flexing as he works, his thick hair curled on his collar.

She pushes the door to behind her. 'Hi,' she says.

He turns, startled, then smiles broadly at the sight of her. 'Hi to you too.' He places the chisel on the workbench. 'How is he?' he asks.

'He'll be fine, poor lad. It's been a shock but he'll be alright. He's with Elena this afternoon and she will cheer him up I'm sure.'

He nods. 'Good,' he says, adding, 'He's lucky to have you both.'

'He's no trouble,' she replies.

'And how are you?' he asks, stepping closer to her. She moves away.

'I'm as well as can be expected I suppose. For someone who's been deserted by their husband and been a willing party to adultery.'

'Marianna. Don't. Leon was a fool to leave you for Amelia. As for adultery, I was just as much to blame.' He gazes at her intently. 'It was inevitable after all.'

She shakes her head.

He continues. 'I knew it would happen the moment I met you. We both did.'

Stefan retrieves his letter from its hiding place and presses it into her hand.

'Here, take this. Read it carefully and believe this, Marianna. I mean every word.' He presses the letter into her hand.

'It's no good, Stefan. I can't be responsible for another woman's misery. I just can't.'

'Truda makes her own misery I'm sorry to say. Always has.'

'Nevertheless, I've made up my mind. However much we feel for each other, we mustn't ever do that again. Not ever. Promise me, Stefan.'

'It'll be impossible and we both know it.'

He cups her face in his hands and kisses her mouth. 'Just read the letter. Promise me you will?'

Marianna nods. She can sense her resolve is weakening and pulls away from him. She slips the letter in her pocket and rushes from the room, back to the safety of Stanislaw's shop, not one little bit sure that she'll be able to carry through her good intentions.

*

Tomas is happier when he returns from Elena's but insists he's likely to have nightmares about Eryk once he's left alone in his sleep cupboard. Marianna says he can spend the night with her.

'I'll make you a bed on the sofa. In case you need me.'

He does need her and not long after midnight she's

woken by the sound of crying. He's a sorry sight, hunched over and hugging himself fearfully as the tears stream down his face.

'Oh, Tomas, please don't upset yourself, my love. Come. Slide in next to me.' She pulls him close and he lies sniffing in the dark. 'That's it. Have a good cry. You'll be fine. You'll see.'

'I wish… I wish…' he stutters between sobs.

'What do you wish?' she asks gently.

'I wish you was my mum.'

*

Tomas barely moves during the night, but Marianna has been restless and is awake as dawn breaks, her mind buzzing with the unexpected revelations about Tomas's family. She leaves him to sleep and tiptoes from the room, closing the door behind her.

Stefan's letter is still tucked in the pocket of her skirt. She longs to read it but is afraid of what it might say. She busies herself making coffee and spends a little time watching the pigeons on the rooftops opposite, folds and refolds the towels drying above the stove until she can bear the suspense no longer and, clutching the letter, slowly peels the envelope flap open, pulls out the folded sheet and reads. It's everything she'd hoped it would be.

# Seventeen

Feliks' life has changed dramatically since Marianna left for Zalipie and he's longing to tell her his news, but having heard about the trouble with Eryk, feels he should leave it a couple of days. But he has underestimated Marianna's enthusiasm for their joint project and she rushes to see him as soon as her morning shift at the shop is over.

'Oh, darling girl!' he exclaims, hugging her tight. 'Fancy that bastard leaving you like that. He didn't deserve you. But now you're back so how are you?'

Marianna is determined not to go into detail. 'I don't want to talk about it, Feliks. He's been relegated to my past and I'm starting again. Now tell me what you've been up to. I can't wait to hear.'

'There's so much to tell. So much!'

'I've got an hour, so come on let's hear it. Why don't you start with Lidka? I hear you two are seeing a lot of each other.'

'Ah. Lidka. My salvation. Where would I be without her? She's organised my space as you can see,' he laughs affectionately. 'She's become my manager and chief spokesperson, negotiator and,' he winks at her, 'other things too. But we won't go into that! Most importantly she's escaped the clutches of that dreadful woman. Her mother has been such a drain on Lidka's confidence, I can't tell you.'

'I've heard she spends a lot of time organising you,' Marianna grins. 'Just goes to show that still waters run deep and all this because of a chance tango lesson. Well, I'm pleased. She's just what you needed. So tell me about the artwork.'

'All finished and those that haven't sold are still on display at the restaurant. Have a look at this!' With a flourish he removes the cotton sheet covering a large canvas.

'Goodness! That's beautiful, Feliks. The colours are stunning. Very Spanish.'

'I worked from the drawings I made of you before you disappeared. Poof! Like a magic trick.'

'I know. I'm sorry I didn't say goodbye. It was very rude of me. Hopefully I'm forgiven?'

'You are. Of course you are.'

'So where is this painting going? Who's bought it?'

Feliks looks smug. 'This, my dear, is my first commission from a very wealthy Spanish gallery owner.' Feliks is still unable to believe his luck. 'Very wealthy,' he repeats. 'His name is Pedro. No, I promise you, that's not a joke. Pedro Gonzalez. He owns a gallery in Barcelona. He saw my work at the restaurant and wants some larger pieces. Six paintings! And that's just for starters. I tell you, Marianna, one day I'll wake up and this will all be a dream.'

'That's marvellous, Feliks. You've been so lucky that somebody like him came along when there's so much bankruptcy and hardship going on. Things are getting worse by the week apparently, so Stanislaw tells me.'

'I know. Someone must be looking down on me and now I must take care of you too. Now that I'm actually earning it's only right that you should receive some monetary compensation for all those hours you so willingly sat freezing in my studio.'

Marianna shakes her head. 'That's not necessary, Feliks. I'm just pleased you're being recognised for your talent at last. Stefan must be thrilled.'

'He seems pleased enough. Though he's very quiet lately. Not sure what's troubling him.' He glances at Marianna. 'Have you two fallen out?'

'No. Certainly not.'

'Well, I hope not. You're good for each other, though I shouldn't say so. Anyway, I want you to have this. It's not much but there'll be more to come, and I hope you'll feel you can help me out again if I ever need you.' He hands her an envelope and she takes it reluctantly.

'Really, Feliks, you don't have to do this but thank you. I'd be happy to model for you any time. I've missed our conversations.'

Stefan isn't mentioned again until she's leaving.

'One more thing, Marianna. Whatever's happened between you two,' he gestures towards the workshop, 'you're better together than apart. Take it from one who knows about these things.'

# Eighteen

The first golden days of autumn are fading and a distinct chill in the air has curtailed Tomas and Marianna's trips to the park. The cemetery is off limits since the awful episode with Eryk.

Stanislaw has agreed that until they find a new tenant for Amelia's room, Tomas can call it his own. Needless to say he's in seventh heaven. 'I've got a place of me own now,' he tells every customer with pride.

Marianna is grateful to have the shop as a diversion and looks forward to seeing Stefan with the safety of the counter between them. And so it goes on. Snatched conversations, longing looks and total frustration.

With their wedding day drawing closer, Elena and Stanislaw have had their first row, throwing temporary doubts on the wisdom of remarrying at such a great age. It blew up when Elena suggested that her much cherished cat, Boris, would be an asset in the shop. Stanislaw, never fond of cats, was adamant that the cat would not be coming with her.

'Wherever I go Boris goes too,' Elena told him, astonished that she was unaware of his aversion to anything four-legged. 'Take my word for it, Stanislaw Novak, at night this cat turns into an alert stealthy killer. He has all the necessary equipment to secure the position of resident mouser.'

'We'll see,' he'd replied.

'Well, Boris, what do you think about that?' she said to the cat when Stanislaw had gone. Boris glanced half-heartedly over his shoulder, blinked slowly and turned away, disgusted. He flicked his tail. Just once. He had, of course, heard every word. She picked him up and his legs dangled like a set of furry bagpipes. She squashed her face against his stuffy tabby head and kissed him. He flattened his ears and growled.

'Oh, stop that, you grump,' she said, tapping his nose with her forefinger.

Boris wriggled free and jumped down. It had been hours since he'd eaten. He looked up at her pleadingly and meowed, rubbing his back against her ankles and twitching his tail with impatience.

'Well, I'll not leave you behind, my lovely,' she'd insisted. 'We'll just have to show the old devil that you're worth your weight in mice. Now come along. Eat this. It's your favourite.'

He sniffed the contents of the bowl, looked at her with contempt and sniffed again. It clearly wasn't right and he slinked away to sulk from his favourite spot on the windowsill.

'I'll take you for a visit tomorrow,' she'd told him. 'He'll see you're no trouble.'

Boris turned his back on her and gazed out of the window, salivating at the sight of a lone pigeon on the ledge outside.

*

Boris can hardly believe his eyes when Elena unceremoniously plonks him on the shop counter the next morning. The place is full of nooks and crannies and things to explore like paper bags dangling on strings and open sacks with contents ripe for investigation. Crouching low to the ground he stalks the cloth covering Truda's baking table, makes a sudden dash with his claws extended like a set of mini knives and leaps. Hanging momentarily, he looks around frantically until the cloth slips and a dozen crusty rolls fall on his head.

'Bloody cat!' Stanislaw yells, swatting him with a cloth. 'Get him out of here.'

Boris makes a dash for it, yowling as he crashes into a bag of dried peas. They scatter across the shop floor. Elena, busy making tea in the living room, hears the commotion and is soon on the scene. 'Dear oh dear! What *is* going on?'

'It's that pesky cat of yours. Just look at this mess. I knew he'd be trouble.'

Boris skids to a halt. Elena scoops him up. He glares and spits at Stanislaw from the safety of her arms. His green eyes speak of evil as he pushes his paws against her chest in an effort to escape. 'Come on, my pet,' she coos. 'Let's get you something to eat.'

'You'd better keep him out of my sight,' Stanislaw grumbles. 'He's nothing but trouble.'

'If it makes you happy I'll lock him in the stock room until we leave,' she replies.

Later in the day Elena goes to check on the cat. His afternoon has been productive; Boris is standing guard next to three very fat and very dead mice.

'Good boy. Oh, you *are* a clever boy,' Elena purrs. She calls to Stanislaw. 'Look, Daddy! Look what Boris has caught you.'

Stanislaw pretends not to be impressed and shuffles back to the shop, muttering under his breath. Smiling triumphantly, Elena waddles towards the kitchen. 'Come on, Boris. You deserve something nice to eat. Let's see what we can find.' Boris's mouth twitches. He grumbles from somewhere deep within and follows. He may have secured his place for the future but Stanislaw, far from magnanimous in defeat, is perfecting his own version of hissing for the next time he sets eyes on the moggy.

*

Stanislaw has reluctantly agreed that Boris can stay. His mousing skills are not to be sniffed at and it's agreed that Tomas will take care of the cat. Before the week is out Boris has become his roommate.

'He's a crafty devil that one,' Elena told him. 'He'll be running rings round you before you know it.'

Stanislaw has Boris on permanent trial. 'One false move and he'll be out,' he insists. Tomas is fearful of losing his new furry friend so takes the threats seriously. There's something about the cat's wily ways that strike a chord with Tomas, who quickly rectifies any trouble caused during Boris's mouse-hunting sessions before Stanislaw has a chance to add a black mark against the cat's name.

Boris had Tomas in his sights as a potential 'sucker' from day one. Whilst the boy is waiting for his day's instructions, Boris jumps onto the counter and tiptoes towards him, his bushy tail held high, and bumps his head against his shoulder affectionately. He knows where the next treat is coming from and needs to keep in his good books. He sits outside Tomas's bedroom door for hours, waiting for his return, and darts through the smallest of gaps the moment the door is ajar, making a beeline for his favourite resting place on Tomas's bed. It's an arrangement that suits them both nicely.

Within a week the two became inseparable. 'I do believe you have been adopted Tomas's Elena tells him, and chuckles at the thought that at least her beloved moggy will be out of Stanislaw's sight.

# Nineteen

Stanislaw and Elena's marriage vows are taken in a simple civil ceremony one bright autumn afternoon. Under Stanislaw's instructions the shop is shut for the day and Truda has been tasked with the job of laying on a meal for a dozen invited guests. She's laid out tables in the back room and they're laden with baskets of bread and casseroles filled with Elena's speciality stew. It has taken her days to assemble the ingredients but she's managed. It's very much a help-yourself supper, the stew to be followed by apple strudel. Stanislaw has been generous, much to everyone's amazement, and the vodka is flowing. Before long the room is buzzing with loud conversation and laughter.

Stanislaw has appointed Stefan as his chief barman, and as such he spends much of the evening getting up and down to refill glasses. Marianna is overtly aware of his closeness and the warmth from his body as he leans over her to pour yet another drink. She's desperate for his touch and leans her head back so that he touches her hair in passing. The vodka is taking effect and she's unable to resist making eye contact with him.

'Be careful,' Feliks warns with a look from across the room.

Stanislaw's tango records get a dusting off and Feliks and Lidka, now inseparable, demonstrate their perfected dance moves. Her mother tuts all the while but Sara's disapproval is met with nothing but amusement from her liberated daughter.

Tomas has never been to a wedding and sits with his hands clasped in a state of constant delight. The evening is a great success and most of the guests have stumbled home when Elena finds Stanislaw fast asleep with his head on his chest.

'Oh Lord!' Elena sighs. 'I think I've married a drunkard!'

'There's a few of them about tonight,' Marianna agrees, feeling more than a little lightheaded herself.

'Still, as long as he's enjoyed himself,' Elena muses. 'You only get married twice.'

Stefan conceals his own inebriation poorly and Marianna wishes he would stop looking at her with such longing. 'Come on, you. Stop staring at me like that and give me a hand to stack these chairs in the storeroom.'

The corridor and storeroom are in darkness and out of the sight of the last stragglers. Marianna reaches round the door, fumbling for the light switch.

'Don't,' Stefan urges as his hand covers hers and he pulls her into the room, pushing the door closed. The folded chairs he's carrying crash to the floor as he takes her in his arms.

'Let me kiss you, you witch. I'll die if I don't.'

'Sshh. Someone will hear you,' she says, giggling like a schoolgirl.

'Just kiss me then and I'll be quiet,' he demands.

It's been weeks since that day in the workshop but it's as if they've never been apart. He presses against her, raises her arms above her head and they stand like this with their hands clasped and fingers entwined. He kisses her neck, her cheeks and her eyes. Her mouth searches for his in the dark and then Truda calls.

'Stefan! Come and help with these tables, will you. They're too heavy for Elena and me.'

They break apart. Marianna smooths her dress, breathing heavily and pats her hair back into place.

'I'm coming,' he calls and mutters, 'Damn her.'

Marianna picks up the chairs with shaking hands and stacks them neatly back in the storeroom.

*

The following morning she's feeling decidedly nauseous. *That'll teach me for drinking so much vodka and eating so much dessert* she concludes. Gluttony is bad both for the body and soul. She struggles through the rest of the morning feeling limp and listless and promises herself an early night.

Stefan calls into the shop just before lunchtime. 'I was hoping I'd catch you. You look pale. Are you alright?' he asks, looking concerned.

'I'm fine. Got a headache, that's all. Self-inflicted as they say.'

'I know the feeling, I feel like I've been kicked in the head. It was good fun though, wasn't it? Where are the newlyweds?' he asks.

'Stanislaw is suffering rather badly. Elena thinks he should know better at his age.'

Stefan nods in agreement. 'Probably should, but we never learn, do we? About lots of things.' His tone changes abruptly. 'When can I see you alone?'

'You can't.'

He looks dejected. 'Well, we can't go on like this.'

'Think of Truda.'

'Truda and I hardly converse anymore and that's not just because of you.'

'That doesn't make it right for you to have sex with me.' She's getting annoyed.

'For God's sake, Marianna. It's not just sex. Surely you know that.'

'It still doesn't make it right.'

The shop bell rings and Sara enters.

'Morning, how can I help you, Sara?' Marianna turns to Stefan and asks, 'Was there anything else I can get you?' He has no option but to say, 'No thanks, that's all for now,' and leaves feeling like a child who has been dismissed.

*

Elena eventually surfaces having slept till late.

'Oh dear, you still look peaky, my dear,' she says to Marianna.

'Do I look as bad as I feel? I feel so... sick.'

'It'll take a while for your system to get back to normal. You'll be fine tomorrow.'

But she isn't. Her stomach's on a rollercoaster of nausea, and although customers have been few and far between and she's had plenty of time to relax she's exhausted. She can't bear the thought of eating, and even the smell of brewing tea causes her to heave as another wave of sickness engulfs her. She makes a dash for the sink clutching her stomach, vomits violently and collapses into the chair, limp and shaking. It crosses her mind that she might have food poisoning, but she knows this is unlikely as none of the other guests have been ill. Come to think of it she's been feeling sick quite often lately.

The retching starts again and between the gut-wrenching spasms comes the dreadful realisation that she may be pregnant. She covers her face with her hands. Please God no. She must stay calm. She may be wrong. She hasn't been with Leon for months; she can't be pregnant by him and this surely can't be the result of that one time with Stefan. Her head spins. No, she can't accept that, but deep in her heart she knows it to be true.

*

'Marianna's late this morning,' Stanislaw says to Elena as they prepare for another busy day. By ten o'clock there's still no sign of her and Elena is concerned.

'She wasn't feeling well yesterday, I think I'd better pop upstairs and check on her.'

She taps on Marianna's door. There's no answer. She taps again, places her ear against the door and strains to hear any sounds from within. If she's not mistaken she can hear sobbing. She turns the handle and opens the door far enough to call through the gap, 'Marianna, are you alright?' The sobbing gets louder. She opens the door a little wider and peers in. Marianna is slumped on the sofa, her eyes swollen, her face pink and blotchy. She's dressed in her nightwear but from her appearance Elena suspects she's had little sleep.

'Can I come in?' Elena asks, uncertain of her welcome.

Marianna blows her nose and nods pathetically.

'Whatever's the matter?' Elena asks, flopping down heavily beside her and placing a chubby arm around her shoulder. 'Do tell me. I know things are hard for you at the moment but I hate to see you so upset. Is there anything I can do?'

Marianna sniffs. 'I'm afraid there's nothing anybody can do, Elena. I think I'm pregnant.'

'Oh Lord. Oh dear oh dear. And that awful Leon has left you at such a time. My dear, he should be ashamed of himself.'

'But he doesn't know,' Marianna grabs her arm, 'and he mustn't. I don't want him to know, Elena. I'll deal with this on my own.'

'Whatever you say, but you must take care of yourself and you should get it checked out. It may just be a stomach upset.'

Marianna is relieved that Elena believes its Leon's baby and there's no reason for her to doubt it. There's no reason for anybody else to doubt it either, except perhaps for one person. She places her hands protectively on her abdomen. *He must never know. I will let everyone think it's Leon's. I may never have Stefan,* she thinks, *but I will have his baby.*

The pregnancy is confirmed and before long most of Szeroka Street knows that not only has her hapless husband run off with another woman but he's left her with the daunting task of bringing up a baby on her own. Sympathy for Marianna knows no bounds. She feels a fraud but the truth must never be known. It's her secret and hers alone.

*

Truda removes her apron and sighs as she stomps into the hallway and calls upstairs.

'Stefan! Are you coming down! Coffee is made!'

Her mother always insisted the way to a man's heart is through his stomach, so today she's taken her at her word and has made more of an effort. Their finances are becoming increasingly tight, but having reluctantly pawned one of her mother's pearl necklaces there's a little money to spare and she's indulged them with a breakfast the likes of which they haven't had for a while. After all, she tells herself, what use are pearls if you can't eat properly. She has risen early to bake a sourdough rye loaf and the warm smell of baking fills the room. She has purchased a block of Stefan's favourite smoked cheese, a small piece of ham and boiled some eggs. She surveys the scene with satisfaction. It looks good and she feels sure he'll be impressed. Wandering to the window she looks down at the neighbours going about their daily business in the street below. Young mothers are pushing prams with small children running alongside, a scene she's imagined herself inhabiting but wonders if she ever will.

Stefan ambles into the room yawning and as usual his appearance prompts a disapproving frown from his wife.

'Oh, there you are!' Truda huffs. 'I thought you were never coming down. You promised Stanislaw you'd see him about his cupboard repairs and it would be rude to be late.'

Mornings aren't the best for Stefan. A heavy sleeper, he takes a while to get into the rhythm of a new day. 'You've gone to a lot of trouble,' he says sleepily, rubbing his eyes and dragging his fingers through tousled hair. 'It's a while since we ate this well in the morning.'

*At least he's noticed,* Truda thinks, pleased with herself. She moves to and fro between the table and the stove, pours steaming coffee into heavy mugs whilst bombarding him with the latest mundane local news. Stefan concentrates on his food, spreading a chunky portion of bread with margarine and slapping a sliver of cheese on top. He sips quietly at his coffee, his mind elsewhere, while Truda drones on in the background, her voice now a distant blur.

She glances sideways at him. 'Are you listening, Stefan?'

'I'm hanging on your every word,' he replies.

The sarcastic tone in his voice goes unnoticed and she carries on, 'Oh, and here's a bit of news that'll surprise you. Marianna's having a baby.'

The shock is like a lightning bolt. He stares at her unblinking and stony-faced, unable to find a suitable response.

'Well? What d'you think about that?' she asks.

Truda sits opposite him, studying his reaction, a smug look on her face. 'Don't you think it's awful for her?'

Stefan stays silent, frantically collecting his thoughts.

'Nothing to say?' Truda asks.

He leans back in his chair and places his trembling hands on his lap out of her sight.

'Apparently she's very upset,' Truda continues. 'Not surprising in the circumstances. What with Leon gone and with her parents so far away and goodness knows what they'll think.'

Stefan feels obliged to respond. 'It'll be difficult, that's for sure. Still, there's not much we can do about it. It's her problem,' he says dismissively.

Truda seems puzzled. 'I thought you'd have more to say about it as you two seem to be on particularly good terms. Not sure you can call the joy of having a baby a problem.'

'It's irrelevant whether I'm pleased or not.'

Truda pushes her chair back and stomps to the stove like a sullen child. She refills the coffee pot and slams it down on the table.

'At least she'll have a baby!' An uncomfortable silence follows, broken only by the frantic buzzing of a fly as it bashes against the window in vain and finally submits to suicide. A bubbling pan on the stove boils over. Truda grabs it and throws it in the sink.

Stefan winces. 'Let's change the subject, shall we? All this baby talk is bound to upset you. Tell me what delicious bakes you're making for Stanislaw.'

Truda is sulking but she can't resist telling him.

'If you must know,' she says petulantly, 'I've made a whole tray of *rugelach*, three dozen bagels and two dozen cinnamon *babka*.'

Stefan picks up his apron and turns to go. 'Then it's lucky for them, and me, that you're such a wonderful baker. Thank you for this,' he says, gesturing towards the table.

Things haven't gone quite as she'd planned. They're no closer to being reconciled. She clears the dishes, brushes away a handful of crumbs from the freshly scrubbed table and prepares for another day of baking.

*

Stefan can hear Truda pounding away at her kneading and judges he can nip next door without fear of her coming to the workshop while he's out.

There's no sign of Marianna so Stefan mouths to Stanislaw who is busy with a customer, 'Where is she?' Pointing towards the stairs Stanislaw mouths back, 'Resting.'

He climbs the stairs two at a time and waits outside the door for a few seconds before tapping quietly. 'Marianna. It's me. Can I come in?'

The door opens an inch. 'What d'you want?' she mutters, head bowed.

'Let me in, for God's sake. I need to speak to you.'

He pushes the door open and takes her hand. 'Why didn't you tell me?'

'Why would I? It's nothing to do with you.'

'Are you sure about that?' he asks.

'Yes. I'm sure!' she shouts at him.

'For goodness' sake, calm down,' he says, taking her by the arm. He leads her away from the door and pushes it shut behind him. This needs to be a private conversation and he can't risk anyone overhearing. 'Why are you treating me like this?'

She doesn't answer.

His tone is gentler now, hopeful even. 'I thought that maybe, after what happened in the workshop, it could be mine?'

She cuts him short. 'No! Absolutely not and don't mention that again.'

'Please don't treat me as though you don't care, Marianna. It's not entirely impossible, but if you say it's not the case then I'll have to take your word for it.'

She weakens and takes his hand in hers. 'Oh, Stefan. I care. Of course I do. I care too much and that's the trouble. There's no future for us. And now I've this and I refuse to involve Leon after what he did to me,' she touches her stomach, 'and I have to make a life for myself without you. I've always known that, but it won't stop me loving you.'

He kisses her face, the fire within him relit. 'Do you know what you've done to me? Do you? I've been sleepwalking through my life, Marianna. Please believe me when I say I came alive when I met you.' He presses himself against her. 'I'm flooded with feelings I never knew existed and I refuse to lose you from my life. One thing is for sure: I won't be leaving you to deal with this on your own.'

Marianna starts to cry and Stefan wraps his arms around her. 'Ssssh, darling girl. Everything will be alright. Just say you love me and I'll never let you go.'

*

Stanislaw is alone when Stefan reappears. 'How is she?' he asks.

'She's fine. It's good of you to let her take some time off. I've told her we'll do what we can to help. We're very fond of her after all.' He cringes inwardly at his own deception. Stanislaw places a hand on Stefan's shoulder.

'Elena and I have had an idea and wonder how you'd feel about making something for the baby. It would be a gift from all of us and we'd pay you of course. Elena came up with the idea of a cradle, though nothing too fancy. We wouldn't want to take up too much of your time. How'd you feel about that?'

Stefan is delighted. 'I don't have much work at the moment, so yes, of course. I'd love to.'

Stanislaw is pleased. 'Why don't you scribble down a few ideas and we'll have a look and come to some agreement over the cost.'

'Consider it done,' Stefan enthuses.

*

Stefan is bent over the plan for the cradle when Truda appears with his lunch.

'How are you getting on with the chairs?' she asks.

'Not doing the chairs today.'

'Oh?'

'Stanislaw has asked me to make a cradle for Marianna. It's to be a gift from all of us. All the neighbours, that is.'

Truda freezes and glares at him but says nothing.

'You clearly have something to say, Truda. Why don't you spit it out?'

She raises her eyes and sighs.

'So you're spending valuable time working on a cradle for her when you should be doing other things?'

'I don't understand why you're so upset about it. Marianna is our friend and Stanislaw has asked me to make her a personal gift. I haven't got that much work at the moment and I'd have thought you'd be pleased for her. We're all chipping in so it isn't costing a lot.'

'You know very well why I'm so upset, but you just don't care!'

'That's an unfair comment, Truda, and I'm beginning to think you can be quite uncharitable at times.'

Truda has gone pale.

Stefan turns his back to her. 'I'm sorry, Truda, but I really don't have time for this.'

Truda explodes, waving her arms about wildly.

'So Marianna's cradle is more important than you having a conversation with your wife!'

Stefan grimaces and sighs.

She rants on. 'Just how insensitive are you? You know how much I want a baby and here you are making a cradle for somebody else! You said you wanted a family but you lied to me, Stefan. You lied! My mother warned me. She said, "Truda you won't always get what you want from him!" She was right. My mother was always right! I'm glad she's not alive to see me suffering so much. At this rate I'll be too old to be a mother. I'll be a barren old maid.' She stamps her foot and a shaking finger stabs at him.

'Behaving like this won't get you a child,' he says. 'For goodness' sake calm down, you'll give yourself a headache.'

'I've already got a headache! You've given it to me!'

Truda starts to cry and Stefan sighs.

'D'you really think we should be starting a family when we do nothing but row? Believe me, Truda, it's beginning to get to me. I suggest you think long and hard about where our relationship is going.'

Truda does think about it. She thinks about it all day and long into the following night, and not until dawn is breaking does she fall into a disturbed sleep.

*

With her duties at the shop on temporary hold Marianna spends most of her time writing or sleeping, and now that her nausea has eased at last she's able to venture outside. With the weather unusually mild for the time of year she spends most mornings at the park wandering contentedly among the amber blanket of fallen leaves that clothe the ground.

Stefan has walked with her twice on the pretext of visiting clients and she cherishes the precious hours they spend together as they stroll arms linked, chatting and laughing.

'The sad thing about autumn,' Marianna says one day when the air is a little chillier, 'is that it inevitably leads to winter and I can't stand the relentless cold and wet. I always feel a dampening of spirits when it arrives.'

Stefan agrees. 'I dislike winter too. It's like an unwanted guest who arrives with nothing but bad news, stays too long and then leaves when they've worn you down.'

She smiles. 'Here's a random thought. If autumn were a person would it be a voluptuous woman? I think so. She'd bear all the characteristics of the season, be boundless in her generosity, with an outward appearance of quiet confidence punctuated with moments of sheer abandoned exuberance. Cheeks like peaches, luscious and ripe for the picking, skin kissed golden by the summer sun, honey sweet, generous and kind.'

Stefan laughs. 'Sounds like you. And what does this imaginary woman do when winter comes?'

She considers for a moment. 'I would imagine that her mood ebbs and flows between joyful and restless, and then, when the golden days turn to cool nights, she wraps herself in a rich cloak of velvet cloth embroidered with leaves of crimson, ochre and saffron and stays cocooned in its warmth until winter is ushered out by the return of spring.'

'Lovely description,' he says, squeezing her arm. 'You've a way with words.'

'And what kind of person do you think winter would be like?' she asks him, teasing.

He stops. 'Hmm. Let me think about it for a moment.'

They stroll on.

'Right. I've got it. Picture this. Autumn is at home and winter knocks at her door. She's exhausted but she drags herself across the room and, opening the door, sighs deeply as the embers of happy times fade and her heart goes cold.'

Marianna's eyes widen with mock surprise. 'Goodness. Carry on. I'm impressed.'

Stefan continues, 'There he stands, as he does every year, unblinking, thin and stooped, pale-faced and white-lipped. An unwanted, depressing presence, miserly and cruel with nothing to give save an occasional unexpected burst of brilliance.'

He smiles now, enjoying her reaction. 'That was a sunny day, by the way.'

'And?' She wants more.

'Oh. You want an ending? Okay, let me see.'

They walk on for a while.

'I've got it!'

'Let's hear it then,' Marianna urges.

'Well, reluctantly, autumn steps aside to let him in. She has no choice.'

Marianna reaches up and kisses his cheek.

'Sheer genius.'

He laughs. 'I'll never have your imagination. You should write more. Promise me you will?'

'I promise,' she says and kisses him again.

# Twenty

The photo of Tomas's grandparents takes pride of place on the small chest of drawers beside his bed. Those of his parents are tucked inside a drawer along with Eryk's watch. His annoying habit of asking the time so often throughout the day prompts Stanislaw to suggest he may like to wear it, but Tomas adopts an expression Stanislaw is becoming familiar with and stubbornly replies that he doesn't want to.

'I know it's a little large for you but I could alter the strap if it helps.'

'No thanks, I'm not wearing it. Not yet,' is his curt reply.

Marianna and Elena take it in turns to give him a meal at the end of the day and this gives each of them some respite from his endless questions.

'Your brain's like a sponge,' Elena declares. 'A great big squishy sponge that never fills up. You're going to be cleverer than the three of us put together if your memory's as active as your tongue.'

He pokes his tongue in and out at high speed, and

rolls his eyes. 'Yeah. You're right. Look how quick my tongue is!'

Tomas loves Elena's company and whenever he has a spare hour he joins her in the kitchen.

'Mind you don't fall off that stool, young man,' she warns one morning when she finds him wobbling from side to side, stirring a huge pot of stew with a ladle as long as his arm.

'I ain't gonna fall,' he says, removing the ladle and wiping his hands on the heavy apron that hangs loosely around his neck. 'I'm gettin' the 'ang of this now.'

'Getting the hang, Tomas. Please try and remember.'

A delicious aroma wafts along the corridor, enticing Stanislaw to pay a visit. He dips a spoon into the pot and slurps the contents greedily.

'Not bad, young man, not bad.'

Tomas has become increasingly interested in the workings of Elena's kitchen. 'I'm not always gonna deliver groceries, ya know. One day I'll be a chef in charge of a big hotel or a posh 'ouse.'

'House,' Elena corrects. 'Yes, I'm sure you are but there's a load of washing up here that needs doin'.'

'Doing!' he shouts back at her and ducks as she swipes at him with a cloth.

Elena shakes her head. 'I give up. You aren't even trying, are you, and what's all this about selling food?'

He removes his apron and jumps down from the stool. 'I got this idea, see. I could make soup and sell it outside when it gets real cold.'

'Oh yes. And who's going to pay for the ingredients?'

'I am. I can buy leftover veg at the market. Pay 'em somefing. Better than them getting nuffing. I've thought it through. It's all planned out in me head.'

Elena is speechless and can't understand why Stanislaw hasn't thought of the idea himself.

'And how d'you intend to pay for the ingredients?'

'I got money I saved. Money Mrs Cohen and others paid me for doin' jobs. I'll start wiv that and when I sell the first lot it'll pay for itself. See, your 'rifmatic lessons have come in right 'andy.'

Elena chuckles. 'I always knew there was more to you than meets the eye, young man. You'd better go and tell Stanislaw that he's got competition. Then get yourself back 'ere as quick as you like and finish stirring that stew.'

'Here!' he says, correcting her for the second time, and runs off to sow the seeds of the idea with his boss.

Stanislaw is equally flabbergasted.

'Good on you, boy, it's a great idea. When are you starting this venture?'

'I thought I'd check wiv you first and if it's alright to use your stove, I'll give you somefing for the heat. I'll start tomorrow, go to the market at closing time and make the soup in the evening ready for the next day. What d'ya fink?'

'I fink... think, you've thought of everything. You've got a deal. And what will you serve this soup in?'

'In a mug, I s'pose. We could charge for the mug and they'll get that back when they return it.'

'You can't expect people to stand about in the cold,' Stanislaw says. 'I could put a few chairs round the shop. They might even be encouraged to buy something they didn't know they needed.'

Tomas is beside himself with excitement. He can't believe it's been so easy to put his plan into action.

'That's just great. Fank you, Stanislaw,' and like a real businessman he shakes his hand to seal the deal.

*

The following afternoon he changes into some old clothes, roughs his hair up and waits nervously for the market traders to start packing away their goods. It won't do to look too smart, not for the yarn he's about to spin.

He strolls up one side of the street and back down the other, noting who has the best produce and who has the most left over. Soup is only as good as the ingredients you use, and he's no intention of filling the pot with manky bits and pieces.

He lurks about until the carts are brought up for reloading then picks his victim and adopts a hungry look.

'You throwing that stuff away?' he asks the stallholder. 'It don't look that bad to me.'

The street trader doesn't reply but Tomas persists.

'How much do you want for it? I'll take a load off yer 'ands if ya like.'

He has caught the stallholder's attention. 'Really? And

what would a young whippersnapper like you want with a load of old veg?'

'I got a big family. Three bruvvers and two sisters and they need feedin'. Me dad is dead. Fell down the stairs he did and me mum ran off.' This part is at least true. 'I'm in charge now. I 'ave to do what I can to keep 'em alive.'

The stallholder is a soft touch and takes pity on him. 'I tell you what, I'll let you have a box of mixed veg.' He piles a selection of vegetables into the box and it's soon filled with onions and carrots, turnips and cabbage, root celery and leeks.

'You'll be able to make a good soup with that, you will. It'll keep you going for a week. Now get yourself over to the slaughterhouse quick and pick up some bones for your broth.'

'How much d'you want for these?' Tomas asks.

'Forget it,' the stallholder says, waving him away. 'You look like you could do with a good feed.'

Tomas can hardly believe his luck. Next time he'll start at the opposite end of the market and with any luck he'll be able to spin the same story. He scrounges a bag of bones, collects the vegetables and struggles back to the shop.

Tomas clears his throat, adopts a gruff voice and approaches Stanislaw.

'I'd like to purchase some of your best pearl barley please, Mr Shopkeeper.'

Stanislaw admires the boy's resolve. 'It'll be a pleasure to serve you, young man,' he says in a suitably business-like voice.

Tomas takes a handful of coins from his pocket and Stanislaw counts out the correct amount. 'I'm afraid I'll have to charge for this,' he explains, 'it wouldn't be right for you to think you'll always get your ingredients for free.'

'No problem,' Tomas says.

Stanislaw ruffles his hair. 'Off you go now. I can't wait to try this soup.'

That evening while the bones are boiling for the stock he scrubs, peels and chops the veg into chunky pieces then adds them to the drained liquid along with the bag of pearl barley, periodically checking its progress and adding more salt and herbs as required. The soup smells and tastes delicious and he's happy with the result.

Elena lends a hand and keeps an eye on the stove. The last thing they want is an accident. Satisfied that it's cooked for long enough, he covers the pot with a heavy lid and joins Elena for a cup of hot chocolate.

'You've done well.' Elena pats his shoulder. 'I might even buy a mug myself.'

'If it goes well,' Tomas is already thinking ahead, 'I'm gonna make some bread next time and charge them extra.'

Elena chuckles. 'There's no stopping you, is there? Go on, off you trot. I'll see you in the morning.'

*

Tomas's little scheme of working the stallholders with his sob story works a treat and it's some time before they realise they're being duped. Before long he has expanded his business and bakes bread to accompany the soup, upping the price of a mug accordingly. Things are going well. Stanislaw is cashing in on the presence of all those partaking of the Tomas special, and at the end of each day there's just enough left for everyone to have a bowl for tea.

Tomas's jacket pocket is full of jingling zloty and his head is full of dreams.

'What are you going to do with all that money?' Stanislaw asks, ever so slightly envious of the amount that Tomas has made during the week.

'I'm saving up for my restaurant,' he says with self-assurance.

# Twenty-One

The chilly damp air of oncoming winter has curtailed Marianna's early morning walks and now she spends her time writing until it's time to join Stanislaw in the shop.

Stefan's encouragement has motivated her and words pour from her pen onto the page with ease.

He sets her a challenge each week. 'Write me a story about…' and comes up with some random subject with which her imagination can run riot. Spurred on by his enthusiasm and praise there are few days when she doesn't put pen to paper. When Truda is out he comes to the flat and listens while she reads aloud her latest piece, taking on board his constructive criticism.

'Write about paradise,' he suggests one morning.

'Then I'll write about you and I sitting here,' she says, curled into his shoulder, her fingers stroking the golden hairs on his forearm as though it were a sleeping creature.

Stefan sighs and becomes serious. 'Being here with you is like living in a parallel world, a kind of paradise. We're lucky to have each other and we can pretend when we're together that life is good. But it's not reality, is it? Everywhere you look people are struggling to make ends meet. I don't know how you manage on the money that Stanislaw pays you and I wish I could help you out, but Truda and I are struggling too and I think I may have to consider getting some extra work to supplement our income. My carpentry skills are less in demand. Our money situation is not looking good at all.'

'I'm alright,' Marianna says. 'Stanislaw has been so kind about the rent now that I'm on my own and there are always perks left over from the shop at the end of the day. Something'll turn up for you, I'm sure. Perhaps Mr Cohen will want more pieces from you. He was thrilled with your work, wasn't he?'

'He certainly seemed to be, but clients like him don't come along every day sadly and so far I've had no further word from him.'

Stefan kisses her forehead.

'Better go now. Truda will be back shortly. I should be working or we'll have another row.'

'Poor you,' Marianna sympathises, resisting the temptation to criticise Truda, although sometimes she wishes he wouldn't be so compliant. She's beginning to realise that Truda is a demanding and possessive woman who's only happy when things are going her way.

'Right. I'm off then and don't forget, paradise awaits. I look forward to reading your next masterpiece.'

Paradise is easy to conjure up after an hour in his company, so Marianna puts pen to paper immediately. In no time at all she has filled a page with her vision of the perfect hideaway.

*Do you believe in paradise?*
*Does it actually exist?*
*If there is such a place*
*Would it be just like this?*

*The gardens resemble a lush jungle, full of flowering shrubs and dramatic sculptural foliage. Exotic blooms of red and magenta cover the dense canopy and coconut palms rustle in the warm breeze.*

*I enter my secret hideaway via a stepping-stone path that winds down through a steep rocky gulley and leads to a clearing where a crystal clear pool sparkles in the morning sun and upon which flowers float like stranded butterflies. I trail my fingers through the cool water as it tumbles over smooth rocks to a deep pool below. The smooth silver bark of a frangipani tree is outlined sharply against the indigo sky and occasionally a vanilla bloom floats silently down to the pool below like an exotic offering from above.*

*On an area paved with pebbles, a large shallow carved bowl filled with water is home to a thousand floating rose petals. A canopy of jasmine encloses the space above my head and its heady scent fills the air. I take a seat in the shade.*

*My writing book is open.*
*My pen is ready, poised.*
*But for now I sit enchanted*
*This moment truly golden*
*Until the spell is broken.*

*

November slides inexorably and depressingly into December as a cold wind blows from the Baltic.

With her belly swelling, Marianna is reluctant to venture out on the icy pavements, but Tomas is more than happy to run errands and has become Marianna and Stefan's go-between. With little to fill the hours of the day, she has taken to writing each morning – sometimes a poem, sometimes a short story – and sends them via Tomas for Stefan to read.

Stanislaw and Elena are happy working side by side in the shop. Elena's floristry business has lost customers since the move, but her time is filled looking after her new husband, feeding him and pandering to his every need. 'I know I spoil him but he deserves it,' she croons at a pinch-faced Sara quibbling over the price of Michal's favourite sausage.

Feliks' Spanish benefactor has purchased all the artwork in the restaurant and is demanding more. Lidka has taken charge of negotiations.

'Don't undersell yourself, Feliks,' she scolds him one day when he's in a quandary about pricing. 'If your work is so much in demand, you should be charging more. You know you're worth it and think of the money Mr Gonzalez is making at the gallery. Twice what he pays you, I'm sure.' Feliks agrees and has yet another reason to adore Lidka.

The month slips by, but the relentless cold persists and sleet falls intermittently, adding to the lethal frozen layers on the pavements. Horses struggle to pull their heavy loads with heads bowed against the wind, their breath rising in steamy clouds around them. Stallholders at the market look shrivelled and grey. They stamp their feet and blow into their cupped, frozen hands in a futile attempt to keep warm. The shorter hours of daylight are filled with activity, but as darkness falls the streets empty and doors close against the relentless cold.

Truda's barrage of complaints and criticisms is relentless and Stefan is reaching breaking point.

'Oh please, Truda, for God's sake leave me alone for five minutes?' he snaps one day.

She niggles persistently about the baby situation, and the constant antagonism inevitably leads to a mighty row culminating in slammed doors, tears and a deathly silence that lasts all evening.

The next morning Stefan's head is throbbing from lack of sleep and his entire body aches under the strain of lying rigid for hours. Downstairs the table is stacked with baking ingredients. 'Bloody baking!' he exclaims, irrationally sweeping aside bags of flour. One hits the floor and explodes in a cloud of white powder. Stefan's eyes squeeze shut. When he opens them Truda is there, manically kneading a glutinous mountain of dough, reaching out to him with flour-coated arms and grasping hands. Kneading and needing, forever needing and shrieking silently through a paper-thin shroud of filo pastry. His exhausted brain is playing tricks on him. He gulps down some cold coffee left from the night before and minutes later is out on the street with a small brown suitcase in hand. His departure has been impulsive and he has no idea where he's going, but he just can't face her today.

He passes shuttered shops, their doors still closed to customers. The streets of silent homes, in endless rows, like grey barricades to his escape. A woman passes him pushing a pram. The baby is crying and the woman looks harassed. He closes his ears to the deafening noise, peers in and recoils in horror. Its toothless mouth is open, forming a cavernous space filled with yet more babies. He looks back fearfully to see them crawling after him, their tiny arms outstretched. He shakes his head to clear the image and breaks into a run until he reaches the Podgorski Bridge. His impetus is flagging but his mind is racing as he leans on the parapet gasping for breath, head throbbing, and stares at the slow flowing river below. A barge makes its way towards him. There's a brightly painted figurehead of a woman on the bow, with a smiling face and glossy auburn hair. She looks up at him as the boat glides from view below and calls his name.

'Marianna,' he calls back, and runs to the other side, desperate to catch another glimpse of her, but the barge is already through and Truda, hands on hips, laughs from the deck as it slowly moves from view. He collapses onto a seat, head in hands. Men shuffle past him towards their place of work, their heads down, oblivious to his torment.

'Stefan?'

A half-glance sees only black woollen stockings and laced shoes beneath a heavy brown coat. Marianna bends over him and places a hand on his arm.

'Stefan. Whatever's wrong?' The spinning in his head slows. He takes a deep breath and grasps her hand, finally able to compose himself.

'I've been living a nightmare. Tell me I'm awake. Tell me you're real.'

Marianna gestures for him to move along so she can sit beside him. She wraps her coat around her belly and sits awkwardly with her legs splayed out at the knee.

'Where are you going?' she asks gently.

A weary frown crosses his face. 'I've no idea. I just had to get out.'

'And the suitcase?'

'Open it.'

Marianna tentatively lifts the lid and the clasp opens with a vicious click. A small brown parcel tied with fraying blue ribbon and a paper bag showing the telltale greasy stains of the pastries within are its only contents. 'You won't go hungry for a while,' she quips, attempting to make him smile.

'The gift is for you. I couldn't leave it at home.'

She unwraps a wooden rattle. There's a tiny bee carved on the handle. She shakes it gently and the dried beans inside jingle and echo their own sound. He watches her face light up as she opens it. In Stefan's eyes Marianna is joy personified. She kisses his cheek. Lays her head on his shoulder.

'So what's wrong?'

Stefan leans forward, elbows on knees, rocking from side to side, agitated. He drags his hands through his hair and blurts out, 'I can't go on like this. We row all the time. We've little money and yet Truda just won't let the subject of a baby drop.'

'Is that really the reason why you don't want to have a child, Stefan?'

He sighs deeply. 'Well, it's a good enough reason.'

"That's not what I asked though, is it?'

'Weren't you going somewhere? Stefan asks her, avoiding the question.

'Yes. But it can wait. Come on,' she says, pulling him to his feet. 'Let's get you home. You can't sit here all day.'

*

Truda wanders downstairs yawning and stretching. There's no sign of Stefan, though he has drunk last night's leftover coffee so she guesses he must already be in the workshop.

She searches amongst the shelves of opened packets and tins, finds an elegant, much-cherished tea caddy, flips open the lid and instinctively draws it towards her nose, closes her eyes and inhales the sweet raspberry and rose aroma.

Tea made, she flops into a chair and waits for it to brew. She gazes at the caddy reflectively. Was it really only a year since Stefan bought it for her on a rare trip to a client in Warsaw? It was an expensive gift and she'd been annoyed that he went alone and was gone longer than she'd thought necessary.

'It's elegant. Just like you,' he'd flattered.

She doesn't feel very elegant today in her plain nightwear, her hair straggly and matted from a disturbed night's sleep. If she's honest, it's been a long time since she made any effort to look elegant; she's always up to her elbows in dough. Their relationship is in a mess but it's his fault. All he has to do is provide her with a baby and everything will be fine.

She's indulgently starting a second cup when the door bursts open and he appears looking pale and tired, the suitcase clasped in one hand.

'What the hell's going on, Stefan?' She looks from him to the case.

He drops it and throws off his coat.

'I've something to say and it's important. Sit down and don't interrupt.'

Truda is stunned into silence by his unusually authoritarian tone.

'I've thought about it long and hard and, although I know it's what you want, we're not starting a family, Truda. Not until we're in a more financially stable position and I can't see how that can happen, not with things as they are. There's little factory work available but perhaps we should both look. We may get lucky.'

She butts in, horrified at the thought. 'A factory! I can't work in a factory! I love my baking and I won't do dirty manual work and that's an end to it! You do what you like, but don't count me in!'

'Then if that's your answer and you're not prepared to make sacrifices or compromise in any way, neither am I.'

As far as Stefan is concerned that's the end of the subject. Turning on his heel he leaves, slamming the door behind him.

# Twenty-Two

'I ain't never celebrated Christmas before,' Tomas tells Marianna as they sit planning the forthcoming celebrations.

'This will be my first Christmas away from home and I'm excited too,' she says. 'There's a lot to plan and it would be good to have some help. Are you up for that?'

'Course I am,' he replies readily. 'Who's coming and can I tell them yet?'

'They already know, Tomas. There'll be eight of us including a new addition to our usual party.'

'Oh. Who's that?'

'Lidka.'

'Lidka!'

'Yes. Apparently being apart from Feliks on Christmas Eve is not an option.'

Tomas sniggers. 'Are they girlfriend and boyfriend now then?'

Marianna winks. 'Yes, I believe they are.'

'Won't her mum be cross about it? I don't think she likes Feliks very much.'

'Maybe she will, but Lidka has made up her mind.'

'What about Chajim and his mum?' he asks.

'They've already celebrated Hanukkah, but if they want to join us of course they'll be welcome.'

In accordance with Polish tradition it's imperative that the flat is spotless. Windows are polished until they shine, carpets beaten and floors scrubbed, and Tomas helps enthusiastically.

On Christmas Eve morning Stefan and Stanislaw lug a tree up the two flights of stairs and they decorate it with home-made baubles, gingerbread courtesy of Truda and candles from Stanislaw's stockroom. Tomas has made a huge star for the top and Stefan, holding him round the legs, lifts him onto his shoulders so he can fix it in place. Truda arrives later in the morning with some fresh pastries but leaves almost immediately to deliver the last of her Christmas orders. Elena brings a floral arrangement of holly and berries, and together she and Marianna lay the table after Tomas has spread hay under the cloth.

'Wos the hay for?' he asks, puzzled.

'The hay represents Jesus' birth in a stable,' Elena explains and points out that it's these traditions that make a Polish Christmas so special.

'Don't forget the extra chair,' she says, as Tomas jiggles them into place round the kitchen table.

'Why? Is someone else coming?'

Marianna laughs. 'No. But it's tradition that there's always a spare chair for a stranger to fill.'

Truda has made a batch of *oplatek,* a thin star-shaped wafer made from flour and water and similar to those used for communion during Mass.

'This is the most ancient and beloved of all Christmas traditions,' Marianna tells Tomas. 'The head of the household starts by breaking the wafer and then shares it with everyone else at the table. Even pets are given a piece, if you have a pet of course, and legend has it that if animals eat *oplatek* on Christmas Eve, they'll be able to speak in human voices at midnight, although only those who are pure of spirit will be able to hear them.'

Tomas laughs, disbelieving. 'That's nearly as daft as your Petronella pigeon story,' and not wishing to be disrespectful adds, 'but I like the idea.'

Tomas is more impressed by Stefan's nativity scene.

'I made this when I was ten years old,' Stefan tells him. 'With my father's help of course.' A beautifully crafted version of St Mary's Basilica in Krakow's main square provides the backdrop for the intricately carved wooden figures. It's a fanciful version of the nativity scene that has become unique to Krakow. The church spires have been enhanced with the use of foil sweet wrappers, pressed flat and glued to the wooden structure, the rest being painted with bright colours.

'You should be proud of this,' Tomas tells him, examining the tiny figures.

Stefan smiles, recalling the many happy hours he spent working on the scene with his father. 'I am, Tomas. I am indeed,' he replies.

At the agreed time everyone arrives and there's much kissing under the mistletoe, strategically placed by Tomas, just inside the door. He declares there are to be no escapees from this tradition and lines people up ready for their turn. Stefan and Marianna's kiss is fleeting, but although their lips barely touch, their eyes say a whole lot more.

It's a day full of traditions and the festive meal doesn't start until the first star is seen in the night sky. Tomas is put on lookout and stands on a stool with his nose pressed against the window.

'Let us know when you see it. Don't look away. We are relying on you, Tomas.' Stanislaw is teasing him a little but Tomas is so caught up in the excitement he doesn't notice.

'Hurry up, star,' he calls, 'I'm hungry.'

At last the cry goes up, 'There it is, it's arrived!' Everyone takes their place and a parade of dishes is brought to the table. Marianna has had more than a little help from her guests, and with great generosity on Stanislaw's part they have managed to pull together a sumptuous celebratory meal. It's compulsory to try every dish and Tomas, who has never seen so much food in one place, has spent hours making a written menu with a drawing beside each item. There are twelve different dishes to represent the twelve apostles, starting with beetroot soup served with tiny dumplings, then herring fillets with sour apple and chopped onions, cabbage rolls stuffed with rice and mushrooms, gingerbread, dried fruit compote and poppy seed cake to name just a few.

Wine is served and '*Smacznego!*' echoes around the table. The meal is eventually over and modest gifts are exchanged, then shortly after eleven thirty the party assemble in the shop dressed for the cold night and make their way to the Corpus Christi Basilica for midnight mass. Elena, Stanislaw, Lidka and Truda are regular churchgoers, but Stefan, Feliks and Marianna usually only attend on special occasions. Tomas has never been to church and is excited but nervous.

'What if I get it wrong?' he asks Marianna as they walk behind the others.

'You won't. Just copy what I do and if you make a mistake I'm sure God will forgive you.'

He squeezes her hand. 'Fank goodness for that.'

Tomas can't believe how often people move around in church, constantly standing up, sitting down, kneeling and then standing up again. The priest doesn't say when to do what, so Tomas keeps his eye on the others and copies what they do. Sometimes they say the same thing over and over again but despite the repetition he has no idea what it means. He likes the singing and although unable to read all the words joins in where he can.

When the congregation make the sign of the cross he gets a little confused but by the end of the service has mastered the technique. Right hand to forehead, then to the middle of his breast, then his left shoulder, and finally his right shoulder.

'What was all that confession stuff about?' he asks Marianna on the way home. 'I ain't done nuffinck bad for ages.'

'It's a way for people to unburden themselves of their guilt,' she explains, wondering if Leon has ever felt the need to spend time in the confession box and at the same time, chastising herself for being so judgmental. Who is she to criticise when she'd spent the entire service deliberately brushing against Stefan's arm and at one point they'd actually linked fingers. She should be on her knees asking for forgiveness and reciting Hail Marys for her irreverence in the house of God. The alternative option is altogether more appealing. She and Tomas will have a warming mug of hot chocolate, curl up on the sofa and relive the entire wonderful day.

*

Tomas runs upstairs as fast as his legs will carry him.

'Marianna! Marianna! Quick! Look out the window.'

'Goodness, what's all this?' she cries as he bursts into the room, although she already knows. There's a deep covering of virgin, crystalline snow outside. The muffled street sounds and unusual light drew her to the window on waking.

'It's snowin'. Everything's white. Every single thing!' He clambers onto a chair and looks out the window at the storm of feathered crystals falling slowly from the grey sky and soundlessly coating the world in a blanket of white.

'S'weird,' he says. 'If you stare at the snow falling it feels like it's you that's going up and not it that's coming down.'

'So it does,' Marianna agrees, starting to feel dizzy. They watch the snowfall from the safety and warmth of indoors, though Tomas is urging Marianna to join him outside for a snowball fight.

'Not wise in my condition,' she says, pointing to her ever-growing bump.

'Oh yes. I forgot. D'you think Stefan will come out?'

'He might. Why don't you go and ask him?'

Tomas grabs his coat and gloves and is tapping on the workshop window before Marianna has closed the door behind him. Stefan obliges and the pair venture outside, the virgin snow compressing and creaking underfoot. They duck and dodge as each takes aim, laughing and shouting and tumbling together in the blanket of white. Marianna, watching from inside, is overcome with a feeling of inexpressible love for them both. The wind increases and a horizontal blur hides them momentarily from view. Her gaze shifts to the rooftops. It's a beautiful sight. The whole world is painted in a palette of grey and white. Fires are lit and smoke rises from chimneys all along the street as the occupants of freezing homes decide to stay put until the worst is past.

*

During the night the temperature drops dramatically and icicles have formed on the overhang outside the window. Frost has formed a magical fern-like pattern on the inside of the glass. Marianna presses her hand against the icy surface, melting a patch through which she gazes out at the clear blue sky and the scene below.

Stanislaw is outside shovelling snow from the pavement in a futile attempt to clear a pathway to the shop. The scrape of his spade echoes around the empty street as he huffs and puffs and the snow piles up, muttering to himself all the while that this may well be pretty to look at but it's bad for business. As if things aren't bad enough, what with his arthritis and failing eyesight, it now looks as if this weather is set to stay for a while. Stanislaw glances up and down the road, but it seems that fearful of the icy conditions his customers are afraid to venture out and the street stays eerily quiet.

Stefan visits Marianna on the pretext of checking on Tomas who has a very small bruise on his cheek, a souvenir of their snowball fight. Marianna, wrapped up against the cold, has her dressing gown on over her clothes and is wearing thick socks and fingerless gloves. A kettle is steaming away on the stove and she's toasting yesterday's dry bread in front of an inadequate, smoky fire in the grate. Things may be hard, what with the relentless cold and shortages of food becoming more apparent, but her skin is glowing and her hair glossy. Pregnancy suits her.

'My God you look magnificent. Positively glowing,' Stefan tells her as he takes her in his arms. 'I can barely keep my hands off you.'

'You don't have to try too hard,' she says, taking his face in her hands and kissing his mouth greedily. 'I've been thinking about you all night. I'm exhausted with thinking about you. You are my guilty secret. How long can you stay?' she asks, sliding his coat over his shoulders.

'As long as it takes. Put the catch on the door,' he urges.

Somehow they find themselves on the bed and she abandons herself to his dexterity as he undresses her.

'I had no idea you were such an expert,' she teases.

'Only with you,' he responds, seriously.

She is soon undressed down to her underwear, and her breasts, firm against the silky fabric, appear fuller and more voluptuous than ever, her swollen belly smooth and hard. He pulls her slip up and over her head and they lie back. She whispers urgently, 'I want your hands all over me.' His hands shake as he strokes her smooth skin and buries his face in her. She cradles his head, her fingers rake his hair and her nails scrape seductively across his shoulders. The muscles in his stomach tense with anticipation as she encourages him to turn onto his back, sliding her hands down his arms and holding him still as she sits astride him. She lowers herself onto him and he cries out as slowly they move against each other and indulge in the sheer joy of it. Her sweet-smelling hair falls silky against his cheeks.

'Kiss me,' he demands, desperate to feel her tongue on his. Their mouths meet with an urgency that won't be denied and in perfect time they fall into that deep fathomless place that is love.

*

For two weeks the Arctic weather grips the entire country. Roads are blocked and journeys cancelled. The population has been in virtual lockdown and frustrations are surfacing on every front.

Stanislaw is fretting about the lack of business and has relieved Marianna of her duties in the shop. 'There's absolutely no point in both of us standing around doing nothing all day, and judging by the size of you, you could do with sitting down more often.' As a result she's been revelling in the opportunity to spend more time writing.

Stefan is equally content. The design for the cradle has been approved and he's happy carving away for hours each day in the solitude of his beloved workshop. In the freezing studio beyond, Lidka has hunkered down with Feliks and his output has increased under her organised regime.

'What cold?' she questions one day when Sara asks how on earth she can spend so much time in that 'pit of a studio'.

'We don't notice the cold. We've got each other now Mother,' she purrs triumphantly.

Sara's eyes rise heavenwards. Michal, hunched behind his newspaper, smiles. 'That's my girl,' he chuckles to himself.

Truda, frustrated that she's been unable to fulfil orders, is worse-tempered than usual, and her complaints and disapproval of everything Stefan does, or doesn't do, have reached fever pitch.

'It's alright for you in your cosy workshop' she grumbles. 'You don't need to go anywhere, but I have to deliver this cake to the Bartkiewiczs' whatever happens. There's two days' worth of work down the drain if I don't.'

She's been making a special cake for Mrs Bartkiewicz's mother whose ninetieth birthday is the next day, and Truda has promised them that come hell or high water the cake will be there.

'You'd be a fool to go out in this weather. Can't they celebrate her birthday without it?'

Truda slams about the kitchen. 'Who asked for your opinion?' she snaps at him. 'Don't interfere; it's none of your business. I'll take the wretched cake if it's the last thing I do.'

'Well, don't say I didn't warn you. If you drop it, you'll be furious. I don't understand why you didn't ask them to collect it if they want it so badly, after all Dr Bartkiewicz has his own car.'

'Because that's not how it works, now shut up about it, will you.'

Stefan obliges and they don't speak for the rest of the day.

*

The next day dawns with a clear blue sky. There's been a partial thaw overnight and from the relative comfort of indoors the conditions outside appear less treacherous. As soon as Truda leaves home she realises she's made a mistake. The Bartkiewicz's live a good twenty minutes' walk away and although Stefan has offered to go with her, she has declined on the grounds that work on Marianna's cradle must be far more important and should clearly take precedence over anything he does for her.

The cake is heavy, the large box cumbersome and her leather-soled boots unsuitable. She slips frequently but manages to stay upright, and once out on the main road, where the snow has turned to slush, the going is easier, although passing trams surge dirty water onto the pavement, soaking her legs and feet. Truda arrives red-faced, her arms aching.

Mrs Bartkiewicz is thrilled with the cake and offers Truda a warming drink. 'You must be frozen, dear. It's very kind of you to deliver it but I'm sure Mr B would have been happy to collect it if you'd asked.' Mrs Bartkiewicz is full of interesting gossip that's new to Truda and she soaks up the details with relish, making a mental note to pass it on to Sara. The time has flown and, glancing out of the window, she notices that snow is falling again.

'Oh! Goodness I'd better get going. I'd no idea it was that late and the weather appears to be closing in again.'

Mrs Bartkiewicz is concerned. 'It's such a long walk, dear. Why don't you wait for my husband to return? He won't be long, I'm sure. He's gone to collect an order of oysters. It's our weekly treat, you know.' But Truda insists she leave before the weather worsens.

The wind is near horizontal and the snow, now sleet-like, stings her face. Pulling her collar up tight around her chin she strides purposefully towards home.

*

The driver of tram number forty-nine whistles quietly to himself as he turns the final corner on his route, relieved that he's nearing the end of another gruelling shift. With just one more stop to make, the bus terminal is almost in sight.

Black ice covers the pavement like death's doormat, and in the moments between loss of balance and impact, Truda's face registers nothing but annoyance.

A small crowd gathers round and watches in horror as a pool of blood spreads across the ground from the back of her head. Silence descends on the scene as shocked onlookers move a discreet distance away and speak in hushed voices. An ambulance eventually arrives but a doctor, passing the scene, has already covered Truda's face. The tram driver, severely traumatised, sits ashen at the side of the road, drawing repeatedly on a cigarette. The police arrive and Truda is taken away. The snowfall intensifies, covering the ground swiftly, and within minutes a white shroud covers all evidence of her untimely demise.

*

The priest greets mourners at the door of the church and sprinkles Truda's coffin with holy water. Stefan, Stanislaw, Feliks and Michal carry the coffin into the church. The congregation consists of a dozen neighbours and a few of Truda's regular customers. Elena has provided a wreath made with ears of dried corn and wheat, a fitting tribute to Truda's love of baking. Lidka places the Bible and a crucifix next to a photo of a smiling Truda. Stanislaw says the bidding prayers, Stefan reads the eulogy and is in charge of the readings, and Elena brings up bread and wine at the funeral mass. They perform each task with solemn dignity.

Afterwards there's a short ceremony at the cemetery and the mourners return to Stefan's flat for a reception where he greets his family and friends with quiet deference. A private man, his grief will be borne with stoicism in public, but privately he'll be awash with waves of sadness, anger and guilt. Marianna's love for Stefan manifests itself as physical pain as she watches him struggle with the challenge of greeting them. He gazes from one to the other, grey-faced and vacant. Photographs of Truda have been placed around the room and memories are exchanged. Marianna keeps herself occupied helping Elena with food and drink. Stefan looks exhausted as the mourners finally take their leave and he thanks each one of them for their kind words.

'Such a lovely woman... I'm sorry for your loss... we're all here for you... if you need anything... such a tragedy...' and so on.

Stefan asks Marianna to stay a while.

'No. It wouldn't be right. But you know where I'll be when you're ready.'

He nods in agreement and touches her arm. She kisses his cheek briefly. 'I'm so sorry, Stefan.'

Stanislaw offers to stay and the two men partake of a few vodkas. They skirt round emotions and talk only of practicalities and finances before finally retiring to bed, Stanislaw uncomfortably to the sofa, shortly after midnight.

*

A week later the snow has melted. The old familiar townscape has emerged and Szeroka Street is back to normal. Stefan has stayed away, but a short note, sent via Tomas, puts her mind at rest.

Elena and Marianna make sure he's supplied with hot meals and Tomas takes great pride in being the go-between. Plates are returned empty and this is a good sign.

Marianna is sitting quietly one afternoon when there's a barely discernible tap at the door. She creeps across the room, turns the handle carefully and pulls it open with a jerk.

'Got you!'

Stefan takes a step backwards.

Covering her mouth she whispers, 'I'm so sorry. I thought you were Tomas. That was stupid of me. I apologise.'

'There's no need. Really.'

She takes his hand and leads him to the sofa, sits him down like a child and arranges the cushions around him as if he's an invalid.

He smiles. She groans. 'Sorry, I just can't get this right, can I?'

'Stop trying so hard, it'll be better that way.'

'Okay. Let's start again. Would you like some coffee?'

'I'd love some. And thank you for the meals, I would have starved without you.'

The coffee is good and strong and they sip at the scalding liquid as she waits for him to speak.

'I've been doing a lot of thinking these last few days and the truth is, Marianna, I'm bloody angry!' He takes a gulp of coffee, turns to face her and continues, 'Death is a thief! Do you know that? It stole the chance for me to make things right. Although if I'm honest, I know we wouldn't have worked it out, we both wanted different things.'

She instinctively knows what he means and takes his hand.

'The thing is, in the beginning we were in love. At least I think we were. Not the all-consuming love that I now know is possible, but we were happy for a while.' He shakes his head. 'Then things went wrong and in the end, and this is the bit I hate the most, in the end I was so worn down by her whining and moaning that I was just ... done with her.'

'Perhaps you should focus more on the happier times. You won't forget her faults, but in time you will forgive them and remember her for how things used to be rather than how they became.'

'I'm so angry with her. She was so obstinate. She insisted on taking the bloody cake that day.'

'Of course she did. She was an independent woman and determined to do things her way.'

'I suppose so. I just don't want to think about her resentfully. Will I get over that, do you think?'

'I'm sure you will, it's not in your character to bear a grudge, but it'll take time, she was a big part of your life.'

'She was certainly always there, marking out the path we would take, where it would lead. But it was what *she* wanted, they were her horizons, not mine. Now I can follow my own path. I have to move on. Don't I?'

'You do and you will, but in the meantime you'll be caught up in a whirlwind of emotions. It's all perfectly normal.'

Stefan drops his head into his hands. Marianna wraps her arms around him and holds him tight while he sobs and sobs.

# Twenty-Three

In late January a letter arrives from Leon.

*Darling wife,*
*You will undoubtedly be surprised to receive this letter. I know I've been awful to you but I can't undo what's been done. Amelia was fun to be with and it was good for a while, but things didn't work out. She has left me and gone home to her parents. I can no longer afford the rent for the rooms and have no idea what I will do or where I'll go. Work has been patchy to say the least, as nobody wants to employ a lone violinist. I hope you aren't bearing a grudge; you were always so easy-going. Will you find it in your heart to forgive me and allow me to return? I've searched my conscience and forgiven myself. I hope you can do the same. Please reply as soon as you can. I do miss you.*
*Yours*
*Leon*

'The audacity of the man!' Marianna is pacing about, furious. 'How could he? Darling wife! He's forgiven himself! Huh!' Her eyes are wide with disbelief as she waves the letter agitatedly above her head. 'Does he seriously expect me to take him back?'

Stefan's about to answer but she cuts him short.

'Well, I won't. Never! Not in a million years!' She plonks herself down on the sofa. 'The bastard! What a total and utter bastard!'

Stefan grasps her hand in his and squeezes it reassuringly while Marianna continues to rant. 'There's no way he's ever setting foot in this flat again and one thing's for certain. He's never to know about the baby.'

Stefan has stayed quiet so far, but he wonders if she should, perhaps, reconsider this particular point.

'Are you sure about that, Marianna? He is the father after all. Do you think that, perhaps, he has a right to know?'

She stands abruptly and walks away. 'No! He has no right. Absolutely none and don't mention it again. Please.'

Stefan changes the subject. 'How about some coffee then?'

'Coffee is no problem at all.' She smiles at him now. 'And then I'll write and tell him never to darken my path again.'

*

Leon holds Marianna's letter in one hand, thrusts the other into his trouser pocket and jiggles his leg with annoyance. His teeth grind in exasperation. He's a man used to getting his own way and this is not the reply he expected.

The bare-boarded apartment is cold and evidence of Amelia's departure is apparent. Dirty washing and an unmade bed, stale food and unwashed dishes, cupboards emptied of her belongings. His chest tightens as he is overcome by a crushing defeat the like of which he has never known and suddenly, unable to breathe, he rushes from the building.

Sitting on the kerb he folds his arms across his heaving chest. The grey building bears down on him from behind. The grey road stretches out in front. Grey people pass by, living their own grey lives.

The situation is of his own doing, although he'll never admit it. He tilts his chin in denial and mutters out loud to himself. 'She knew what I was like when she married me. I made no pretence and was honest from the start! She was smitten from the moment she saw me. I was a fool to think we could make a go of it. All she ever thought about was her ridiculous writing. Her time spent daydreaming; drifting off to some imaginary world.' He searches around for justifications for his behaviour. 'She used me to leave that wretched pit in the country. Cared more about that urchin kid and pandered to Feliks' needs. And all this when I spoilt her rotten. Flowers on her birthday and…' He can think of nothing else. 'What do women want? It's beyond me. Amelia never complained or criticised. No one else played with her like I did.' He sniggers at his own innuendo. 'She'd have had no work without me. Ungrateful bitch.'

Leon drops his head into his hands. It's time to face realities and with Amelia gone his former contacts are no longer interested in employing him. 'Sorry but a lone violinist holds little appeal,' they'd told him. He has no idea how he'll earn enough to pay the rent. Damn them. Damn them all!

He unfolds the crumpled letter and reads again. 'My life will be better without you… your constant lies… you are a selfish man, Leon… uncaring and cold-hearted.' The damning accusations shout out from the page but he knows no remorse. Hurling the letter into the gutter he strides indoors. He's made a decision. It's time to move on!

# Twenty-Four

Pedro Gonzalez has offered Feliks the opportunity of a lifetime.

'Come to Barcelona and paint all day. Make a name for yourself,' he says when the pair are enjoying a casual conversation over coffee one morning. Feliks is stunned by the suggestion and Pedro senses why he's stalling. 'Bring your young lady if you want. There's a place to stay and I've a gallery nearby. What's to stop you?' Feliks is unsure but Pedro is convinced his art will sell. 'Take my word for it, Feliks. Even during these hard times there are people with money to spend, the kind of people who view art as an investment. There's nothing to lose and if things don't work out you can always come back.'

Feliks rushes back to the studio. His own mind is made up and he's buzzing with excitement. All he has to do is convince Lidka. 'Picture this,' he says, squeezing her hands. 'You and I bronzed golden by the sun. Flamenco. Paella. Siestas.'

Lidka flops into a chair. 'We can't, Feliks. It's too big a step.'

He pulls her to her feet and swings her round.

'Lidka, you and I can do anything. We've proved we're a great team and we'll only look back with regret if we don't go. Come on, nothing ventured and all that. What d'you say?'

Lidka is finding it hard to visualise herself anywhere other than Kazimierz, although she's come a long way in other areas of her life in the last six months. 'I'm not sure I can, Feliks, I've never been further than Krakow. Barcelona is a world away.'

'Exactly. Think how exciting it'll be to discover a new country.'

She bites her lip and sighs.

'I really don't know.'

Feliks grips her arms.

'Listen to me, Lidka. You can do anything if you put your mind to it. Remember you told me once you couldn't tango and you did that with great panache. This is just another bigger adventure. And don't forget, you'll be with me.'

He kisses her and looks at her with puppy dog eyes.

'Pleeeease. Don't leave me to survive without you.'

'Don't blackmail me with that look. You know I can't resist you. At least give me until tomorrow.'

*

The day Lidka and Feliks leave for Spain is the first day of spring and outside the rain is pouring down. Lidka looks pensive. Feliks is trying to keep her spirits up, afraid she'll have a last-minute change of mind.

'It's an omen. What do they say? The rain in Spain falls mainly on the plain? Well, Barcelona is miles from any plain.'

He smiles broadly. 'In a few days' time we'll have forgotten what rain looks like.'

A small farewell party has assembled at the studio. Michal and Sara are fussing round. Michal tightens the straps on Lidka's luggage for the umpteenth time. He'll miss her but is thrilled she's taking such a bold step, becoming independent. It's all he's ever wanted for her.

'I'm proud of you, Lidka, now just get out there and experience a bit of the world. Take a few chances.'

Sara, on the other hand, has spent hours out of Michal's earshot trying to talk Lidka out of going.

'I probably shouldn't be telling you this but it is possible to die of heatstroke. You're fair-skinned, Lidka, you really shouldn't go. You won't be able to cope and shouldn't you be getting married? Running off like this without a ring on your finger. Whatever are you thinking? Whatever will people say?' She has resorted to tears and almost to blackmail, but to no avail.

Lidka has made up her mind and there's no going back.

'I'll be absolutely fine. Please stop worrying.' She tries to placate her mother. 'It's only for a year. The time will fly by.'

Marianna is slumped on the sofa, her size getting the better of her.

'Darling girl!' Feliks gushes. 'You look magnificent. I wish I could paint you right now. You're a Rembrandt in the making.' She laughs. She'll miss Feliks and his endearing overacting. He kisses her fondly. 'Now you make sure you take care of both of you. We can't wait to meet this little one.' He pats her belly tenderly.

Their journey will be a long arduous one, crossing borders and changing trains several times, but the trip has been organised like clockwork and they have all the details that will deliver them safely to their destination.

Stanislaw slaps Feliks on the back. 'Good luck. You've come a long way, Feliks, and I'm proud of you.'

It's time to go. There's much kissing and crying. Feliks is determined to keep the mood upbeat, and waving his hat high above his head he whoops, '*Adios, Amigos. Deseame suerte.*'

'What does that mean?' queries Tomas who has been watching, bemused by the emotional outpouring.

'It means, wish us luck.'

# Twenty-Five

Stefan has made good progress, although there are days when he would swear there's an actual black cloud hanging over his head, the feelings of anger and guilt are so overwhelming. It's little things that spark a downturn in his mood. The smell of baking bread, the sight of a young woman carrying a basket, the silence in the flat at the end of each day. But it's during the night when his conscience troubles him most and he wrestles with the enormity of the changes in his life. Sleeping badly has resulted in a lack of concentration and long daytime naps in the workshop have become habitual. Until recently he's been unable to work for any length of time, but now with Marianna's baby due within weeks, he has a goal as the cradle must be finished in time.

Marianna has been Stefan's greatest support. She enjoys cooking him meals and encouraging him to get plenty of fresh air and exercise. They stroll to town once or twice each week where they spend time wandering among the stalls of the old Cloth Hall. A break away from the workshop and his familiar surroundings is proving beneficial and as the weeks go by his mood lightens.

Tomas's soup business has been a success throughout the winter months, and now that warmer weather has arrived, he has diversified to become an expert at pastry for his new line in vegetable pies. The money he earns is squirrelled away in his restaurant fund. Stanislaw worries there's too much cash around, but Tomas assures him he's constructed a thief-proof storage place.

Since the devastating shock of losing her best friend and Lidka's sudden departure for Spain, Sara has changed her gossiping ways and makes increasingly frequent visits to Marianna's flat to discuss the imminent arrival of the baby and lend a hand with the daily chores.

Despite the hardships brought on by the financial crisis, life in Szeroka Street has adopted a new but comfortable routine.

# Twenty-Six

April is awash with sunshine and showers, trees are bursting into life and the sweet smell of spring fills the air. Unable to believe that her belly can get any bigger without bursting open, Marianna is becoming increasingly anxious about giving birth, despite Elena's assurance that everything will be fine.

Marianna's mother has been unwell so is unable to be with her for the birth, but Elena has stepped in and offered her services. 'Don't you worry, my girl, I'll be here for you when the time comes. The midwife is on standby so there's nothing to worry about.' This is only partially comforting, bearing in mind that Elena has never had a baby and therefore no experience in the matter whatsoever.

Marianna is helping Elena with her flower order when her waters break. The shock of so much fluid whooshing from her body leaves her standing open-mouthed and terrified. 'Oh my God! What do I do now?'

Elena takes matters in hand immediately.

'Here we go. Baby has decided it's time to join us. Come on, let's get you upstairs.'

Holding her belly as if it were about to detach itself from the rest of her body she gingerly makes her way to the flat. Elena jokes as they pass Stanislaw, who is weighing out coffee beans behind the counter.

'You'd better give those scales a polish. There'll be something very important to weigh before this day is done.' Stanislaw looks aghast. The last time he experienced the trauma of childbirth was a very long time ago.

Elena fusses about, covering the bed with fresh linen and collecting towels. 'Don't panic,' she instructs, doing just that. 'It'll be hours before anything happens. Why don't you have a nice warm bath? It'll help you relax.'

Marianna is slumped on the sofa, scared to move, but nods in agreement. 'That sounds nice.' A while later she's heaving herself over the edge of the bath, wondering how she'll ever get out again and more than a little anxious about what's to come. 'I must be brave,' she mutters to herself, feeling anything but.

She hears Tomas stomping up the stairs at breakneck speed. 'Is the baby born yet?' he asks. She winces as she hears Elena's reply.

'Of course not, you silly boy, it's going to be a long time before we see any baby. Now get out, this is no place for a young lad. Go and tell Sara it's started, she's bound to want to help.'

Tomas hops from one leg to the other. 'Can't I watch?'

Elena bustles towards him waving her arms in the air. 'You most certainly cannot. Now go on, go and make yourself useful.'

He tumbles downstairs and, dashing through the shop at breakneck speed, is in Stefan's workshop in less than a minute.

'It's coming! The baby is coming!'

Stefan is asleep in the rocking chair. His eyes pop open with a start. 'What! What's going on?'

'The baby is coming!' Tomas repeats, breathless and wide-eyed.

Stefan jumps to his feet. 'Oh! Good heavens above. We'd better go and see then.'

Tomas steps forward and thrusts out a hand. 'No! Boys aren't allowed. Elena said so.'

Stefan is flustered. 'No. I suppose not. Well, we'll just have to wait then.'

'Gotta go. Gotta tell Sara,' Tomas says, and with that he's gone and Stefan is left pacing around the workbench, hands raking through his hair, his head filled with confused emotions.

The day slips by and there's little progress.

'Is this normal?' Marianna asks Elena.

'Oh yes,' she replies confidently. 'I'm sure it is, dear. I've heard it sometimes takes a while before contractions start but I've sent for the midwife to have a look at you.'

The midwife comes. 'Not much going on here,' she grumbles. 'Call me when her contractions are five minutes apart,' she instructs with business-like efficiency. 'I've got my hands full tonight. Three mums on the go at once,' and with that she leaves.

At midnight Marianna is racked with acute cramping in her abdomen. It's over almost before it's begun, but a dull ache lingers in her back and around her groin and she declares she feels happier now she knows what to expect.

'Not so bad as I thought.'

Elena says nothing.

Sara makes more tea.

By three in the morning the contractions are so powerful she fears her body will split in two. An hour later they're five minutes apart and she's exhausted. The midwife dutifully returns and takes control of the situation. 'My, we are doing well. I think we're nearly there. The baby's head is engaged.'

Marianna interrupts with a groan that seems to come from the very depths of her.

'Excellent,' the midwife encourages, rubbing her back.

Marianna is gripping Elena's hand, her face racked with pain. She squeezes so tightly Elena is tempted to join in the yelling, but resists on the grounds that a bruised hand pales into insignificance in comparison to the agony that Marianna is enduring.

'Okay. Time to get this baby into the world,' the midwife announces, rolling up her sleeves.

Stanislaw, Stefan and Tomas are in the shop displaying varying signs of anxiety. Stefan is pacing about nibbling at his fingernails. A bottle of Stanislaw's best vodka is half empty and Tomas has drunk so much fizzy Oranzada his belly is quite round.

'God almighty,' Stefan mutters as Marianna lets out a sound like a wounded animal. 'How much longer is this going to take?'

Stanislaw shrugs and downs another vodka.

'It must hurt an awful lot,' Tomas says, wide-eyed, and takes another swig of his drink. 'I'm glad I'm not a girl.'

At the sound of a baby's cry, all three drop into their seats with a collective sigh.

'Thank God for that.' Stanislaw crosses himself.

'Thank God,' repeats Stefan.

'Fank God,' Tomas agrees. 'Is that the baby? It sounds like a cat meowing,' he says, clearly disappointed that such immense effort on Marianna's part has culminated in such a disappointing cry.

Elena appears at the top of the stairs, leans over the banister and announces, 'It's a girl! It's an absolutely beautiful baby girl.'

An hour later the midwife leaves with a cursory glance over her shoulder. 'I'll call in tomorrow and check on you. Get some sleep. You've earned it.'

Marianna sits propped against a wall of pillows with the baby in her arms while Sara and Elena stand either side of the bed cooing in unison. 'Tell the boys they can come and see her now,' Marianna tells them, 'and please get yourselves something to eat, you must be famished. I don't know how I'd have coped without you. You've both been wonderful.'

*

The three traumatised men (Tomas considers himself a man now) stand awkwardly by the end of the bed.

Marianna laughs. 'Come closer, she won't bite.'

Tomas steps forward and perches on the bed but makes sure he is an arm's length away.

'Would you like to hold her?' Marianna asks.

He shakes his head then quickly adds, in case he misses his chance, 'Okay. If ya like.'

She shows him how to hold the baby and he nervously wraps his arms around the warm bundle. He touches the soft blond down on her head and she makes a snuffling sound. He gently rocks her back and forth. 'Ssshhhh,' he says. 'It's alright.' He beams at Marianna. 'Ain't she pretty?' he says, and the baby wriggles in his arms. 'Sshhhh, little one' he whispers, kissing her cheek. 'How long before I can take her for a walk?' he asks, wiggling her toes one by one.

Marianna laughs. 'Not for quite a while, I'm sorry to tell you. First she has to learn to sit and then crawl and then stand. You'll have to be patient.'

'What if I help her?' he says eagerly. 'It'll speed things up a bit.'

'You're welcome to give her all the help she needs, when the time is right.' Marianna smiles at the thought. 'You will be like her big brother.'

Stanislaw is all bravado as he paces about the room with Lilliana in his arms. 'I've done this before, you know. I have a way with babies.'

'Then you'll make a great babysitter,' she teases.

Stefan has been watching silently and Stanislaw suggests he and Tomas leave. 'Can't have too many big men around, we don't want to frighten her, do we? Come on, young man, let's go and get something to eat and let Stefan have a hug. We've missed our tea what with all the excitement.'

Stefan looks down at the woman he loves more than words can say. She pats the bed beside her and passes the baby to him. He holds her close, allowing his lips to brush the top of her head. She exudes the intoxicating scent of warm new baby and, closing his eyes, he breathes in the very essence of her. 'She's very beautiful. What are you going to call her?'

'Lilliana. My grandmother was called Lilliana and Lily is still lovely if people shorten it. What do you think? Do you like it?'

A hand, like a miniature starfish, escapes from the blanket and clutches Stefan's thumb, the tiny fingers clasping and releasing and clasping again as if to confirm he's there. Lilliana opens her eyes and appears to look straight into his.

'I think it suits her very well. You've chosen a beautiful name for your daughter.' He kisses the tiny fingertips as Lilliana squeezes his finger again. 'She looks just like you,' he says, looking from one to the other, 'she has your pretty nose.'

'Do you think so?' she queries. 'I think she looks more like you.' She waits for his reaction and he looks up slowly, realisation dawning. 'Yes, Stefan, it's true. She's ours. We have a beautiful daughter.'

*

They break the news to those closest to them that Lilliana's father is Stefan. Whilst the news is a shock the general consensus is that it's the best thing that could have happened and Elena insists that she knew it all along. Stanislaw chooses a quiet moment when he can be alone with Marianna.

'She's wonderful,' he says, peering at Lilliana with dewy eyes. 'I wish she were my granddaughter.'

'I'm so sorry, Stanislaw,' she replies. 'I feel you've been deceived.'

'Not at all. I never would have seen you this happy with Leon. I know that. He and I have history, and though it grieves me to say it, Stefan is a far better man.'

Tomas's reaction is best of all. 'I flippin' knew it. I seen the way she looks at him and I said to myself, she thinks he's her dad!'

Stefan can hardly believe how he feels and has a grin as wide as a crescent moon. 'One thing I don't understand is why you didn't tell me.'

Marianna raises her eyes in disbelief.

'It would hardly have been right in the circumstances.'

'And what if Truda hadn't died?'

'You never would have known,' she replies seriously, certain that it's the truth.

'What now?' he asks.

'That's up to you.'

He doesn't hesitate. 'I think, when the time is right of course, we should get married. If you want to.'

'If I want to?' she says. 'I'll have to see about that.' She's laughing at him now.

He knows she's teasing him but continues, his tone becoming serious. 'The flat has nothing but unhappy memories and I'll be able to help look after Lilliana, though I will keep up the rent on the workshop. I can't work anywhere else.'

Marianna smiles broadly. 'Sounds like the perfect plan,' she says. Lilliana kicks her legs and her blanket slides to the floor. 'I think we'd better put her down for a while. We don't want her to be spoilt,' Marianna says, tucking her safely back in the cradle her father so lovingly made.

# Twenty-Seven

The harsh winter has taken its toll on Stanislaw and his arthritis has reached incapacitating levels. No longer spritely, he puffs and groans his way around the shop. Elena has infinite patience but insists his poor old bones need a rest.

'You've got to ease off, Stanislaw,' she scolds one day when she finds him stuck halfway up a ladder unable to move.

'Can't do that. Who'll keep the shop going?'

'I've no idea, my love, but you can't keep this up. Now come on down please before you have an accident.' She fusses round him. 'I'm no youngster either and I'd love a little break. Can't we visit your sister? You've kept in touch with her all these years and I'm sure she'd like to see you again.'

'I don't know. She's not well off and we'd have to sacrifice some of these luxuries.' He points vaguely towards his deli counter. 'I hope you like vegetable soup,' he adds as a flippant afterthought.

'Well, I've heard things aren't so bad in Tarnow,' she says.

Stanislaw leans against the counter, puffing. 'Think of the business we'll lose if we shut the shop. Once your customers go elsewhere they never come back. That's a fact.'

'That's not true and you know it. Your customers have always been loyal and maybe, if we can find a way to keep the shop open, they'll be fine about you going away for a while.'

'Well, it isn't going to happen so forget it.'

But Elena doesn't forget it. As far as she's concerned, they're going and that's that. One day, whilst cooing over the baby, she mentions it to Marianna. 'I wish someone would convince him.' Marianna sips her coffee. 'I'll have a word if you like, or Stefan can.'

Stefan is happy to speak to him and after discussing the situation with Marianna takes it a step further and offers to run the shop in their absence.

Stanislaw looks unsure. 'I couldn't expect you to do that. Absolutely not.'

But Stefan insists. 'Go, it'll do you good and give me something to do. I've little work at the moment. The only thing I'd ask in return is that you allow me to close for two days each week so I can keep up with any odd jobs that come in for the workshop. Any larger commissions for bespoke work, not that it's likely I'll get any, can wait.'

Rubbing his chin, Stanislaw paces about.

Stefan can tell the idea is beginning to appeal. 'Think how pleased Elena will be.'

'Yes she will, won't she.'

'And don't forget I'll have Tomas to help me,' Stefan adds. 'What would he do if you close? The shop is his life.'

Stanislaw nods. 'Yes. Yes. I know. I'd hate to let the boy down when he's worked so hard.' Stanislaw blows out his breath through pursed lips. 'I can guess who's had a hand in this and you're making it very hard for me to refuse.' He shakes his head and smiles. 'Okay. You win. Two weeks, mind. No more.'

Stefan grips his hand. 'It's a deal. You won't regret it. All I need are a couple of sessions learning the ropes and some tips on how to avoid being disabled by that till of yours and you're on your way.'

*

The arrangements work well but unforeseen bad news isn't far away and days before Stanislaw is due to return, his sister becomes ill. He writes to Stefan that it's impossible for him to return and leave her alone. It's his duty to look after her and having given the situation a lot of thought thinks it best that Stefan close the shop. It's asking too much that it's kept going until he returns and the last thing he wants is for their friendly arrangement to turn into a commitment far beyond its original intentions.

Marianna and Stefan discuss alternative ways of keeping both businesses viable but reluctantly come to the conclusion that it isn't possible. Stefan agrees to run the stock down and two weeks later the closed sign is hung in the window, with a notice announcing that the shop will re-open when Stanislaw returns.

Shortly afterwards, and much to Stefan's surprise, Mr Cohen, thrilled with his initial commission, orders a set of furniture and Stefan sets to, working all hours to meet the deadline. 'Thank God for those who still have money to spend,' he comments to Marianna, 'and he's such a decent chap. I consider him a valued friend as well as a customer.'

'He is that,' Marianna agrees.

Another financial boost arrives in the form of a cheque from Feliks. 'I promised I would pay you well for your contribution to my success, dear girl, and here it is. Please accept it with my deepest gratitude.'

*

Summer is fast approaching when Marianna receives word via Ania that her ageing parents are finding it difficult to manage and writes in great detail about how the village is coping with the deepening effects of the depression. 'I've heard things aren't so bad in the big towns and cities and we are lucky here compared to the rural villages. They say cattle farmers are being forced to sell their dairy products to buy other staple items such as salt, matches and kerosene, while the luxuries of meat and sugar are becoming a distant memory. Daily rations consist of basic ingredients such as wheat porridge, potatoes, borscht or sourdough soup and sauerkraut. We're so lucky to have a plentiful supply of eggs from our chickens, honey from our bees and the vegetable and fruit harvests from the garden.'

Much discussion takes place, and despite the obvious drawbacks the decision is taken that once Stefan's outstanding work is completed they will close the workshop for the summer and travel to the countryside.

'I'm sure they will appreciate some help and they'll be so excited to meet Lilliana and Tomas,' Marianna adds.

Tomas is thrilled that he's to be part of this adventure, but Marianna warns him that life in the country won't be easy. Tomas seems undaunted by her tales of hardship and he dismisses them with a shrug of his shoulders. 'Won't bovver me. I've had a hard life.'

Marianna suppresses a grin and replies in sympathy, 'I know you have, my love. I know.'

A month later they leave Szeroka Street laden with luggage and head for the bus station. Marianna carries Lilliana and a large holdall, Tomas walks alongside pushing a small cart piled with precariously balanced bags and Stefan follows behind, a suitcase in each hand.

When they reach the terminal, their luggage is stowed securely on the roof of the bus while Tomas, who has taken charge of Lilliana, is already settled in a window seat.

'Are you sure you're happy to hold her, Tomas? This is going to be a very long and uncomfortable journey and she'll get very heavy,' Marianna says.

'Don't matter about me,' he replies, 'as long as she's happy I'll be alright.'

Stefan and Marianna sit behind him with their hands

clasped together. With her head resting comfortably on his shoulder her thoughts inevitably drift back to the journey that brought her here only a year ago.

'Isn't it funny?' she says wistfully. 'We spend all our lives travelling from one place to another, but in the end the real journey is the one that happens in our hearts.'

Stefan smiles. 'I love the way you make everything sound so poetic and of course it's true, although sometimes the right path can't be found without first getting a little lost.'

She laughs. 'And you call me poetic?'

He kisses her forehead as the bus jerks into motion and pulls away. 'Here we go,' he says, 'we're off. Another journey has begun.'

# Autumn

## *Zalipie 1975*

The notebook with the painted lovebirds given to Marianna so long ago is full to overflowing and countless loose sheets have been added. She flicks through the pages, satisfied that her story is almost finished, leans back and stretches.

'How's it going?' Stefan asks, resting his hand on her shoulder.

'Almost there.' She smiles up at him.

'You've said that a thousand times,' he responds.

'I know, but it has to be absolutely right.'

'And when will I be allowed to read this masterpiece?'

'Have a little patience, my love, there's just one loose end to tie up and it'll be done.'

*

The previous week a letter from a family friend arrived.

> *Dear Stefan,*
> *I enclose the details of a number of properties in Szeroka Street where I believe you once had a workshop? It seems too much of a coincidence to see your name above one of the units. The owners are looking for a new tenant and I thought you might be interested in the details.*
> *Hope you are all well.*
> *Much love to Marianna.*
> *Best regards,*
> *Adam*

Stefan had laughed. 'As if I'd want to go back to city life. I'm far too old to start again and my heart lies here in the country.' But Tomas is captivated by an idea that is rapidly forming in his mind and after dinner that evening the two men spend hours in discussion. Later on Tomas puts forward the idea to his wife. 'This could be the opportunity we've been waiting for. Think about it, Lilliana, what a great opportunity to do something different!'

But Lilliana has reservations about his plan. 'The properties must be dilapidated after all this time and Adam says they're filled with furniture and fittings from before the war.'

Tomas's imagination is one step ahead. 'Yes, but if we used them as part of the décor, think what a fantastic unique interior it could be. The place has such wonderful memories for me. It's where your mother changed the course of my life and I would probably have amounted to nothing if she hadn't taken me under her wing. I would get satisfaction from bringing the old place back to life.'

She snuggles into his shoulder, his enthusiasm winning her over. 'I know, but let's sleep on it and chat again tomorrow.'

*

Tomas and Lilliana are relocating the beehives for winter. This year has been a bumper one for honey and the jars of liquid amber are stored ready for use.

Lilliana removes her beekeeper's veil and reaches up to remove Tomas's. They stand together for a while, deep in conversation. A young girl skips along the path towards them calling, 'Daddy, Daddy,' and Tomas lifts her onto his shoulders.

Stefan and Marianna are waiting when they return to the house. 'Well?' Stefan asks eagerly.

'It's decided,' Tomas smiles broadly. 'We're taking a chance. We're going to rent three of the shop units and turn them into a restaurant serving traditional Polish dishes. We'll create an intimate atmosphere with candlelit tables and have musicians playing every night. We'll make good use of all those old knick-knacks and objects. Your old rocking horse will feature somewhere and Michal's sewing table will be utilised as a serving space. Some of Chajim's shop fittings will provide us with shelving and Stanislaw's stove will be a centrepiece at the entrance. I've so many ideas I could burst! It's so exciting to have a new beginning, an adventure and I can't wait to get started.'

Marianna is swept along with his enthusiasm. 'It sounds quite wonderful. How exciting for you both. And what will this restaurant be called?'

'We've spent a long time discussing this point,' Tomas says seriously, 'and you may think this a little unusual for the name of a restaurant, but as far as we're concerned it can only be called one thing.' He takes Lilliana's hand in his and squeezes it affectionately. 'We're going to call it Once Upon a Time in Kazimierz.'

# Epilogue

After the death of her parents, Marianna, Stefan and the family stayed in Zalipie and never returned to Kazimierz.

Marianna resumed her friendship with Ania and was initiated into the art of decorative painting, although her lifelong passion remained writing.

The simplicity of country life suited Stefan, and in time he became an enthusiastic gardener, providing the family with their staple needs. He transformed Marianna's father's old woodshed into a workshop and continued to provide his expert carpentry skills whenever needed.

In 1939 the Germans invaded Krakow and with them came the horrors of World War II and the Holocaust. In 1941, when Lilliana was six, German soldiers scoured the countryside looking for fair-haired blue-eyed children. Many were forcibly removed from their homes and eventually adopted by German families. Stefan built a hiding place in the roof of the chicken coop that was impossible to distinguish from the outside and here they hid Lilliana whenever soldiers were in the area. A dozen clucking hens were distraction enough and she was never discovered.

The Polish resistance movement was the largest in all of occupied Europe, collecting and supplying valuable intelligence to the Allies and causing disruption with disinformation and other forms of sabotage. As an active member of the Home Army, Stefan played a key role in their underground activities.

*

Tomas was fourteen at the outbreak of war. He was responsible for looking after the bees, chickens and geese and helped Stefan in his workshop. He was inevitably drawn into local underground activities and became adept at steering clear of trouble. The locals nicknamed him 'the invisible boy'. He worked his way up to the position of sous chef in a restaurant in Tarnow, eventually realising a lifelong ambition of owning his own small café. Tomas and Lilliana became inseparable and when she was eighteen they married in the chapel where Marianna had found such peace. They have a daughter, Olga, named after Marianna's mother.

*

After receiving Marianna's letter, Leon stayed on in Warsaw for a while earning a little money here and there. He was eventually forced to pawn his precious violin and a watch given to him by Stanislaw in order to raise enough cash to make the journey to London.

He found cheap lodgings advertised on a grubby card in a telephone box in Camden Town and rented a room in a dilapidated three-storey Victorian house. The basic facilities consisted of a draughty outside toilet and a damp bathroom shared with six other people. The landlady, a middle-aged but not unattractive actress/singer, was easy-going and entertained her tenants, all of them musicians, with tales from the theatre. Previously top of the bill in a small East End variety theatre, she embellished her colourful stories with an active imagination and had them begging for more. Meals weren't included in the rent but Olive Ginger, named on account of her greasy orange hair, would occasionally entertain them with a dubious meal. With mediocre food and cheap alcohol. These evenings were famous for their lively and often promiscuous outcomes.

Olive secured Leon a job at The Dorchester House Hotel where he worked up to and throughout the war years. The hotel was frequented by the likes of General de Gaulle, General Patton and Eisenhower. Leon revelled in the close proximity of such eminent people, and an endless parade of glamorous young ladies, who danced the night away in sequin-dusted shoes and slinky satin dresses, added to the attraction. In the uncertain climate of Blitz-ravaged London they were happy to throw caution to the wind and Leon took every advantage of this. His position centre stage provided an uninterrupted view of the dance floor and allowed him to choose his next dalliance unobserved.

According to Cecil Beaton, the iconic fashion portrait and war photographer of the time, the Dorchester was a place to which the respectable and dubious flocked and mingled, partaking of copious amounts of alcohol and indulging in careless talk. By now a proficient seducer, Leon was able to indulge himself in the way he loved most. He is still looking for the right woman.

*

And what of Feliks and Lidka?

They married and had a son, Pedro, and daughter, Lucia.

As Pedro Gonzalez predicted, Feliks' work became sought after. After Pedro's death Lidka took on the role of gallery manager, and with her prudent management of their finances they survived one of the darkest periods in Spain's history, the 1940s decade of impoverishment. They eventually abandoned city life for a small villa in Cadaques, a fishing town with steep cobblestone lanes and whitewashed houses where Feliks was thrilled to find himself in the illustrious company of artists such as Marcel Duchamp and Salvador Dali.

The nearby Tudela National Park became a frequent destination, his work having taken a different direction after he became entranced by its rugged landscape. He would fill his battered Seat 600 with empty canvases and all the paraphernalia required for a day's painting and drive up into the mountains for inspiration.

Lidka, who by now turned her hand to anything, was almost solely responsible for repairs and improvements to their home and courtyard garden, which she filled with lemon trees and bougainvillea. As visitor numbers to the area increased she saw a money-making opportunity when an elderly neighbour offered to sell her his olive grove. She enthusiastically took ownership, harvesting the olives and bottling the oil for sale to tourists at the local market. Feliks accredited a huge amount of his success to the tireless work and support he received throughout his life from his 'darling girl,' Lidka.

*

Stanislaw and Elena lived in Tarnow for the rest of their lives. He never lost the urge to keep shop, and whilst starting afresh was out of the question he spent all his spare time assisting and giving valuable advice to the owner of the local grocer shop, becoming a much-loved character in the town.

The war years brought the constant threat of reprisals from the German army, and the terrible roundups that resulted in the disappearance of so many of their Jewish neighbours took its toll on Stanislaw emotionally. Riddled with arthritis he eventually became housebound. Elena spent the rest of her life looking after him and tending her beloved flower-filled garden.

Marianna and Stefan remained close to the couple until they passed away. Stanislaw died at the grand age of eighty-eight and Elena followed five years later.

*

After the Germans invaded Krakow, life for those living in Szeroka Street became intolerable. In 1941 all Jewish inhabitants of Krakow were ordered to relocate to the ghetto in the Podgorski district. Michal, Sara, Chajim and his mother, Sofia, were forced to leave their homes and businesses, taking little in the way of belongings. Sofia was shot in front of her doting son before they had reached the end of Szeroka Street. Sara, virtually a prisoner in the ghetto, was determined to help as many people as possible but was murdered for stealing a loaf of bread intended for a starving family. Michal died alongside Chajim at Auschwitz having endured the most horrific treatment at the hands of the SS. The pair stayed together until their deaths in 1943.

*

The village of Zalipie is now a famous tourist attraction.

# About the Author

Barbara lives in Buckinghamshire and is a practising artist with a degree in Fine Art Practice. She has exhibited in London and throughout the South East of England and run various art groups and workshops both privately and for various organisations, recently including cruise ships to her CV. Four years ago she joined a creative writing class and began to paint with words, swapping her paintbrush for a pen. Led by an inspirational tutor the classes led to her first published piece appearing in Hi2020, one of a prize-winning collection of twenty short stories chosen from over a thousand new writer entrants.

Her artwork can be viewed at www.barbarapearmanart.co.uk

For exclusive discounts on Matador titles,
sign up to our occasional newsletter at
troubador.co.uk/bookshop